The Critics on Graham Hurley

'Intricate, pacey and thrilling, this is a book to keep you awake all night – even after you have finished it'
Harpers & Queen

'First class'   *Sunday Express*

'A compelling narrative with an unexpected twist in the tail'   *Books Magazine*

'Hurley's twists and action are electrifying'
Daily Telegraph

'Pick him up for the kind of book you thought was no longer written. Or you will be sorry'
Alex Dickson, *Radio Clyde*

'An eye for character and fluid, intelligent prose'
The Times

'As good a read as you'll ever get . . . A wonderful, wonderful thriller writer'   *Daily Mirror*

'With a deftness that is sharp and painful, Hurley entices you into the terrified and confused mind of his heroine. This spooky novel is utterly gripping'   *Daily Telegraph*

Graham Hurley is an award-winning documentary producer who now writes full time. Away from the typewriter, he pursues a lifetime's ambition to master windsurfing, colloquial Spanish and the perfect chicken bhuna. He lives, blissfully, with his wife, Lin, in Portsmouth.

Also by Graham Hurley

RULES OF ENGAGEMENT
REAPER
THE DEVIL'S BREATH
THUNDER IN THE BLOOD
SABBATHMAN
THE PERFECT SOLDIER
HEAVEN'S LIGHT

NOCTURNE

Graham Hurley

ORION

An Orion Paperback
First published in Great Britain by Orion in 1998
This paperback edition published in 1999 by
Orion Books Ltd,
Orion House, 5 Upper St Martin's Lane,
London WC2H 9EA

Second impression 1999

A CIP catalogue record for this book
is available from the British Library.

ISBN: 0 75281 749 3

Typeset at The Spartan Press Ltd,
Lymington, Hants
Printed and bound in Great Britain by
Clays Ltd, St Ives plc

For Jane and Simon
with love

'La nuit bien-aimée. La nuit, la raison dort, et simplement les choses sont.'

'Pilote de Guerre'
Antoine de Saint Exupéry

Prologue

If this were a film, the opening sequence would find me in bed.

It's half past four in the morning, still dark. I've been awake all night, worried sick about Billie. Billie is my baby daughter. She's nearly three months old. This afternoon, in a local park, someone took her away.

I'd been in the café for maybe a second or two longer than usual. I was buying myself a sticky bun and a can of Diet Coke. There were lots of people and I had to push my way through to get back outside. The pram was still there, hard up against the window. But Billie had gone.

In the flat upstairs, I can hear Gilbert on patrol, six steps across, nine steps up and down. He's been walking the circuit for hours on end, caged in his own back room, as helpless and as desperate as I am. I broke the news this afternoon. It was obvious he didn't believe it and neither can I. I thought that finding Billie gone was the worst moment of my life but every hour that passes makes the feeling worse. What kind of monster takes a baby like that? What kind of mother lets it happen?

I think guilt must wall you off from the world because it takes me longer than usual to pick up the sound of movement outside my bedroom window. I first put the footsteps down to party-goers from the squat across the back. Then, very distinctly, I hear a squeaking hinge. It belongs to the kitchen door that leads to the garden. There's a whispered conversation, two people at least,

3

then silence again. Even Gilbert's footsteps overhead have stopped.

Given what I've been through these last few hours – indeed, these last few months – I suppose I should be hardened to excitements like these but sadly I'm not. I pull the sheet up to my chin. I shut my eyes. I say a prayer. Dear God, please let all this stop.

Seconds later, my bedroom door is opening. I search for the light beside my bed but the torch has already found me. I hear a voice, male, urgent.

'Miss?'

I'm shielding my eyes. I expect the worst. It doesn't happen.

'Get dressed. Quick as you can, love.'

At last I've found the light switch. My visitor is wearing a black jump suit. His hands are gloved. Across the buttoned pocket on his chest, a velcroed strip reads DC Flowers. I should ask him how he forced the door, what right he's got to be here, but this list of sensible questions is the last thing on my mind.

It's about Billie, I say. It's about my baby. Have they found her? Has he come with news? It's obvious he hasn't a clue what I'm talking about. He tells me again to get dressed, to keep calm. The street is being evacuated.

'Evacuated?'

He nods, backing towards the door.

'You've got two minutes,' he says. 'Then you're out of here.'

Outside, it's freezing. At the far end of the street, a double-decker bus is filling with other residents. I join them on board. Faces I recognise: families, babies, students, drop-outs, old folk. We're all half-asleep, wall-eyed, bewildered. The place is swarming with police. Everywhere you look there are men and women

4

murmuring into radios. They seem watchful, keyed up. Of Gilbert, I realise, there's absolutely no sign.

A couple of minutes later, after a head count, they drive us away. The local library has obviously been opened specially. There are mattresses on the floor and a pile of neatly folded blankets. A woman behind the issuing counter is dispensing mugs of cocoa from a big urn.

We whisper to each other, neighbour to neighbour, wondering what possibly might have happened. No one seems to have any information. After a while, curled up beside Fiction G–J, I try to sleep but Billie won't let me. I want her back. I want her in my arms. Nothing else in the world matters.

Later, I'm not sure when, I feel a hand on my shoulder. It's Gaynor. She squats beside me, as sane and sensible as ever, a radio in her hand. I've never seen her in black before. It suits her.

'You OK?' she says.

I blink. What a silly question.

'Have they found her?'

She shakes her head and says there's been no news. I explain about the park, and the café, and the way it had happened, so abrupt, so sudden, but I can tell from the look in her eyes that she's got something else on her mind.

'Why didn't you tell me?' she asks.

'Tell you what?'

She stares at me a moment, the kind of look my mother used to give me as a child when I'd done something wicked.

'Gilbert?' Gaynor says softly. 'Are you really telling me you didn't know?'

One

Film-making brought me to London. I was twenty-three years old. I had a degree in media production from Bournemouth University, a cardboard box full of windsurfing trophies, and a debt that – by October, 1996 – was nudging £6,000. Most of this money I owed my father and after his abrupt death – a stroke followed, mercifully, by a massive heart attack – my mother was nice enough to call it quits. He'd left her a modest sum in various stocks and shares and I suspect it softened her grief to think that his passing returned me to solvency.

At the time, I'm ashamed to say that I was less grateful for this gesture than perhaps I should have been. I had my own problems with losing my dad like that and whether or not I still owed him £6,000 was the last thing on my mind. In any case, money was irrelevant, merely the preoccupation of a society I was desperate to expose as greedy, self-centred, and in most cases bloody unfair. Unlike the vast majority of my buddies at Bournemouth, I wanted to change the world.

Was I naive? Probably. At Bournemouth, a large part of your final year is devoted to what they call 'the major project'. This is a ten-minute video and it counts thirty-five per cent towards the degree. They give you a word or a phrase, like a chord on the piano, and you develop it in whatever direction you like. Our theme was 'Letting Go'. Bournemouth isn't California, but there are lots of young people in the town, and a great beach, and sunshine, and most of the final year opted for various

9

combinations of rave music, soft drugs, and moodily-lit raunch.

To no one's surprise, I went for something altogether more gritty. I wanted to explore the urban wastelands, those scruffy inner-city Bantustans where the underclass had been cast adrift. The link with 'Letting Go' was a bit tenuous but the invitation was there to explore the phrase at every level and it seemed to me that poverty and a general sense of lostness could drive weaker individuals over the brink. In retrospect, of course, I was dead right, prescient even, but at the time my theory was pretty half-baked, an undergraduate mix of Irvine Welsh, *The Big Issue*, and the songs of Billy Bragg.

Bournemouth, alas, was quite the wrong setting for what I had in mind. It has its share of Nineties blight – there's an alarming heroin problem – but images are everything in video and the town looks far too leafy and prosperous to sustain even ten minutes of inner-city grief. I wanted rain-stained concrete, drifts of sodden chip wrappers, vandalised cars, abandoned supermarket trolleys, flattened cans of Special Brew. I wanted drug dealers, teenage mums, gangs of rampaging kids, huddles of bent pensioners, faces and lives hollowed out by the blessings of the Thatcher years. None of them were available in Bournemouth in quite the right combination but after a three day recce I found the council estate of my dreams in Southampton, the next city up the coast.

The estate overlooked Southampton Water. Every wall had been spray-painted with graffiti and the man from the Social Services warned me about leaving my borrowed car unlocked. The estate even had tower blocks, wonderfully gaunt, where the lifts never worked, the windows leaked, and no one in their right mind ventured out after dark. I spent most of the day there and afterwards I sat on the crescent of tarry pebbles by the water, committing my impressions to paper. Behind me, the tower blocks threw long shadows across the bleak expanse of windswept concrete and when I got back to the car I found kids loitering nearby, waiting for me to find the flattened scabs of chewing gum over the keyhole on the driver's door. 'Brilliant,' I remember scribbling at the bottom of my location notes, under-lining the word three times.

Making the video was harder going than I expected. For one thing, the people I wanted to feature wouldn't let me anywhere near them. I'd pick up gossip about battered women or schoolgirls on the game or – in one block – rumours of a black guy who was dealing huge quantities of stolen amphetamine. Yet when I knocked on the relevant door, or ambushed a particular indivi-dual in the lift, I got nothing but silence or a shake of the head. However hard I earbashed them, these people just didn't want to know. They were, I told myself, totally alienated, totally out of it. In the spirit of our final year project, society had let them go and this was the result.

Happy that I was on track, I abandoned documentary and settled for actors and a script, threading a number of my precious storylines through the video, cutting the grainy black and white pictures to a track from my favourite Counting Crows album. The finished piece was wonderfully depressing, a sour cocktail of Nineties angst, exactly the kind of personal statement I wanted to put in front of my fellow cineastes. Already, I knew I was tipped for a First. When the summons to appear for a viva arrived, I looked the external examiner in the eye, warming up our encounter with my usual rant about the iniquities of capitalism. He listened with great courtesy, making the odd note, and when I finished by asking him what he felt about the piece, it was his turn to be direct.

'You've got a good eye for a shot and I like the music

very much,' he smiled. 'Maybe you should think about MTV.'

I got the First but what stuck in my mind was the line about MTV. Was he serious? Had I really condemned myself to an eternity of music videos? Was I kidding myself trying to carve out a career as the new Ken Loach? For three months, like a couple of thousand other media graduates, I wrote to every address I could find, enclosing my CV, pitching my ideas, begging for work. The main stream broadcasting companies didn't want to know. The smaller production houses mostly didn't answer. Even when I descended to the level of provincial advertising agencies, the replies were less than encouraging. I was beginning to think seriously about wedding videos when a letter arrived with a London NI postmark.

It came from a man called Brendan Quayle. He was one of the founding partners of Doubleact, a biggish London production company. He'd seen my letter and my CV and my eight outlines for various documentary series, and he wanted to meet me with a view to discussing a job. I read the letter twice then looked for my mother to share the good news. Our patience with each other was beginning to run out. Only the previous week she'd been making serious noises about secretarial work or trying to find a job where I could use what she termed 'my looks'.

My looks, incidentally, are nothing special, at least not according to the evidence I see in the mirror. My mouth is slightly crooked, giving my face a lop-sided look, my chest is unfashionably large, and I'd kill to be another couple of inches taller. Put these items together, and I totally fail to understand the effect I seem to have on men. They talk of my long blonde hair, and my 'Scandinavian' cheekbones and the sexy way I'm supposed to wave my hands about. One ex-boyfriend even likened me to a Victoria plum. I was, he said, 'ripe'.

Doubleact operated from a handsome three-storied house in Islington. I waited for forty minutes in a cubby hole on the ground floor, listening to the girl on the switchboard trying to cope with floods of incoming calls. Doubleact had made themselves a nice little corner in late-night entertainment. Most of their stuff went out on BBC2 or Channel Four, mildly anarchic quiz shows, fuelled by barbed wit and close-quarters nastiness. Their latest offering, *Don't Call Me Luvvie, Luvvie*, had been one of the surprise hits of the summer season. Guest actors slagged each other off for half an hour while the quizmaster drove the wagon forward at breakneck speed. It was news to me that Doubleact should be remotely interested in my sort of documentary work, but I certainly wasn't there to complain.

Brendan Quayle had an office on the top floor. Autumn sunshine flooded in through the big sash windows and he seemed to have angled the desk so that most of it landed on the huge pile of scripts beside his telephone. On the wall behind the desk he'd hung framed press ads for some of Doubleact's shows. *Luvvies* featured a blow-up of the best weekly audience figure, a big fat 5.6 million.

'I watched this.' He tossed me the video I'd sent. 'Twice.'

'And?'

'Crap.'

He was a freckled, lean, intense-looking man. He wore a pair of baggy cords and a rather nice collarless shirt. His sandy hair was beginning to thin and he looked knackered but there was mischief in his eyes and I liked that.

I looked down at the video in my lap. After my signed Van Morrison CD, my Bournemouth major project was the most precious thing in my life.

'Crap?' I inquired mildly.

'Yep. Every cliché in the book. Plus one or two I'd never seen before.'

'Isn't that a contradiction in terms? A cliché you've never seen before?'

He studied me a moment then conceded the point with a grin. Instinctively, I had the feeling I'd passed some kind of test. He rummaged in a drawer and produced my CV.

'I went through this, too. Impressive.'

'Thanks.'

'You liked it down in Bournemouth?'

'Sometimes. Half and half really.'

'What does that mean?'

I thought about the question, wondering whether he was serious. In the end I decided there was nothing wrong with the truth.

'It was OK,' I said. 'I had a good time, good mates, all that stuff, but I think we were a bit pleased with ourselves.'

'Socially?'

'Politically. We were all too lazy, too complacent, too . . . I dunno . . .' I frowned, trying to find the right word.

'Middle class?'

'Yes, and privileged. Hard times were when you couldn't find the mobile phone. You know what I'm saying?'

He put his head back, barking with laughter, then he

14

began to flick through the CV again. I'd sent a photo, too, paperclipped to the front page, but that seemed to have disappeared. His finger had stopped halfway down page two.

'Tell me about the Politics Society. How come you ended up President?'

'I wanted it,' I said simply. 'So I lobbied hard.'

'Big majority?'

'Best ever.'

'And did it live up to your expectations? Did you enjoy it?'

'Very much.'

'Get lots of the big guys down? For the debates?'

I nodded, naming half a dozen prominent politicians. Under my stewardship, the left had been more heavily represented than usual, a fact that seemed to amuse him.

'You feel comfortable in that kind of company?'

'Yes, very.'

'How about the Tories?'

'Loathsome. Pond life with ties.'

He smiled.

'Are you always this candid?'

'Yes.'

He pressed me for more names. I listed a couple of junior ministers who'd deigned to appear for our end-of-term thrash. One of them he evidently knew well.

'How did you get on?'

'We didn't.'

'Why not?'

For the second time, I wondered just how candid he wanted me to be. A couple of minutes' banter had altered my first impressions. Behind the seeming arrogance and the blunt one-liners, he was a good deal more perceptive than I'd thought. He also paid me the compliment of serious eye contact, something that few men – in my experience – will risk.

He still wanted to know about the junior minister.

'He was infantile,' I said, 'in every conceivable respect.'

'Like?'

'Like politically. Like socially. Like conversationally. Women belonged on a different planet. He was barely out of the egg.'

'Did he try it on?'

I raised an eyebrow, not bothering to suppress a laugh.

'Yes,' I said. 'Since you ask.'

'And?'

I looked away for a moment. The houses across the street were in deep shadow.

'We put these guys up for the night,' I said, 'if they really insist. There's a little private hotel we use. It isn't the Ritz but I don't think he was interested in room service.'

'So how did you handle it?'

'I told him to fuck off, politely of course.'

'And did he?'

'He had no choice.'

'Why not?'

I shook my head at last, refusing to go any further. It wasn't my job to fuel this inquisitive man's fantasies, though his Tory chum had been so legless that even a child could have fought him off.

Brendan was back in the CV again, his interest in my sex life evidently at an end.

'Windsurfing,' he mused. 'What does it take to get to the nationals?'

'Practice.'

'And?'

'More practice.'

'Are you always so forthcoming?'

'No, it's just . . .' I was still thinking about his previous line of questioning, '. . . how much do you really want to know?'

'I'm not sure.' The sudden grin transformed his face again. 'I've never tried it. It looks bloody wonderful and I always tell myself I'll have a go but somehow never get round to it. I need a bit of incentive, someone who knows what they're doing . . .'

He let the sentence trail away. I grinned back, playing dumb.

'It's like riding a bike,' I told him. 'You do it, and you do it, and you do it, and one day it just happens.'

'Just like that?'

'Yes. It's about balance. And confidence, too. You'd be fine.'

I began to warm to the subject, moving briskly through the stages that had taken me from novice to runner-up in the National Slalom. In this respect, Poole Harbour had been heaven-sent, God's gift to board-crazies like me.

Brendan had abandoned the CV and was leaning back in the chair, his hands behind his head, his feet on the desk. His eyes had an extraordinary frankness and he couldn't have made it plainer that he fancied me. I was telling him about a friend of mine, a serious contender for the Sydney Olympics, when he interrupted.

'We're doing a new series,' he said, 'and we're looking for a researcher.'

'A what?'

'A researcher. A fixer. A gofer. A meeter and greeter.' A languid hand indicated the *Luvvies* poster on the wall behind his right shoulder. 'It's a political version of that. Thought you might be interested.'

I heard myself stalling, playing for time, asking for more details. I'd come to London to change the face of social documentary. This man wanted me to tart around while politicians made fools of themselves. He was telling me about the meeting he'd just had with some commissioning executive. The working title for the new programme was *Members Only* and the people at the Beeb thought the concept was brilliant. Politicians would role-play their way through carefully scripted situations, each tailored to their particular foibles. The risks were pretty obvious but, politicians being what they were, they'd gamble anything for the exposure. The series, said Brendan, would roar away. The bloody thing couldn't fail.

'I'm not quite sure I . . .'

Brendan leaned forward across the desk.

'You can,' he said, 'I know you can.'

'But I'm not sure I want to.'

'Why not?' He had his hand out for the video. I gave it to him. 'This is OK, as far as it goes, but if you're serious, really serious, then you have to be around these guys, understand the way they work, what drives them, what keeps them at it.'

'Ego,' I said at once. 'And money.'

'Of course, of course.' He was smiling now, indulgent this time, the kindly uncle. 'But it doesn't end there, believe me. These guys are more complex than they seem and, like it or not, they matter.' He tapped the cassette. 'If you're really interested in change, in doing something, then you have to start at the top. You want to change the world? Fine. You think the guys we elect are a load of wankers? Terrific. But get to know them first.

Time spent in reconnaissance is seldom wasted. Rule number one.'

Listening to him, it occurred to me that we appeared to have swopped roles. He was pitching. I was playing hard to get.

'What about afterwards?' I said carefully.

'We do another series.'

'I meant me,' I nodded at the cassette. 'And all those ideas I sent you.'

Brendan looked at me for a long time. Then the smile was back.

'We'll see,' he said softly. 'But first things first, eh?'

Back home, in Petersfield, my mother was delighted. So delighted, she offered to pay for the van I'd need to hire to ship my stuff up to London. Thus far, I hadn't given much thought to where I might live, but once the Doubleact offer was in writing, I knew I had to get myself organised. The series was already in pre-production. Brendan Quayle was insisting I start no later than 1st November. Time was short.

I spent the best part of the next week in London, camping out on Nikki's living-room floor. Nikki was my best girlfriend. We'd been together down in Bournemouth and – lucky thing – she'd already got herself a job on a new fashion magazine. Her flat was over in Chiswick and I left every morning after breakfast, taking the tube to the Angel and schlepping from estate agent to estate agent, looking for a place to rent.

The first shock was financial. Down in Bournemouth, I'd been used to paying £150 a month for a room. Up here, that kind of money wouldn't buy me a bus shelter. By lunchtime on day one, my dreams of a studio flat in Islington had withered on the vine. They were certainly available, and some of them sounded really nice, but at £650 a month they were way past my limit. With my trusty *A–Z*, I began to work north, neighbourhood by neighbourhood, amazed at how slowly the rents came down. Even one-bedroomed flats in Stoke Newington would have stretched me to the limit. Finally, depressed by yet another afternoon of trudging round damp, badly converted bedsits, I phoned my mother. It might, I suggested, be cheaper to commute.

'Have you thought about buying?' she said at once.

'I can't.'

'Why not?'

'I haven't got the money. For the deposit.'

'How much would you need?'

I did the calculations. Up around Tottenham, only that day, I'd seen places going for £48,000.

'They normally ask for five per cent.' I said. 'That's £2,400.'

'When would you want it?'

'Now.'

My mother gave the proposition a moment or two's thought then told me the money was mine. I could pay her back on a monthly basis. We'd work the figures out later.

Next morning, newly bold, I was back in Tottenham Green. The streets off the High Road were full of 'For Sale' signs but most of the places looked grim. I was beginning to wonder whether I couldn't afford a bigger mortgage when – late in the afternoon – I found exactly what I'd been looking for.

The street was a cul-de-sac, a hundred metres or so from end to end. At the top was a major road; at the bottom, sealing the street off from the cemetery beyond, a pitted brick wall. Adjoining the brick wall, on the north side of the street, was an end-of-terrace house, two stories, with big square bays up and down. The foot or two of garden between the house and the front wall had been covered with crudely poured concrete, and the 'For Sale' board was sagging where someone had nicked the loop of wire securing it to the gatepost, but I liked the warm red colour of the bricks and the double bays were capped with a nice piece of stonework in the shape of a Dutch gable.

I stepped back into the road, consulting the details I'd picked up at the estate agents. The house had been subdivided into two flats and it was the bottom half that was for sale. The window frames needed a lick of paint, and the front door had seen better days but the road was unquestionably quiet and I liked very much the idea of being in a cul-de-sac. Best of all was the price. For a living room, two bedrooms, a kitchen and a bathroom, the agents were asking just £43,000.

I returned an hour and a half later with the key. Inside, while the woman from the estate agency did her best to secure a broken window catch at the back of the house, I prowled from room to room, my initial hunch confirmed. Like so many terrace houses, the property was bigger than it seemed, stretching back along a dark, narrow hall that smelled, very faintly, of disinfectant. The two bedrooms were a bit of a cheat, a crude subdivision of a once-larger room, but the kitchen was a good size and whoever had done the conversion had known a thing or two about bathroom suites. This one was in egg-yolk yellow, one of my all-time favourite colours, and it even boasted a bidet between the pedestal washbasin and the big scalloped bath. By the time the estate agent had finished wrestling with the window catch, I'd made up my mind.

'Yes,' I told her. 'Very definitely yes.'

We stepped out into the street and she locked the door

behind us. It was nearly dark by now but I could see a blur of little black faces behind the curtains in the house next door. One of them offered a shy wave. I waved back.

'Know anything about the neighbours?' I inquired.

The woman from the estate agency looked blank. She couldn't find her car keys.

'Nothing,' she said. 'Apparently there's some bloke up top but that's about the size of it.'

I nodded, another little query answered. Nice to have company, I thought, waving at the kids again and wondering vaguely about the man upstairs.

It took longer than I'd thought to move in. The mortgage people demanded a survey and the surveyor's insistence on various 'structural adjustments' took my mother's loan to £4,850 before 31 Napier Road was legally mine.

By now it was early December and I'd seen enough of the realities of mainstream television to make the prospect of my little hideaway all the more enticing. Doubleact had become a nightmare, a never-ending series of deadlines that seemed to stretch onwards and onwards into some infinite future. Not once at university had it occurred to me that broadcast television might be nothing more than an assembly line, a machine for turning bad ideas into fat profits, but the more people I talked to, the more I realised that this was exactly the way it was. I was working in a factory – exhaustion salted with moments of blind panic – and what made it worse was the fact that I'd finally recognised the logic behind Brendan Quayle's offer of a job. He'd always made it pretty plain that he badly wanted to shag me. That I could cope with, but what came as a surprise was the realisation that he was offering the same challenge to more or less anyone else who'd demean themselves by appearing on his wretched show. In part, poor sad man, he was using me as a kind of company come-on, a role for which three years at Bournemouth most definitely hadn't prepared me. Not that I had any intention of playing along.

I moved into Napier Road on a Saturday, the week before Christmas. We'd partied late on the Friday after a particularly boisterous recording and I'd spent the small hours fighting off a predatory staffer from Conservative Central Office. Because he was so much younger than the rest of them, he seemed to think that conferred special privileges and he'd raised the stakes to a weekend in New York *and* a chance to meet Michael Portillo before it dawned on him that my knickers were staying on. When I finally got out of his flat he was very drunk and very angry.

'Why the fuck not?' he shouted down the stairs. 'Why make it all so bloody personal?'

Next morning, I left for Petersfield at dawn, badly hungover. I was driving a hire van and had Nikki for company. My brother met us at the other end to help load one or two bits of the heavier stuff and by late morning we were bowling back up the A3, feeling a good deal better. The previous weekend I'd scrubbed the flat out, every single room, and one of the reasons for bringing so little furniture was my determination to strip the doors and sand the floorboards. In my mind's eye, by early spring, I'd be living in a little minimalist bubble, all varnished pine and fresh flowers, plotting anew my assault on the world of documentary film-making.

We got to Napier Road in the early afternoon. The heavens had opened and we sat in the van until the shower passed. I remember looking up at the house, wondering why the curtains were never pulled back in the bay window on the top floor. I'd heard someone moving in the top flat the previous weekend, and I'd toyed with going up there and introducing myself, but by the time I got round to it my new neighbour had evidently gone out because there was no answer at his door. Odd, I'd thought at the time, because we had a shared hallway and front door, and I'd heard nothing.

When the rain stopped, we began to unload the van, carting the cardboard boxes into the house and stacking them in the smaller of the two bedrooms. The house faced south-west. After midday, the front room was flooded with sunshine and this particular afternoon, the clouds gone and the van emptied, we sat on the floor demolishing cheese rolls and toasting the move with a bottle of Côte du Rhone I'd lifted from what my dad used to call his 'cellar'. Nikki and I were still arguing about my plans for rearranging the kitchen when, for the first time, I became aware of music overhead. It was exquisite, a piece of something classical, light, melodic, almost jaunty.

Nikki was listening too. She knows much more about music than I do.

'Flute,' she said. 'And I think it's the real thing.'

'What do you mean?'

'Someone's playing. It's not recorded.'

On cue, as if we'd been overheard, the playing stopped, then started again, picking up a particular phrase, repeating it in a different tempo, first quicker, then slower before returning to the original interpretation, busying along, a perfect musical echo of the way we happened to be feeling.

We were drinking the wine out of plastic picnic mugs, the only ones I could find. Nikki raised hers.

'Trust you,' she said. 'Most of us have to put up with head bangers and ghetto blasters.'

I grinned, touching mugs. Everything was slipping nicely into place. I don't think I'd felt so happy for years.

Nikki left late that night. We'd got the back bedroom into some kind of order and unpacked most of the cardboard boxes. I'd already hired a guy to put a couple of extra shelves up in the kitchen and we'd distributed my meagre collection of spices and pickle jars to add a bit of colour to the bare white walls. Tomorrow, Nikki would be back with her two cats. She was off to South Africa for six months on a fashion assignment and I'd volunteered to look after them while she was away. After putting up with me for nearly six weeks, it was the least I could do.

Way past midnight, I went to bed. Even with the few bits and pieces I'd brought up from Petersfield, the place already felt like home. Like a favourite old sweater, it fitted beautifully, snug and warm and unaccountably familiar, and I lay under the duvet, listening to the ticking of the central heating pipes, wondering just what I'd done to deserve such a perfect landfall. The second bedroom, I'd decided, would make an ideal study. I'd buy a flatpack desk, and line the walls with all the books I'd never had time to read at university, and if I played my cards right with Brendan, I was sure I could borrow one of the Doubleact laptops. At that point, with the door closed on the world, I could get down to some serious work, developing various documentary ideas, lashing together a raft of submissions that would float me away from the cesspit of late-night adult entertainment. I smiled, tallying the ideas in my head, getting them into some kind of order, and the last thing I remember before drifting off to sleep was the sound of the flute again, somewhere overhead, two notes only, the softest imaginable touch.

I awoke late, pulling on a pair of old tracksuit bottoms and a sweatshirt before filling the electric kettle in the kitchen. At the top of the road, by the bus stop, I'd noticed a newsagent's that was bound to sell milk and I was out of my flat and halfway down the communal hall before I registered the flowers. They were lying on the floor outside my door, a bunch of blue flag iris, beautifully wrapped, ribboned and bowed. I picked them up. There was a plain white card tucked inside. In purple italic script, it read 'Welcome Home'. I turned the card over. There was no name, just the message.

I looked upstairs, knowing they must have come from the flautist in the top flat. Only he had access to the hall. Anyone else would have needed to ring at the front door. I hesitated a moment. Should I go up there now? Introduce myself? Say thank you? Or should I leave it until later? Get myself showered and half-decent? I looked at the card again, struck by the rightness of the message. Home. How come he could echo my own thoughts so exactly? How come he *knew*? I grinned, not knowing the answer but recognising that little tingle of anticipatory excitement which occasionally signalled something special in my life.

Nikki came later with the cats, Pinot and Noir. We shut them in the kitchen with saucers of milk and a big fat mountain of boiled fish, and spent lunchtime in a pub in Stamford Hill. Afterwards, Nikki braced herself for a tearful parting from the cats then pushed off. By midafternoon I was alone again, buried in the Sunday papers, promising myself an evening with the sander. I'd make a real start on the floorboards. With luck, I could have the front room finished by Christmas.

I was halfway through an article on flamenco dancing when I heard a door closing overhead and the sound of footsteps on the stairs. By the time I got to the hall, he was standing by the front door, his back to me. He was wearing jeans and an old suede jacket and a nice pair of desert boots. His tousled hair was beginning to grey in exactly the way you'd associate with soulful flute music, and when he turned round, the low winter sunshine through the glass panes of the front door rimmed his face in gold.

I thanked him for the flowers and told him it was a lovely gesture. At first, I wondered whether he'd heard me but then he shrugged and made a loose, eloquent movement with his hand and said it was nothing.

'I hope you'll be happy here,' he murmured.

He had the door open now and with the sunshine pouring down the hall it was even harder to see his face but I thought I detected the remains of a bruise under his left eye, the flesh yellowed and purpled. I heard myself asking about milk deliveries, and which day of the week the dustmen called, anything to prolong the conversation. He gave me the name of a local dairy. He spoke softly, taking his time. An educated man, I thought, trying to guess at his age. Forty-five? Fifty?

'We were listening to you playing the flute yesterday,' I said. 'You play wonderfully.'

'We?'

I nodded, explaining about Nikki. She was my best friend. She was off to South Africa. I paused, expecting a comment. None came.

'Do you mind cats?' I asked him.

'Not at all.'

'You like them?'

'Very much.'

'Thank God for that.'

27

He looked at me with a quizzical smile, saying nothing. He had a big broad face and the fact that he hadn't shaved for several days gave it a strange depth. His eyes were slightly sunken, and his nose was a little bent, and I remember thinking it was the kind of face that belonged on the moodier book covers. It spoke of a life lived to the limits, of numberless experiences barely survived. It fascinated me.

I was telling him about Pinot and Noir, how much they meant to Nikki, what a responsibility I'd taken on.

'It'll work out,' he told me. 'I know it will.'

'How do you mean?'

'I can see it in your face. You have an aura, an affinity. The cats will know that. They'll sense it.'

Something in his voice snagged, just the tiniest tremor on the nerve ends, and I asked him what he meant, relieved when he explained about his own cats. He'd adopted two strays. They'd been old and fat and he'd spoiled them to death.

'Literally.' He frowned.

'You mean they died?'

'I'm afraid so.'

'Don't you miss them?'

'Sometimes.'

'Why don't you get a couple more?'

'Good idea.'

We looked at each other for a moment longer and then he stepped out into the sunshine and pulled the door shut behind him. The abruptness of his departure took me a bit by surprise and left me wondering whether, in some subtle way, I'd offended him. Maybe it was uncool to get so effusive about a bunch of flowers. Maybe they should have gone unacknowledged. I frowned, retreating back into my flat, and I went into the front room and stood in the bay window for a full minute, watching him walk to the top of the road. He walked slowly, with a great deliberation, his head bent. My father had been like that, for a year or so before he'd died, and I found myself revising my estimate of his age. Definitely fifty. Probably older. Nice, though, in that mysterious, rather enticing way that goes with the unexpected and the unusual.

Christmas came and went – I spent most of it with my mother – and over the next month or so my new neighbour and I saw less of each other than you'd probably imagine. For one thing, I'd become maniacally busy at work, filling in for another girl called Solange who'd got whiplash in a traffic accident and spent hours visiting some far-flung chiropractor. This, oddly enough, turned out to be a blessing. My computer skills are pretty good and the stuff they gave me – booking contracts and production schedules – got churned out quicker than usual with the result that I began to lose my bimbo image. The last thing that Brendan Quayle would ever do was take me seriously but there were a couple of occasions when yours truly dug him out of nasty corners and the little notes he took the trouble to send me afterwards seemed genuinely grateful.

With my usual insight, it had taken me the best part of my first month to realise that Brendan was in fact married to the other partner in the company, a savage blonde called Sandra Merricks, and the more I saw of her, the more I understood Brendan's incessant womanising. The extravagant plays he made for me, and for more or less anyone else in a skirt, were obviously pleas for help. How else could he survive a marriage to someone who'd long ago abandoned real life for the tyranny of the Sage spreadsheet?

We were friends enough by now for me occasionally to say yes to the constant invitations for meals or a drink, and over a bowl of noodles in mid-January he dropped his guard long enough for me to glimpse a little of the bewilderment that lay behind.

'When we go public,' he told me, 'I'll be worth nearly three million quid. I've done the sums. It's kosher. No bullshit. Three million quid.'

'So when does that happen?'

'It won't. Not if I've got anything to do with it.'

'Why not?'

'Because then we'd be together all the time. It would be like early retirement, only worse. Can you imagine?'

To be frank, I couldn't, and I told him so. It was a symptom of the kind of company Sandra Merricks ran that everyone, including her husband, put her in the same category as Saddam Hussein or bowel cancer.

'Wait for the three million,' I suggested. 'Then leave her.'

'It's not that simple.'

'Why not?'

He shook his head, refusing to elaborate, and for weeks afterwards, in those milliseconds when I wasn't doing anything else at Doubleact, I'd try and work out exactly what it was that she had on him. Was it great sex? Some amazing kink of his that only she could unfold? Or was it something altogether more prosaic? Like the fact that he was too terrified of reprisals to even contemplate digging the tunnel? Either way, bottom line, I didn't much care, and although the pressures at Doubleact were crippling there were parts of me – terrible confession – that were beginning to thrive on eighteen-hour days and a non-stop succession of crises that no one else seemed able to sort out.

Thus it was, for week after week, that I'd get back to Napier Road the wrong side of midnight only to disappear again for nine o'clock next morning. And thus it was that I began to depend on the dozens of little kindnesses that my neighbour upstairs extended to me.

By now, I knew his name. According to the post that landed on our shared mat every morning, he was a Mr G. Phillips. G. could have meant anything, of course, but the second time we met he introduced himself as Gilbert, extending a hand and offering the lightest touch of flesh on flesh. It was on this occasion that he suggested he might field my milk for me, an offer I was only too happy to accept. The milkman delivered daily, mid-morning, by which time I'd been bent over a Doubleact keyboard for several hours, but Gilbert retrieved my two pints from the doorstep, keeping it in his fridge upstairs, then leaving it outside my door an hour or so before I returned.

After the milk, he took it upon himself to do the odd bit of shopping – cat food especially – leaving me a list in the hall to which I'd add any little items I might be needing. We'd settle up afterwards, often days afterwards, and I took to inviting him in for coffee while I tried to find the right change. He was very easy to have around – polite, interested, gently amusing – and what I especially liked about him at this stage was the way he preserved the distance between us. Having a neighbour on top of you all the time can be a real pain but it seemed to me that Gilbert had a rare talent for discretion. Almost to the inch, he sensed the exact limits of the friendship we both wanted to establish. He never crowded me. He never intruded. Yet he was always there with those tiny delicate touches on the domestic tiller that can make so much difference. A new brand of Colombian coffee he'd spotted in the delicatessen. A flier for an antiques fair he thought might tickle my fancy. A warning not to bother shopping in Highbury when

Arsenal were playing at home. Little things, but so, so important.

The more we meshed our domestic routines in this way, the more intrigued I became about his background. It was the obvious things, really, like work, and money, and family, and friends. How did he make ends meet? How come he never seemed to have a job? How come no one seemed to visit at weekends? I put the questions in a disguised form one Saturday morning. We were drinking coffee in the front room after I'd hung a new pair of curtains.

'It must be hard getting work as a musician,' I mused. 'I know how tough the competition can be.'

'Work?' Gilbert savoured the word, as if it belonged to a language he didn't entirely understand.

'Yes. I thought you must play for a living.'

'No, not at all. In fact never.'

I waited for him to elaborate. When nothing happened, I tried another tack.

'Did you learn as a child? Were you taught, you know, properly?'

'Of course.'

'With a view to . . .' I shrugged, '. . . playing in an orchestra? Or a jazz band? Or by yourself, as a soloist?'

'By myself.' He nodded. 'Yes.'

There was a long silence. I'd noticed that this was a habit of his, pausing a conversation at a place that intrigued him, or made him think, or perhaps even puzzled him. He seemed totally unembarrassed by silence, and that I rather liked. After the clamour and madness of another week at Doubleact, silence was a godsend.

Finally, he asked whether his playing bothered me. I told him it didn't. On the contrary, I liked it very much.

'Even late at night? After you've got in?'

'Even then.'

'You don't mind?'

'Not at all.'

He was studying me carefully.

'Some people hate it,' he said. 'Your predecessor, for instance.'

'The man who used to live here?'

'Yes.'

'Did he . . .' I shrugged, '. . . . protest?'

'Worse than that.'

'You had words?'

'Worse still.'

I watched his long, bony fingers stray to his face, and I remembered the fading bruise I'd noticed when we first met.

'You're telling me he hit you?'

'Yes.'

He lowered his voice, describing the encounter. There'd been trouble before. The man used to hammer on his ceiling with the end of a billiard cue, the slightest noise, anything. Playing the flute had been the last straw. The attack, when it came, had been unprovoked. They'd met in the hall.

'Smack.'

Gilbert nodded, pale and wide-eyed, driving his fist into his open palm. Then he did it again, and his shoulders sagged at the memory, and his head went down, and for a moment I really thought he was crying. I moved closer to him, meaning to help, but he reached out, fending me off. Like this, vulnerable, he looked about twelve.

'I'm sorry,' I murmured. 'It must have been terrible.'

He nodded, his fingertips back on his face, tracing the ridge of bone beneath his eye.

'Did you go to the police?'

33

'I couldn't.'

'Why not?'

'He said . . .' he began to blink, then shook his head, '. . . he frightened me, Julie.'

He'd never used my name like that before. I patted his hand. It felt cold to the touch.

'It doesn't matter,' I told him. 'He's gone now.'

'And you really like the music?'

'Of course.'

He left shortly afterwards, and the music – when it came – was sweeter than ever.

My mother's birthday is February 4th. Spending it alone, after my father's death, would have been miserable and so my brother and I arranged a surprise weekend for her. My brother runs a pub on the Isle of Wight. On the Friday night, I arranged to take the train down to Petersfield. On the Saturday, mum and I would drive to Portsmouth and ship across to the island. On the Sunday, her birthday, we'd celebrate.

The only problem was what to do about the cats. My mother's allergic to them and my brother keeps a huge Alsatian. For most of the previous week I'd wondered about boarding them out while I was away but doing that seemed a shame, especially since they'd both finally settled in the flat. I was still no closer to a solution when I heard a tap on the door. It was Thursday morning. For once, thanks to a mid-series production lull, I didn't have to be at Doubleact until half past ten.

I opened the door. Gilbert was standing in the hall, holding a white paper sack. Some days he seemed more cheerful, more together, than usual. Today, he was radiant.

'It's called Science Diet,' he said.

I peered at the sack. Science Diet is hi-tech cat food. Gilbert had happened across the stuff at the local pet shop. I was to see what Pinot and Noir would make of it.

I thanked him, taking the sack. Then the obvious occurred to me.

'I'm going away this weekend. It's my mother's birthday.'

I told him about the arrangements, then mentioned the cats. If I gave him the keys to the flat, might he pop in and see they had enough to eat? Change their water? All that?

He nodded.

'Of course,' he said. 'Of course I will.'

The weekend, apart from the weather, was a huge success. My mother, who hates getting her feet wet, even deigned to pull on an old duffle coat and a pair of wellies and tramp the path across Tennyson Down to the Needles. By Sunday night, very late, I was back in London, glowing with fresh air and alcohol.

Next morning, early, I was on the bus to work. After the usual succession of crises, I returned to Napier Road, stopping at an off-licence to pick up a bottle of chilled Chablis. From what little I'd seen, the cats were in wonderful nick. I owed Gilbert, and maybe the Science Diet, a big thank you.

Gilbert was even quieter than usual. We sat in the kitchen with the bottle between us while I told him how my brother's kids had got together and bought their granny an enormous box of fudge. Their present, I'm convinced, had been the highspot of her weekend.

'She was speechless,' I said, 'for once.'

I picked up the bottle and emptied the remains into Gilbert's glass. I could tell from the slightly absent expression on his face that he hadn't been listening. He toyed with the glass, lifting it in a silent toast when I thanked him again for looking after the cats. I was saying something nonsensical about the Science Diet when – unusually – he interrupted. He'd produced my flat keys from the pocket of his jeans, laying them carefully beside my glass.

'I hope you don't mind,' he said matter-of-factly, 'but over the weekend, I slept in your bed.'

I stared at him, chilled to the bone, not believing what I'd just heard.

'You did what?'

'I slept in your bed.' He smiled reflectively. 'And it was lovely.'

I spent that night on a mattress on the floor in the front room, dreading the footsteps that might descend from the flat upstairs, trying to sort out exactly how I felt about Gilbert's little bombshell. At first, more in hope than expectation, I thought I must have misunderstood him, but after he'd commented on how nice and soft my pillows were, and what an unusual pattern I'd chosen for the bottom sheet, I knew he hadn't made it up. At the very least, he'd been poking around my bedroom, and that – in itself – was sinister enough.

Gilbert, on the other hand, seemed completely untroubled by what he'd done, as if it were utterly routine to borrow a stranger's bed, and the more I thought about it, the more inclined I was to give him the benefit of the doubt. We'd been alone together more times than I could count yet not once had he made a move on me. On the contrary, he'd been an absolutely model neighbour, kind, thoughtful, forever inquiring whether there was anything he could do to help. In these and so many other ways, he'd tucked me in and made me feel at home, and if the fault lay anywhere, then maybe it lay with me. I'd been over-friendly, over-trusting. I hadn't realised quite how ambiguous some of my gestures had been. In this light, giving him the keys to the flat might have seemed like an open invitation. Share my life. Make yourself comfortable. Help yourself to everything. Whatever.

Dawn found me back in my bedroom. I circled the bed, the way an animal might, sniffing the air, trying to spot clues. Clues to what? I didn't know. Slowly, I drew back the duvet and the top sheet, all too aware of my heart pumping away. This is where Gilbert said he'd slept. What had he been dreaming about? What might he have done? I bent low over the bed, hunting for evidence. The sheets smelled of me, or more properly of Givenchy, a Christmas present from my mother. Heartened, I slipped into the bed, pulling the duvet up to my chin, resolving to bury the incident. I'd no plans to go away again, not for a while at any rate. We'd just pretend that nothing had ever happened.

I awoke to the trill of the bedside alarm. Rearranging the pillows, I found the audio cassette. It was wrapped in exquisite purple paper. Once again, there was a ribbon and a bow. I looked at it, weighing it in my hand, wondering what on earth to do. However hard I might try and kid myself, Gilbert wasn't in the business of helping me erase history. He had indeed slept in my bed, and he'd left me a little present to prove it.

I listened to the cassette over a pot of tea in the kitchen. I kept the door closed and the volume low, instinctive precautions that made me doubly resentful. Already, Gilbert was turning me into a prisoner in my own flat. Was this the precious freedom I'd come to London to find?

The cassette, on first hearing, was gobbledegook. It featured Gilbert himself, and the moment I recognised his voice I braced myself for something ghastly, like a confession of undying love. Unconsciously, hunting for some explanation of his behaviour, I think I'd settled on the obvious. He didn't go out much. He was lonely. And so he'd fallen head over heels in love, not with me, not with the person I am, but with the idea of me. Upstairs, in that flat of his, he'd had far too much time to dress me up in whatever fantasy turned him on, and his occupation of my bed had been as close as he could get to the real thing. This interpretation, as crass as it was, at least had the merit of proposing an easy solution. In my experience, a passion like that is easy to deal with. You become very hearty, very boisterous, very straightforward. You busy around, and talk perhaps a little too loudly, and make it very plain that a schoolboy crush is no more significant than an attack of hiccoughs or a passing virus. These things are wholly natural. And like a cold in the head, they simply go away. No bad feelings. No harm done. Back to square one.

But Gilbert's cassette wasn't like that. Indeed, it wasn't personal at all except, that is, for the opening ten seconds or so. I'm including them here because I've got what he said to hand, scribbled on the back of a gas bill, one of the many souvenirs of my fourteen months in Napier Road. I wrote it down at the time, there at the kitchen table, mostly because the words might have made more sense on paper.

'It's important for us both that you understand,' Gilbert had begun, 'and it's important that you know you'll be safe. It won't happen, ever, and I guarantee that. Please believe me. We've got so much to lose.'

Lose? Safe? Us both? I mulled over the phrases, testing them this way and that, trying to squeeze out a little meaning, a little sense. The cassette, meanwhile, was still playing, Gilbert flagging a path I found almost impossible to follow. He'd plainly done an enormous amount of reading, an odd mix of current affairs, economic theory, and astrological speculation. He seemed completely on top of all the stuff that had always gone way over my head, and when I tell you it included the GATT agreement, the latest twists in Bosnia, the likelihood of an imminent collapse in global stock markets, and the trajectory of something called Shevelov's Comet, you'll maybe understand what I mean. By the end of the cassette, relieved, I'd even managed to force a smile. If we were really into pillow talk, surely a girl deserved better than this?

I took the cassette to work with me, uncertain what to do next. I'd made a couple of good friends at Doubleact and explaining the problem to others was a real temptation. Even Brendan, I thought, might have an idea or two about just how I should conduct this bizarre relationship, but the longer the day went on, the less inclined I was to share my news. It would be only too easy, I told myself, to turn Gilbert into some kind of sad nutter, to make him the week's office joke, young Julie's live-in loony. That, most emphatically, I didn't want. Until last night, Gilbert had been part of a world I'd managed to preserve from the attentions of the showbiz pack. He'd been, ironically enough, my sanity, a kind of sheet anchor that steadied my little boat. Just because he'd got himself into a state about trade agreements and the Bosnian Serbs was no reason to throw him to the wolves. Indeed, the harder I thought about it, the grosser the betrayal became. Gilbert had been kind to me. He obviously cared. We just needed to have a little chat, get one or two things in perspective. Then we could be friends again.

I got home earlier than usual that night. I'd developed a routine on my return and first stop was always the kitchen. During the day, the cats stayed indoors. They didn't need to use the sandtray by the fridge and by the time I appeared from work they'd be waiting by the back door, their little legs crossed, eager to get out in the garden. This particular night, though, the kitchen was empty. Puzzled, I searched the flat, hurrying from room to room, looking behind chairs, under the bed, wondering what might have happened. Within minutes, it was obvious that they weren't around. Somehow or other, they'd been let out.

The obvious culprit, of course, was Gilbert but this was a conclusion I tried very hard to resist. He'd given me the flat key back. If he'd got in again that could only mean he'd taken duplicate copies. Even the prospect of a break-in – some stranger off the street – was preferable to the thought of that.

I went out to the back garden, standing in the chilly half-darkness, knowing the cats must be out their somewhere but not having a clue why. After a while, still calling their names, I patrolled up and down my thin little oblong of grass, pausing from time to time, listening hard for that scrabbling noise – claws on wood – that would signal their return. I kept at it for ten minutes or so, willing them to return from the gloom, but when nothing happened I turned back to the house. As I did so, I caught a flicker of movement in one of the upstairs windows. I peered up, angry now, convinced I could see Gilbert's thin frame. He was standing several paces back from the window. He had something in his arms, something cat-shaped. He was looking down at me. And I swear he lifted a hand, giving me a little wave, before he turned away.

Thirty seconds later, angrier still, I was up at his door. I banged hard, waiting for a response. Nothing happened. I banged again, and then again. I called his name, then shouted it, only stopping when the sound of my voice came back to me. I stood there for a full minute, appalled. I like to think I'm extremely even-tempered. My friends tell me I have exceptionally low blood pressure. Yet here I was, semi-demented, wound up by some lunatic who – for whatever reason – had chosen to kidnap my best friend's cats.

I knocked again, more gently this time, then gave up. Back in the flat, I double-bolted the front door then sat in the front room for the best part of half an hour, wondering who to phone. What would I tell them? How could I explain? Overhead, I could hear footsteps pacing up and down. Gilbert often passed his time this way, always walking the same pattern, across first, then up and down. The footsteps were often accompanied by mumbling, and little yelps of pleasure or surprise, and to begin with this pantomime had amused me. It went so well with the image I had of the man: the gentle, introspective musician, the wandering solitary, with his furrowed brow and his endless silences and his mysteriously work-free life. The neighbourhood enigma, I wanted to think. So refreshing after the strutting black youths and sullen white faces that occupied the bulk of Tottenham Green.

Now, though, the footsteps had become infinitely more sinister. Nikki's cats were up there. A duplicate set of keys was up there. And just now I couldn't think of a single good reason why my oh-so-perfect neighbour wouldn't turn out to be as predatory and single-minded as the nightmare loners who made the front page of the *Sun*. I shivered at the thought, hearing him pace his exercise yard, then I retreated to the kitchen where I downed the remains of a half-bottle of whisky. By midnight, savagely drunk, I was lying in bed, staring up at the ceiling, searching yet again for an answer. Maybe

I should buy a blow-up mattress and decamp to Double-act. But if I did that, I thought grimly, I'd simply be swopping Gilbert's attentions for Brendan's. Either way, wouldn't it be nicer to be left alone?

Next morning, the cats were in the hall. I heard them when I went to fill the kettle. They were completely unharmed, happy even, and it was several seconds before I realised that their anti-flea collars had changed colour. Yesterday they'd been red. Now they were purple. I picked Pinot up, giving him a cuddle. Why swop collars? What was Gilbert trying to tell me?

At work, mercifully, there'd been another crisis. The next show we were due to record had been built around a prominent Tory politician, who'd resigned from the government when one of his mistresses went to the *News of the World* with a lurid tale about an abandoned love child. The politician's name was Morris Fair-weather. He was way out on the right wing of the party, an intimate friend of a couple of cabinet ministers, and what gave the story legs was yet another outbreak of Tory moralising on the sanctity of traditional family values.

Brendan summoned me to a council of war. Fair-weather had just announced he was refusing all further interviews including – catastrophically – his billed appearance on *Members Only*. A couple of the writers were in Brendan's office and one of them handed me a draft copy of the script. Most of the gags were hope-lessly predictable, schoolboy puns involving Fair-weather's member, but there were one or two deft touches, centred on our new backbencher's penchant for bananas dipped in yoghurt. Details of the latter had been passed to Doubleact by some hack on the *News of the World*, though Brendan wasn't saying how much he'd paid for the material.

'It's an exclusive,' he kept saying. 'They're holding this stuff back for next week. We'll be first on the street.'

I told Brendan he was fantasising, exactly the wrong thing to say. Deep down, I was beginning to suspect he was as committed and angry as I was, though serious money and a couple of double spreads in *TV International* had somewhat blunted his socialism.

He had Fairweather's address and phone number. He scribbled them both down and handed them across.

'Go and see him. Talk him round. If it's the fee, you can go up to £1200. If he wants it paid offshore, tell him it's no problem. Just get him here for the show.' He paused. 'If you do that, I'll be over the fucking moon.'

'Thanks.'

'I mean it. Salary bonus. Company T-shirt. And that's a promise.'

I gazed at him, grinning. Brendan's idea of a salary bonus would probably meet Fairweather's bar bills for a couple of hours but that wasn't the point. The point was that Gilbert, abruptly, was yesterday's news. For today, at least, I had something else to sort out.

Fairweather lived in a big house in Holland Park. When he came to the door, knotting the belt of a terrycloth dressing gown, he looked like a puppy someone had left out in the rain. He was short, fat, and spoke with a broad Lancashire accent.

'Julie? I'm in the shower. Make yourself at home.'

I'd phoned ahead. He'd said to come for coffee. It was nearly eleven o'clock. I sat on a huge sofa, watching a pair of goldfish circling a tank. Trapped, I thought, trying very hard not to dwell on Gilbert again. At length, a woman appeared at the door. She was my age, maybe younger. She was blonde and tousled. She looked gorgeous.

'Has he offered you coffee?'

I settled for black, no sugar. Fairweather reappeared, buttoning his shirt and tucking the bottoms into a pair of pinstripe trousers. He was immensely blunt and immensely friendly. He had ten minutes, and then he had to go. I glanced at the woman. With great good humour, she was trying to run a comb through his thin strands of greying hair and to my shame I began to think seriously about what they'd been up to for the previous hour or so. By now, I'd nearly finished my pitch about the programme: how important it was for us to deliver on last week's big on-screen promotion, how good an opportunity it would be for him to set the record straight.

'We've got five million punters waiting to hear your version,' I suggested, remembering a line of Brendan's. 'Surely that can't be bad?'

Fairweather was halfway through his second cup of coffee. With his jacket on, the transformation was complete, just another businessman hurrying to work. He kissed the woman and gave her a hug and then threw me a sharp look.

'What's it to you whether I say yes or not?' he asked.

The accent took some of the sting from the question but even so, its directness made me miss a beat or two. I was still flannelling about our precious audience profile when he cut in. He'd heard all this before. He had a doctorate in bullshit. What he really wanted to know about was me. How come someone so young, so freshfaced, so obviously *healthy*, was working with a bunch of drunken deadbeats like Doubleact?

I beamed. Freshfaced is a wonderful word. No one

had said that about me, ever. I just don't mix in that kind of company.

'Well?'

I opened my mouth then closed it again. I felt like one of his goldfish.   'It's a start,' I stammered. 'That's all.'

'You like it there?'

'No, if you want the truth.' I frowned. 'Actually, it's getting better. But no, the answer's still no.'

'And they've sent you round? To do the business?'

'Yes, that's my job.'

'Good.' He winked at me, before turning for the door. 'See you at the studio then.'

'You're coming?'

'Of course I bloody am.'

I heard him hurrying down the hall. The front door opened and closed and a shadow ducked into the BMW at the kerbside. Seconds later, he'd gone. I looked at the woman. She was piling the coffee cups onto a tray.

'Is he always like that?'

'Yes,' she laughed, 'ever since I can remember.'

I reached to take the tray, genuinely curious.

'How long's that?'

'Twenty-two years, almost to the day.' She looked up, laughing again when she saw the expression on my face. 'He's my dad, in case you were wondering. And you're right. He's a lunatic.'

When I got back to Doubleact, Brendan couldn't believe it. He'd just had a heavy session with his wife about budget over-runs and the news of Fairweather's defection had been the last straw. After two hours with the spreadsheet, he looked exhausted.

'He said yes? Just like that?'

'Yes,' I nodded.

'So what did it take?'

'Nothing.'

'*Nothing*? You mean he didn't want money? Didn't want . . . ?' He looked wildly around for something else of equal value. Not finding it, he settled for me. 'What did you promise him?'

'Nothing,' I repeated.

At this point, one of the Assistant Producers stuck his head round the door. There'd been a phone call. For me.

'Morris Fairweather,' he mouthed.

'What did he say?'

'He's talking dinner. Tonight. I said I thought you could make it.'

Brendan nodded vigorously.

'Definitely,' he said. 'She can definitely make it.'

The AP disappeared, leaving me and Brendan gazing at each other.

'I guess he's paying, as well,' he said brightly. 'Gets better and better, doesn't it?'

We had dinner at the Caprice. Unlike most politicians I'd met, Fairweather was genuinely comfortable with small talk. He'd made a fortune in estate agency during the Eighties boom and the money seemed to have freed him from the straitjacket of the Tory machine. He didn't care what the Whips thought. He was impervious to the lashing he was getting from the tabloid press. All that, he said, was for the birds. More unusually still, Fairweather seemed to have a real interest in the small print of other people's lives and after the second bottle of Montrachet, I found myself telling him about Gilbert.

When we'd finished at the Caprice, we went to a club he knew in Frith Street for coffees and brandies. There was a jazz quartet on a small, raised stage but we stayed at the bar, perched on stools, tucked into a corner. We were talking about Gilbert again. Fairweather wanted to know exactly what it was that alarmed me.

'His unpredictability,' I said. 'He does strange things. I know him and I don't know him.'

'Do you trust him?'

'I trust the Gilbert I know.' I corrected myself, 'Knew.'

'And now?'

I shrugged, fingering the huge balloon of brandy. Fairweather was still looking at me, still waiting for an answer.

'I don't think he's all there,' I volunteered at last, using a favourite phrase of my father's. 'There's definitely something odd about him, something missing. It wasn't anything I could put my finger on, not until the weekend anyway, but I recognise it now, definitely.'

'And does it frighten you?'

'Yes.'

'And you want advice?'

'Yes.'

'Then move. It's a free world. No one's keeping you there.'

I nodded, acknowledging the logic of what he was saying. Problem was, I didn't want to move. I liked the house. I liked living at the quiet end of a cul-de-sac. And I still liked Gilbert, as long as he behaved himself.

Fairweather was pressing me to do as he suggested. He was very black and white, a businessman for whom a personal fortune had solved more or less everything. Gilbert was someone I could live without. Moving house would simply delete him from my life.

'Well? Don't you think I'm right?'

I said I didn't know. He patted me benignly on the hand and told me I'd be crazy to do anything else. After another brandy, he called me a cab. I was home just after midnight. The cats were in the kitchen, waiting patiently beside the door.

Instead of a salary bonus, Brendan offered me a promotion. So far I'd been employed as a researcher, a catch-all job description that included more or less anything he chose to pass my way. As well as compiling background on the weekly guests, I'd been in and out of various video archives, looking for footage, tracking down stills, and checking out old stories, as well as finding time to speed-read the daily papers and make the odd phone call to the handful of political journalists who would, for a fee, mark our card.

This list of little errands, though trivial enough, had begun to give me a real feel for the way the political world worked, and the deeper I got into it all, the more naive I realised I'd been at university. Politicians weren't just corrupt. Some of them were bloody clever at it. This revelation gave me every incentive to dig deeper still and when Brendan hauled me into his office for a little chat about my infant career, I was wide open to offers.

'Guest researcher,' he repeated. 'Solange's got to have an operation.'

Solange was the girl who'd got her neck half-broken in a traffic shunt on the Hammersmith flyover. She'd been guest researcher on the series, and since the accident, I'd been picking up bits and pieces she couldn't manage. The guest researcher books the weekly invitees. The job involves lots of showbiz networking and high-powered chat to agents. Even politicians, you'd be amazed to know, have agents.

'You think I've got the experience?'

'No, but I know you'll pick it up. Agents are like most

human beings, only worse. Twice as nasty. Twice as ruthless. Twice as susceptible.'

'To what?'

'You'll love it.' He dismissed my query with a wave. 'It's all word of mouth, anyway. Your name gets around, your reputation, the deals you've done, all that stuff.'

'Deals?' I frowned, trying hard to think what he could possibly mean. He smiled back at me in that knowing way men have when they're not quite sure of their facts.

'You're telling me Fairweather's coming in for nothing?' he inquired archly.

'Absolutely.'

'Good dinner, was it?'

'Lovely. And good company, too.'

Brendan looked at me for a moment or two longer, toying with the temptation to take the conversation further, but I foreclosed on him. I wanted to know how long Solange would be away. I wanted to gauge how genuine this offer of his really was.

'Months,' he said vaguely. 'She thinks early summer at the earliest.'

'So I'd be booking for the rest of the series?'

'Definitely.'

'And you'll get another researcher in to replace me?'

He looked at me again, that mischievous smile back on his face. By now, I'd been at Doubleact long enough to recognise what drove the company forward. Greed was pretty high up on the list, Brendan's and the bitch-queen Sandra's. The fewer paid hands at the pump, the more of the production budget slipped effortlessly into their pockets.

'We'll be looking at it,' he said lightly. 'Seeing how you get on.'

'Meaning yours truly does both jobs?'

'Meaning yours truly trusts me.'

The notion of trusting Brendan made me giggle. He looked briefly hurt.

'You don't want the job?'

'Of course I want the job. What I don't want is a heart attack, or a breakdown, or ending up in a traffic queue, not concentrating properly,' I smiled at him. 'Like Solange.'

Brendan sighed and stared out of the window and I knew what was coming next. Out there, he'd say, are ten squillion bright young things, hurting, yes *hurting*, to get into television. Ten minutes on the phone, and he could have the pick of them. Double firsts. Treble firsts. Prizewinners. Sex queens. Wannabe film auteurs. All of them just aching for it. And yet here I was, just a couple of months in, being difficult about the prospect of an extra challenge or two. What was the matter with me? Why didn't I have the stamina for it? Where had my hunger gone?

'Six hundred and fifty,' he said instead. 'A week.'

I blinked. Currently, I was on £350. An extra three hundred quid was a lot of shopping.

'You're serious?'

'Yes.' He nodded. 'And we'll get another researcher, sooner or later.'

The last bit could have meant anything but to my shame I didn't give it a thought. Every girl has her price and Brendan had just named mine.

He was standing up now, one hand extended.

'Shake on it?'

'Deal.'

He held my hand a moment longer than necessary.

'One other thing.' No smile now. 'Can anyone ask you out to dinner, or do you have to be a Tory MP?'

*

I celebrated my promotion with a bottle of gin. I telephoned my mother, who was clueless about the small print but impressed by the money, and several friends, who reacted pretty much the same way. It was nearly ten o'clock before I'd finished boasting and I was looking at the bottle, wondering how I'd sunk so much Gordons, when I heard the ring at the street door.

It was Gilbert. His hair was matted from the rain and his thin coat hung wetly on his gaunt frame. He was carrying a grey, oblong box with a handle. The box looked about the right size for his flute.

'You've been playing,' I said brightly. 'Come in.'

He stared at me for a moment. His other hand was in his jeans pocket, still rummaging for something.

'I can't find them,' he said at last. 'I definitely had them earlier.'

'Keys?'

'Yes.'

I stood back, holding the front door open, letting him in. On impulse, as he headed for the stairs, I called him back. I was having a little celebration. Would he like a gin and tonic? He stopped at once, curiously obedient, and when he turned round and I saw the expression on his face it was suddenly clear to me what I should do. This man was a child. He needed direction. He needed reassurance. I should have known all along.

'Come on,' I said, 'it won't do you any harm.'

In the kitchen, I made him take his coat off. I hung it on the back of the door, spreading yesterday's copy of the *Guardian* to catch the drips. Gilbert had sunk onto one of the kitchen chairs. His hands were blue with cold but he looked cheerful enough and when I asked him again about the flute he said yes, he'd been playing in a little restaurant down in Stoke Newington, a newly opened place called Colcannon's that specialised in Irish cuisine.

'Your idea,' he said.

'Mine?'

'Yes, you told me I should do it professionally. In fact you insisted. You said it was really important. So I thought, why not?'

He told me how nervous he'd been. He'd read about the restaurant in the paper but it had taken him days to muster the courage even to lift the phone. The woman at the other end had been nice enough though, and he'd played for free that first night, a kind of voluntary audition.

'And you're going back?'

'Maybe.'

'Why only maybe?'

'I don't know. I'll see how I feel.'

'Does she want you back?'

'Yes,' he nodded vigorously. 'Oh, yes.'

He seemed pleased, knotting his hands together, and watching him I was glad I'd let the conversation develop, determined not to interpret what he'd said as any kind of threat. Of course I hadn't insisted he get a job. Why should I? But perhaps this pretence of his that I had was his way of saying sorry. He'd intruded. He'd overstepped the mark. And now he was trying to make amends.

I fetched him a glass, splashing in more gin than I'd intended, and he pre-empted my next question by opening his instrument case and taking out the flute. The jig he played me was unusual, a jauntiness suffused with something altogether more plaintive, and the end result was one of those long silences it's difficult to break. At length, he asked me about the cassette. Had I listened to it? Did I understand?

I studied him a moment, remembering the face on the stairs, the glimpse I thought I'd had of the real Gilbert. Children, above all, prefer the truth.

'It puzzled me,' I said. 'And it disturbed me as well.'

'You didn't follow it?'

'It's not that. It's the fact that you left it in the first place. That you stayed here. While I was away.'

I watched my hand reaching for the gin bottle. I couldn't remember finishing my last glass. Gilbert was looking shamefaced. For a moment or two I thought he was going to apologise but he didn't. He still had the flute in his lap and he lifted it to his lips and blew a long, melancholic note.

'What does that mean?'

He shook his head, putting the flute down. Then, abruptly, he changed the subject. He was looking down at Pinot, sprawled at my feet.

'It's clever,' he said, 'how cats find their way to the fridge. It must be something to do with the frequency of the motor. They must sense it. Like bats, really.'

'That's another thing,' I said gently.

'What's another thing?

'Taking my cats like that.'

'I didn't take them. They came.'

'But you must have let them out, opened the door for them.'

'Of course.'

'Then you must have the keys.'

'Yes.' He was frowning now, still studying Pinot.

'You took copies of the keys?'

'Yes, I thought I mentioned it. I thought we talked about it.'

'Never.' I shook my head. 'Why should we? Why should I want you to have a copy of my keys?'

At this point, as if I'd touched a nerve, he suddenly looked up.

'The dark,' he said.

He left an hour and a half later, his gin and tonic barely touched, and as I shepherded him into our shared hall, I felt flooded with relief. It wouldn't, after all, be necessary to change the locks or bar the windows or supplement Pinor and Noir with a Rottweiler. Gilbert was a little simple, certainly, and a little mixed up about one or two things, but at heart he was still the man I thought I'd befriended, the gentle, considerate, neighbourly soul upstairs.

If he had a fault, I thought, then it was the instinct to be over-protective. He was concerned about the world. In fact he was terrified at the direction events were taking. Not just on planet Earth but way out in what I suspect he meant by 'The Dark'. The signs weren't good, he kept telling me. He read all the latest scientific magazines, and it was perfectly obvious that we were facing an impending catastrophe. Quite what he could do to protect me from this kind of disaster wasn't at all clear but listening to him trying to explain it, I had absolutely no doubt about his sincerity.

This man, poor soul, had suffered some kind of ghastly trauma. It had demolished more or less all the personal defences we take so much for granted and as a direct result he was convinced he was in tune with the future, a helpless savant cursed with a knowledge of the horrors to come. These horrors were numberless and beyond description but they were also in some strange way avoidable, and the fact that he counted me amongst those worth saving I took as a compliment.

I watched Gilbert until he disappeared into his flat

upstairs and later, lying in bed, I could hear him walking up and down again, mumbling to himself, patrolling the battlements he'd thrown up around our little house. At worst, I told myself, Gilbert was simply harmless. At best, once I'd learned to cope with his funny little ways, he'd be the perfect antidote to the infinitely less benign lunatics with whom I worked.

A couple of days later, Brendan cornered me on the stairs at Doubleact. He was more determined than ever to drag me out to dinner and my new promotion had given him fresh leverage.

'We need to discuss things,' he said. 'Away from the office.'

He left the choice of restaurant to me and out of curiosity I booked a table at Colcannon's, the place in Stoke Newington where Gilbert had performed. It was a Wednesday evening. Incoming fire at Doubleact had been light to non-existent all day and offhand I couldn't think of anything really pressing that Brendan and I could possibly have to talk about. The last thing I expected was an in-depth analysis of my documentary ideas.

'Are you serious?'

Brendan nodded. He said he'd been going through the stuff I'd sent up with my application and thought it was about time we kicked the odd proposal around. I was astonished and – to be truthful – a wee bit guilty. Just ten weeks ago, I'd had absolutely no doubts about what really mattered in television, promising myself regular evenings at the spare room desk, developing ideas, polishing submissions, plotting my assault on the world of social documentary. None of that, of course, had happened, partly through sheer pressure of work, but partly too because of the growing realisation that I'd chanced upon something that I was good at. I didn't want to spend a lifetime conjuring order out of chaos, and in the shape of people like Brendan I could see exactly where this kind of non-stop madness led, but just now – in mid-series – I was quietly pleased with my own performance. I'd survived. I'd won myself a decent promotion. And the fact that I hadn't even been to Texas or B&Q for the flatpack desk really said it all.

'Documentaries,' I mused. 'What brings this on?'

Brendan mumbled something about taking stock. The restaurant had a bare, unfurnished feel – quite at odds with what you might expect from a place serving Irish food – and the fact that we were virtually the only people there made us mildly self-conscious.

Brendan had lowered his voice to a whisper.

'You get to an age,' he was saying, 'when it isn't bloody funny any more.'

'Change the gags,' I suggested automatically. 'Change the writers.'

Brendan didn't react. He was looking hard at the table placing. His glass, for once, was untouched.

'I mean it, Jules,' he muttered at last. 'I'm in the shit.'

At this point I recognised, rather belatedly, just why he'd been so keen for us to talk. It wasn't about me and my documentary ideas at all. It wasn't even about *Members Only*, or any of the other half-dozen shows churning through the Doubleact production machine. It was about Brendan.

I touched his hand, a gesture of reassurance, and felt him give a little involuntary jump. Maybe the rumours are true, I thought. Maybe he's finally overdone the coke, or the vodka, and any of the other little treats that flag your path to the first million quid.

'What is it?' I asked as gently as I could.

He glanced up, almost furtive. He looked terrible, his face gaunt with exhaustion.

'You want a list?'

'Only if you're offering.'

'OK,' he shrugged. 'Let's start with you.'

I let him get it off his chest. He said he'd fallen in love with me. Right from day one. That's why I'd got the job. That's why I'd slipped so effortlessly into Doubleact. He'd noticed the photo, and he'd heard the voice behind my various submissions, and once I'd turned up in the flesh he was doomed.

He looked up, seeing the expression on my face, sensing my anger at this self-confessional drivel. Hadn't I won the job on merit? Because I was good? Because I deserved it? He stilled my protests, holding up both hands. That was exactly the problem, he said. I *had* been bloody good. I *was* bloody good. And the better I got, the more I got on top of the job, the worse it became.

'Worse?'

'For me. Loving you. Being in love.'

He went on and on, talking about the nights he'd had, not sleeping; the days he'd had, laying little ambushes for me around the office, making sure he got his hourly fix of glimpses, chance meetings, corridors, stairwells, even the fucking kitchen, for Chrissakes. I nodded, afloat on this torrent of self-revelation, wiser now about his obsession with Doubleact's jar of instant coffee. The stuff Sandra gave us was dreadful. Why would anyone want more than one cup a month? Why hadn't I wised up?

'Your desk's outside the kitchen,' he pointed out. 'I use the kitchen to see you, to watch you, to warm my hands at your fire. I know it's adolescent but that's just how fucking appalling it is.'

The bit about warming his hands at my fire made me want to laugh.

'Give it up then,' I suggested. 'Knock it on the head. Cold turkey. Jules Anonymous. I'll give you a phone number.' I was back in Doubleact mode. I couldn't help it. Pure self-defence.

With a little tight-lipped grimace, he mentioned Sandra. She'd noticed. He knew she'd noticed. Next thing, there'd be a confrontation, and that he very definitely couldn't deal with.

He looked up. I returned his gaze. I felt angry again. I didn't want to laugh any more.

'You want me to leave?'

'Christ no, anything but that.'

'What then? How can I help you? What can I suggest?'

He studied me for a long time.

'We could fuck,' he said uncertainly. 'We could fuck and it might be a disaster and then it would be OK again.'

'You'd like me to go to bed with you to have a bad time?'

'Yes. Sort of.'

'You're crazy. What kind of offer is that?'

'You're interested?'

'No.'

'But you understand what I'm trying to say? How bad it is?'

'No.'

He stared at me, not quite knowing where to take the conversation next, and I stared back, equally frustrated. He was obsessed with me.

'Maybe you really should try therapy,' I said slowly. 'People make jokes about it but it's helped friends of mine.'

'I'm in therapy.'

'You are?'

He nodded gravely, telling me about a woman he visited in Hampstead, how perceptive she was, how much she'd begun to help him, but then the waiter arrived and I seized the menu, glad of the interruption. With the greatest reluctance, Brendan turned his attention to the blackboard on the wall. I ordered a plate of sausage and mash and a side salad. While Brendan was still hunting for something to eat, I looked up at the waiter, asking whether he was on every evening. He nodded.

'What did you think of the guy with the flute?' I asked him. 'The one who was playing the other night?'

The waiter looked confused a moment, then shook his head.

'We've had no guy with a flute,' he said. 'The guv'nor prefers to stick with the CDs.'

The meal over, we took a mini-cab back to Napier Road. After three hours at the confessional, Brendan still had a lot to get off his chest and it was obvious that he wanted me to invite him in. I tried to make it equally obvious that it was time to say goodnight and he'd been pleading with me for a couple of minutes before the driver brought things to a head.

'You're up for ten quid,' he muttered. 'Do you want to go somewhere else, or not?'

Brendan was out of the car in seconds, fumbling with his wallet. I'd noticed before how well he responded to deadlines. As he turned towards the house, I took his place on the pavement. The driver was pocketing Brendan's tip.

'Come back in an hour,' I told him pointedly. 'That'll save the cost of the phone call.'

In the kitchen, I busied myself with coffee. Brendan, who'd eaten barely anything in the restaurant, had disappeared into the bathroom. I could hear him being over-emphatic with the loo-flush and the handbasin the way you do when you're trying to cover something up. When he came back into the kitchen, he was grinning, shiny-eyed.

'I apologise,' he said at once. 'I've been fucking silly.'

'Apologise for what?'

'Giving you all that bullshit in the restaurant. God knows what you must think. I'm your boss, for Christ's sake, and probably double your age.'

He took the coffee from my hand. His nose had started to run. I tore off a sheet of kitchen roll and passed it to him, and he eyed me for a moment or two, sniffing.

'You want some? I've got plenty.'

'No, thanks.'

'Never use it?'

'No.'

'Ever tried it?'

'No.'

'Don't think you might be missing out?'

I steered him towards a kitchen chair, sitting myself down at the other end of the table. Whatever else cocaine did for him, it certainly cheered him up. The maudlin depressive I'd just shared a meal with seemed to have disappeared. In his place, there was someone infinitely more self-confident.

On the shelf behind his head was the alarm clock I normally took to bed. It would be fifty minutes before the mini-cab returned so I decided to treat what remained of the evening like a research interview. Most men adore talking about themselves.

'Why Doubleact in the first place?' I asked him. 'How come you got involved?'

Brendan misinterpreted the question, although it took

60

me several seconds to realise he was talking about his marriage. It had been a challenge, he said. He'd done it on impulse, one of those things that feel right at the time, and to be fair the first couple of years had been pretty good.

'So what went wrong?'

'Sex.'

'What?'

'Sex. She lost the taste for it, didn't want it, too busy, too fucking preoccupied, and you know what happens then? You get a bit lonely, and maybe a bit reckless, a bit fuck-you-too, and you know what happens *then*?'

I shook my head, regretting I'd ever started the conversation. We should have stuck to his mid-life crisis and what his therapist thought about it all.

'Tell me,' I said. 'What happens then?'

Brendan had produced a little silver compact. He opened it. On one side was a mirror. On the other, nestling amongst the tiny polythene twists of coke, I counted three condoms. It was a pathetic piece of late-night theatre, at once crude and offensive, and I told him so. He looked at me in genuine bewilderment.

'I didn't mean it that way,' he said. 'Jesus, don't get me wrong.'

'What do you mean, then?'

'I mean that this is what happens. You go off the rails, you flail around. Sex, drugs . . .' he shrugged, '. . . crap quiz shows, it's all part of the same gig.'

'You're telling me it's your wife's fault? She doesn't understand you? Is that it?'

'That's part of it.'

'What else, then?'

'I dunno. Truly, Jules, I don't. All that stuff I was telling you, about you, about what I feel for you, want for you. I meant it, every little bit of it, mean it, present

61

tense. But it's a symptom, isn't it? It means I'm half crazy.' He paused. 'You want me to go? Just say.'

I poured myself another coffee. There were bits of Brendan that were undeniably attractive. Not the bits that he'd be proudest of – the fame, the profile, the money – but his occasional gaucheness, and odd glimpses of a kind of innocence that lay behind it. When he talked about his early career in documentaries – he'd started as a researcher on *World in Action* – I thought I detected a genuine wistfulness that those far-away days were over. He'd stayed with Granada for most of the Seventies, ending up as a Factuals Producer. He seemed to have been good at it. And he seemed to have really cared.

I settled at the table again, reaching for the sugar bowl. Brendan was telling me about *Members Only*. Apparently the BBC apparatchiks loved it.

'We'll get recommissioned,' he sniffed again. 'Definitely.'

'When do they make the decision?'

'It's made.'

I must have looked surprised. I was clueless when it came to the politics of television but the vibe in the *Members Only* production office wasn't that wonderful. The ratings had only recently begun to climb and one of the early reviews had described the series as 'stillborn'. The opening programmes had lacked bite. There was no genuine venom. We'd been too polite, too deferential, a raft of half-funny parlour games lashed together with nods and winks about the week's goings-on at Westminster. Brendan, with his proud talk of the ever-lengthening queue of politicians eager to clamber aboard, seemed to me to be confirming this.

'So how come the Beeb want us back so soon?' I asked.

'Because we're safe. Because we square the circle.'

'What circle?'

'The one they can never crack. They've got a problem with politicians and it's getting worse. Everyone hates them, everyone knows they're at it all the time, fingers in the till, backhanders wherever they can get them, mistresses in love nests, all that. Problem is, what do they do about it in programme terms?'

'Expose it,' I said at once. 'Use *Panorama*. Or *Newsnight*.'

'Of course,' he nodded. 'And that happens. But it's risky. Politicians have long memories. They don't take prisoners, either side. And when they hold the purse strings, licence-wise, it suddenly isn't simple any more.'

'Yes it is,' I insisted. 'You expose it.'

Brendan was looking at me the way he'd done in the restaurant, a great fondness in his eyes. I think he'd accepted by now that a fuck was out of the question but that still left him a number of other options. He could play at being my mentor, my guardian, my friend. The facts of life, after all, was a big, big phrase.

'You need to know how these things work,' he said gently. 'It's not as black and white as you might think.'

'Yes it is. Half the MPs we get on the show are corrupt. Small time, big time, it makes no difference. If we know it, if we can prove it, we should say it.'

'Ridicule's just as effective. They hate being laughed at.'

'I agree.'

'So what's the problem? There are dozens of ways of skinning the cat. Just because we don't happen to go for heavy documentary, does that—?'

'No, of course it doesn't. But that's just the point. We don't ridicule them. We invite them along and let them party. It's all so fucking good-natured, so matey. They come across like actors, only richer.'

'That's because they are actors.'

'No, they're not. They're politicians. They represent us. We trust them with our votes. Democracy? Parliament? The voice of the people? Remember all that?'

I broke off, embarrassed at my own passion, at the way it had tumbled out. We'd had exactly this argument in the office and a couple of us had concluded that there was precious little difference between *Luvvies* and *Members Only*. Both had been risk-free, another twenty-six minutes of late-night wallpaper that no one would ever remember. With actors, that didn't matter. With politicians, it most certainly did.

Brendan was miming applause. I ignored him. One minute he's itching to save the world, I thought bitterly. The next he's counting the money in the bank. One of these was the real Brendan Quayle and it didn't take too many light years to work out which.

'Who can blame you?' I said at last. 'You've got it cracked, you've made it, you can even kid yourself you've tried to make a difference, and *still* be rich. Nice work . . .' I offered him a cold smile, '. . . if you can get it.'

Brendan, chastened, was looking at the open compact and for a second or two I sensed how important it was for him to have someone forceful around. He liked to slip the leash, test the limits, but he liked discipline too. No wonder he'd ended up with someone like Sandra.

I got to my feet, newly businesslike, checking my watch.

'Listen,' I said, 'I'm not being rude but we ought to get one or two things straight.'

'Like what?'

'Like quite where we go from here.' I tried to soften my voice a little. 'You're my boss. I work for you. But we've got a problem, haven't we?'

Brendan shook his head.

'No,' he said, 'I've got a problem. But I've talked about it and you were nice enough to listen. For which, many thanks.'

'You mean that's it?' I was staring at him. 'You're better? You're cured?'

'Of course not, but it's not hole-in-the-wall any more. I'm not creeping around trying to hide it, disguise it, pretend it never happened.'

'You're right,' I said dryly. 'But is that enough?'

'For now, yes.'

'What does that mean?'

'It means I love you, and it means you're guest researcher on the show. I suggest we give it a month, see how it goes. Christ, you might be terrible. Who knows?'

I studied him while he got to his feet, saying nothing. Then I reached down for the compact. It closed with a snap.

'No chance,' I smiled at him. 'Terrible is the last thing I'll be.'

After Brendan had gone, I did a little dance around the kitchen and then demolished the last of the gin. Against the odds, a tacky evening had turned out OK. I'd resisted most of the obvious traps and might even have turned an obsession into the beginnings of a friendship. Best of all, I'd hung on to my new job on terms that were moderately honourable, and as long as I didn't trip over the small print, I saw no reason why I shouldn't go from strength to strength. Beyond guest researcher lay the jobs that really interested me – directing and producing – and I was still fantasising about the series that would take me to the BAFTA awards when I took one last gulp of Gordons, reached for the bedside light switch and drifted off to sleep.

I awoke to a noise. It was pitch black. I lay still, scarcely daring to breathe. I had a pounding headache and the moment I moved it got worse. After a second or two I could make out the shape of the door. The door was open. When I'd come to bed, and turned off the light, I thought the door had been closed. The noise again, the creak of a floorboard, someone moving, someone very close. Was I imagining this? Was it a nightmare? Too much Gordons?

My mouth was dry. I tried to swallow but nothing happened. By now, just, I could make out another shape, something solid, standing absolutely still. I closed my eyes, trying to will the shape away. Definitely a dream, I told myself, making a mental note to go easy on the booze. I opened my eyes again. The shape was still there, anything but spectral. Very slowly, my hand found the light switch. I had no choice. I couldn't just lie there. I had to find out.

The light flicked on and I screamed. Gilbert was standing at the foot of the bed. He had a blanket around his shoulders and a pair of pyjama bottoms on underneath. He stared down at me, motionless.

'Are you all right?'

I nodded, terrified.

'I'm fine.'

'He's gone?'

'Who?'

'Your friend?'

'Yes.' I swallowed hard. I wanted to throw up. 'Yes, he went hours ago.'

'And he didn't hurt you?'

'*Hurt* me?' I stared up at Gilbert, lost for words.

A smile ghosted across his face. Then he nodded twice and began to shuffle backwards towards the door, disappearing into the little hall outside. I heard my front door open and close. Half a minute later there were footsteps overhead, then the lilt of the flute, a reedy jig, celebratory, and the footsteps again, much louder this time, thudding in time to the music, round and round the room, directly over my bed. Gilbert dancing, I thought numbly, crawling out of bed and making it to the bathroom in time to vomit.

An hour later, I was still sitting in the front room, shrouded in the duvet, staring at the phone. I'd double bolted my front door, and wedged the sofa against the door that led to the hall, but no matter what I did the image of Gilbert hung before me. What had brought him downstairs like that? What right had he got to watch over my private life? To make assumptions about the people I chose to come home with? And what, most important of all, might he do next?

The more I thought about it, the more alarming it became. This lunatic, with his recorded messages about approaching doom, had become my self-appointed keeper. He was standing guard over me. He was watching the street outside. Christ, he might even be keeping a record of my movements, counting me in, logging me out. There was still no sign of violence, no definite physical threat, but he plainly had no qualms about trespass, about letting himself into my flat in the middle of the night and scaring me witless in the process.

I tried to calm myself, to tell myself that I was unharmed, untouched, just a bit shaken up, but the truth was that Gilbert had slipped a noose around my life and each time he stepped out of line and did something like this, the noose tightened. Where that might lead terrified me, but trying to work out what steps to take was far from easy.

Changing the locks was an obvious move and tomorrow I vowed to do just that. Phoning the police was another option, but the harder I thought about it, the less certain I became. Would they arrest him? Cart him off somewhere and lock him in a cell? Was that what I really wanted? I closed my eyes, trying to stop myself shivering, trying to imagine the inevitable scene, me trying to explain to some hard-faced cop that Gilbert was harmless really, just a bit odd, a bit funny. Where would that conversation take us? Would they really listen if I suggested they just had a little chat with my nocturnal visitor? Told him to behave himself? Told him to act normal?

I shook my head, knowing it was useless even attempting to explain. The one person who would have listened and would have understood was Nikki, but just now she was on the other side of the world, which left me pretty much on my own. I had other friends, of course – mates from university days, people from work, numbers I could phone – but inviting them into my claustrophobic little world, the on-off saga of me and Gilbert, wasn't a prospect I relished. They'd want to get involved. They'd batter me with advice and good intentions. And just now, all I wanted to do was stop thinking about it. If Gilbert was a headache, please God for a bottle of Nurofen.

Full-length on the sofa, huddled under the duvet, I drifted off to sleep. Dawn brought the cough of a car starting in the street outside. Upstairs, I could hear nothing and, after the car had gone, I shifted the sofa and began to creep around the flat, moving very stealthily, the way you might behave if you found yourself locked up with a wild animal. The image was all too apt and I thought about it while I waited for the kettle to boil. It wasn't Gilbert exactly, not the Gilbert I knew and trusted. It was someone else in there, someone I'd never met, wholly unpredictable, wholly strange, and wholly capable – as I now knew – of terrifying me. Who was this man who'd broken into my flat, and into my bedroom? Who was this man who'd stood by my bed knowing, yes *knowing*, the effect it would have on me? What was his name? And – more to the point – what on earth would he do next?

I went to work. Brendan, sweet irony, was practically invisible. No surprise meetings outside the cubby hole that served as a kitchen. No chance collisions on the staircase or in the corridor. Not a single phone call about something I might – just by chance – have forgotten to do. By midday, dizzy with exhaustion, I went up to his office. He was sitting behind his desk, Sandra at his shoulder. They were going through some budget or other. I stood in the open doorway, staring at them. I hadn't even bothered to confect an excuse for my visit.

Sandra was looking at me.

'Yes?'

I muttered something about one of next week's *Members Only* guests, turned and fled. I had to get on top of this. I knew I had. No one else would help me. No one could. It was down to me. My problem.

I took a cab home. In the hall, fumbling with the key, I looked up to see the message scrawled on my door. The message had been daubed in purple crayon. It read *'Sorry, sorry, sorry. Please change the locks.'* I stared at it a moment, relieved and angry at the same time. This wasn't crazy at all. This made sense. I ran up the stairs to Gilbert's flat. After knocking for the fourth time and calling his name, I gave up. Whether he was in there or not no longer bothered me. I knew exactly what I wanted to say and sooner or later I'd find the time and the place to say it.

Inside my flat, I went straight to the front room. I kept

the *Yellow Pages* beside the phone. I was still hunting for Locksmiths when it occurred to me for the second time in six hours that I wasn't alone. I looked up. Gilbert was sitting in the armchair in the corner. He was wearing jeans and an old sweater and his thin frame was folded into the chair in a position your average psychiatrist might term 'defensive'. His chin was down on his chest. His hands were clasped around his knees. He was watching me warily, like a child expecting the worst.

When my pulse had returned to normal I asked him for the duplicate key he must have used to get in.

'It's on the kitchen table.'

'Get it then.'

Gilbert did what he was told. Back in the armchair he settled himself again, waiting for the next question.

'How do I know you haven't taken another copy?'

'I haven't. I wouldn't. Not without asking.'

I nodded. *Yellow Pages* was still open on the floor and I was determined to phone a locksmith, no matter what Gilbert said. I began to talk about last night, how frightened I'd been, but Gilbert interrupted, one long finger pointing at the window.

'I called them,' he said. 'I called the people.'

'What people?'

'The taxi people.'

I stared at him, the first faint glimmer of logic beginning to appear. Gilbert had seen us in the mini-cab. He must indeed have been watching from his top window.

'And what did they say? The taxi people?'

'Nothing. They wouldn't tell me anything.'

'What did you want to know?'

'His name.'

'Why?'

Gilbert shook his head, refusing to answer. After I'd repeated the question to no effect I came at it another way.

'Who do you think he was?' I asked him.

'I don't know. Your boyfriend?' He shrugged. 'I don't know.'

'He's my boss.'

'Your boss?' He frowned.

'You don't believe me?'

'I don't know.'

'But why? Why does it matter who he is? And even if he is my boyfriend, what's that got to do with you?'

Gilbert was staring out of the window. The word hurt was invented to describe the expression on his face.

'He's my boss,' I repeated. 'And his name's Brendan.'

'Brendan.' He nodded, as if he liked the sound of the word. 'Brendan.'

The smile briefly warmed his face then it went away again. I still had the keys in my hand. I realised I was sweating.

'What would you have done if Brendan had stayed the night?' Gilbert thought about the question for a while and looking at his face it was extraordinary to watch it change and then change again as he struggled to come up with an answer. 'Well?'

Gilbert thought a bit more and then got to his feet. He seemed to have lost weight. His jeans hung loosely around his hips. He looked down at me and I fought the temptation to take the sting from this conversation and make friends again. Gilbert owed me, at the very least, an explanation.

'I didn't want to see you hurt,' he said.

'You were *protecting* me?'

'Yes.'

'By breaking in? In the middle of the night?'

'Yes, I think so.'

'You *think* so?'

I stared up at him. Dear God, if I wanted confirmation that Gilbert was out of his tree, then this was surely it. I'd asked him a straight question. He'd obliged with an answer that at least made sense. But with that last innocent phrase, he'd wrecked it all. I was dealing with a man who wasn't at all sure why he did things. Which made my date with the locksmith even more pressing.

Gilbert was standing by the door now. Time, I thought, for some straight talking.

'I could have you arrested,' I said, 'for what you did last night. I could go to the police and tell them what happened and they'd be round here like a shot. Tell them what you like and it wouldn't make any difference. You trespassed. You broke into my flat. You scared me really badly.' I paused. 'Do you want me to go to the police? Do you really want that to happen?'

Gilbert was shaking his head.

'No,' he whispered.

'But you understand why I might do it? Why anyone might?'

'Yes.'

I waited for him to say something else, increasingly exasperated. I wanted an apology. I wanted a promise that it wouldn't happen again. Failing that, I wanted – at the very least – an acknowledgement that what he'd done was completely unacceptable.

'Just tell me why,' I demanded at last. 'Tell me why you did it, what the point was. Don't you like me? Are you *trying* to frighten me? I've been a wreck all day because of you, because of what you did. It's crazy carrying on like that. It's a horrible thing to do. Don't you see that? Gilbert?' I tried to control myself, tried to keep my voice down, but failed utterly. 'Another thing,' I said. 'Why did you tell me lies about that restaurant the other night? Why did you say you'd been—'

The phone began to ring. We both looked at it, then I picked it up. I recognised the voice at once.

'Brendan,' I said flatly. 'Of course you're not interrupting anything.'

I listened while Brendan rattled through a list of items he wanted to discuss with me. The most important had to do with payment due to a Cabinet minister who'd appeared on one of last month's shows. He wanted the cheque made out to his wife. He made me write her name down. Only then did he inquire what I was doing at home.

I glanced up. Gilbert had disappeared.

'Spot of domestic bother,' I said as brightly as I could.

'Nothing serious, I hope?'

'Not yet.'

'OK, see you this afternoon.' He paused. 'About last night.'

'Yes?'

'I just wanted you to know I appreciated it. Very much.'

Brendan hung up and I took a deep breath, wondering what had happened to Gilbert. I circled the flat, wandering from room to room, dreading what I might find, but the only evidence he'd left was a rather tired bunch of chrysanthemums on the kitchen table. There was no note or card with them and for a moment I wondered whether they were for me. I was out in the hall, wondering whether or not to go up, when I heard the noise. It sounded, to be frank, slightly animal. Muffled as it was, it definitely signalled distress.

I made my way upstairs. Gilbert's door was closed. I

73

stood on the landing for a while, listening, trying to put the sounds together. Twice I called his name but there was no response. The sounds went away, then, more distinct, came a gulping noise and it all started again, unmistakable this time.

I listened for a moment or two longer then made my way downstairs, bewildered and a little guilty, wondering what on earth I'd done to make Gilbert cry.

The big idea for my next move in this strange game came several days later. Work, for once, was going brilliantly. Gilbert, all contrition, had reverted to the model neighbour. And Nikki phoned up from South Africa for a gossip. How were things panning out? How was I doing?

'Fine,' I said. 'How about you?'

She told me about her job. She was working in a fashion house in Cape Town and she'd come up with some promotional ideas that had taken her to Johannesburg for a week. There she'd met a young Afrikaans guy called Henrik and the prospects, in her phrase, were 'yummy'. Only after she'd given me the full story on their first night together did she inquire about life in N17. How was I getting on at the flat? Was Gilbert as interesting a prospect as he'd seemed? Was he still serenading me through the floorboards? I ducked most of these questions but when she persisted, scenting problems, I admitted that Gilbert and I had had one or two minor upsets. It was nothing much, I said, nothing too serious, and now we were the best of friends again. Only this morning, he'd volunteered to get me some more cat litter. Being Nikki, she pressed harder still and though I didn't end up by telling her everything, I did mention the bruise I'd seen on his face. To be frank, I said, I was worried about violence.

'Check it out then,' Nikki said at once.

'Check what out?'

'The bruise. The incident. Go and find the previous owner. He'd know. Bound to.'

It was a brilliant idea but it wasn't, of course, that easy. For one thing, the estate agents weren't keen on releasing his name and it was half a day before it occurred to me that my mother's solicitors, who'd acted for me in the sale, would have all the details in the transfer documents. Their offices were in Petersfield. The senior partner, an old friend of my mum's, dug out the relevant bits for me.

'Kevin Witcher,' he said. '10A Denman's Hill, Crouch End.'

It was Saturday before I made it to Crouch End. I had a phone number for Mr Witcher but when I tried it I got the unavailable signal so in the end there was no alternative to turning up on his doorstep. The more I thought about the idea, the keener I became, not least because – for once – I was taking the initiative. Gilbert had been making the running for far too long. My turn now.

Crouch End is only a couple of miles from Tottenham and I went over on the bus. I'd located Denman's Hill in the *A–Z*, and it was early afternoon when I stepped in through the gate of number 10 and rang the bell. The houses were similar to Napier Road – street after street of redbrick terraces – but the area felt more cared-for. Judging by the extravagant display of blooms in his window boxes, Mr Witcher knew a thing or two about geraniums.

When he came to the door, he was wearing a scarlet dressing gown. He was medium height, early forties. His hair was receding over an enormous head and his eyes were slightly bulbous, as if he had a problem with his thyroid. He wasn't, by any stretch of the imagination, good looking.

I was still explaining the reason for my visit when I noticed the plaster cast on his right arm. It was poking out of the sleeve of the dressing gown, and judging by the state of the plaster, the cast must have been on for a while.

'So what do you want from me?' he asked when I'd finished.

'Just a chat, that's all.'

'Now?'

'If you don't mind.'

He peered at me, uncertain. His toes were curling on the bare lino but there was a nice smell coming from somewhere inside and what little I could see of the hall looked more than interesting. How many people hang glass chandeliers in a shared entry?

With some reluctance, Witcher finally let me in. He led me through to the kitchen. It was neat, spotlessly clean, and extremely chintzy. Amongst the carefully arranged display of cups and saucers on the Welsh dresser was a line of thick ornamental candles, rich blues and reds.

I sat down in a rocking chair beneath a framed black and white poster for a Robert Mapplethorpe exhibition. That was an obvious clue, of course, but I was far too busy trying to put a name to the delicious smells from the casserole pot bubbling on the stove to take much notice.

'Does your wife do the cooking?'

Witcher was draping a cloth over a small mountain of chopped courgettes.

'I don't have a wife,' he said with a tiny frown of concentration.

It occurred to me then that he must be expecting company but he waved aside my apologies for disturbing his arrangements, turning down the gas under the casserole.

He offered me coffee from a cafetière and I said yes. The coffee was a bitter roast, absolutely delicious, but when I asked him where he'd got it, he ignored me. He was sitting at the little kitchen table, plucking at the sleeve of his dressing gown.

'Did he send you? You might as well say.'

'Did who send me?'

'Phillips.'

For a moment I wondered who Phillips was. Then I remembered the name on the envelopes that dropped on the mat for Gilbert.

'God no,' I said. 'He has no idea I'm here.'

'He doesn't have the address?'

'Not as far as I know.'

'And the new phone number?'

'I don't think so.'

Witcher nodded, and I was finally able to put a name to the expression on his face. He was anxious. In fact he was more than that. For some reason, I'd frightened him. Quite badly.

On the doorstep, I'd given him just a hint of the problems I was having with Gilbert. I'd also told him about the bruise I'd noticed, and about Gilbert's version of events. I'm no expert on violence between males but what I'd seen of Kevin Witcher made me wonder about the billiard cue.

'So what happened?' I ventured. 'Between the two of you?'

'I don't intend to talk about that.'

'Why not?'

'It's none of your business.'

'But was there some kind of fight?'

I mentioned Gilbert's black eye again but he shrugged, reaching for a long, thin, wooden ruler hanging from a hook on the wall. He rolled up his sleeve and inserted the ruler into the plaster cast, sawing back and forth.

'Itches,' he said briefly. 'All the damn time.'

I smiled, watching the ruler. He'd rolled up his sleeve and I could see the scrawled signatures mapping the surface of the cast. One of them, much bigger than the rest, was a phone number. 581 7201. I made a mental note.

'Have you had that thing on long?'

'Yes, too long.'

'Is the arm broken?'

'In three places.'

'How awful. Have you been off work?'

Once again, he didn't reply. He'd finished with the ruler now, the relief visible on his face.

'You're quite sure about Phillips?' he said. 'Not knowing?'

'Yes, as sure as I can be.' I paused to sip the coffee. 'Were you there long? Napier Road?'

'Five weeks.'

'Five *weeks*?'

'Yes. It wasn't . . .' he frowned, '. . . quite what I'd expected.'

'The flat?'

'Everything. The area, especially. I expect you've noticed.'

'Noticed what?'

'The blacks. The litter. The state of the place. It's disgusting. I'd no idea.' He frowned. 'Crouch End I find far more acceptable. Have you finished your coffee by any chance? Only I've a great deal to get on with.' He gestured towards the stove and I realised rather belatedly why it was that he'd invited me in. He needed to be

78

sure that Gilbert didn't know where he'd ended up after his five weeks in Napier Road. Now he had a sort of answer, our little chat was plainly at an end.

I stood up, thanking him for his time, and we were back in the hall before I had a chance to ask him the one question that really mattered.

'Did Mr Phillips ever do anything . . .' I shrugged, '. . . unusual?'

Witcher was standing by the front door. I thought, at first, that he was scowling. Only when he answered did I realise that he was attempting a smile.

'*Unusual*?' he said softly. 'Are you serious?'

I phoned the number on Witcher's plaster cast from a call box on Crouch End Hill. The number took a while to answer but when it did it turned out to be a pub. I could hear laughter in the background, and the clink of glasses, and the *ker-ching* of a cash register. Lost for what to say, I mentioned Kevin Witcher's name. I said I was phoning on his behalf. It was a lie, of course, but it seemed to do the trick with the woman at the other end.

'You'll want Frankie,' she said. 'He's busy just now. Call back later. He's off at half four.'

She put the phone down and I stood there in the call box for a good minute, wondering just how far I wanted to take this little adventure. I'd sensed that Witcher had a great deal to say about Gilbert, but it was equally obvious that he wouldn't be confiding in me. I'd done my best to establish that Gilbert and I weren't on the same team but I don't think he'd begun to believe me.

I glanced down at the number I'd scrawled on the palm of my hand and checked my watch. Twenty to three. I picked up the phone and dialled the number again. Mercifully, it was a male voice this time.

'Red Lion?' I asked.

'Queen's, love. Wrong pub.'

'That's the Queen's . . . ?'

'In The Broadway. Dunno a Red Lion.'

I thanked him and put the phone down. According to my *A–Z*, The Broadway was just up the road. I walked slowly in the sunshine, stopping to look in the knick-knack shops. I felt slightly light-headed, as if the power of decision had mysteriously deserted me. A chain of events was unfolding, I told myself, and I had no choice but to be tugged along in their wake. It was a strange feeling, not at all unpleasant, and I marvelled at my compliance. Normally, as you might have gathered, I like to seize life by the lapels and give it a shake or two. I'm not wild about surprises, or losing control. Gilbert, though, seemed to be changing me. Even in this small respect, he'd somehow got the upper hand.

The Queen's was cavernous, a big, high-ceilinged pub with fading curtains and worn upholstery. It was still busy for mid-afternoon and there was a heavy Irish contingent at the bar. They were obviously regulars, big-faced men with baggy jeans and wet eyes. It took me a while to sort out Frankie and I only spotted him for certain when I caught one of the Irish guys calling his name.

He was young, much younger than Witcher. He was wearing black leather trousers and a black shirt and I knew at once that he was gay. You could tell by the way the men treated him, protective, roughly affectionate, and you could tell as well that he didn't care. At the riper remarks, none of them hostile, he'd turn his back, and wiggle his bum, and then play dainty-dainty with his hands when he circled the bar to collect the empties.

I was sitting at a table in the corner when he came for my glass. I moved my bag to let him wipe the table. He did it with a certain deftness, the way a woman might,

80

and I thought at once of Witcher's kitchen, how neat it was, and how pretty.

According to the clock behind the bar, it was twenty past four.

'I'd like to buy you a drink,' I said. 'When you've finished.'

'You would?' Frankie had a lovely smile.

I nodded at the empty chair he'd just tidied into the table.

'Yes,' I said, giving him a £5 note, 'and bring another Pils for me.'

Frankie joined me ten minutes later. In contrast to Witcher, he was a story looking for a willing ear. By six o'clock, I knew where he lived, where he came from, the clubs he liked best for dancing, and the pubs he cruised when he was in the mood for a one-night stand. My only problem was shutting him up.

'There's a man called Keven Witcher,' I managed to say at last.

'Kev?' he nodded, ever eager. 'Yeah, I know Kev. Double vodkas and coke. No ice.'

'You know him well?'

'What do you mean?'

'Is he a friend of yours?'

'Might be, why?'

For the first time, I could feel Frankie touch the brake. There might, after all, be limits to this candour of his. He might even want to know my name.

I extended a hand across the table. I'd already decided to tell him more or less everything and three bottles of Pils confirmed what a wonderful decision that was. This could go on all evening, I thought. Maybe it will.

'Julie,' I said, 'Julie Emerson.'

He touched my hand, giving it a playful little squeeze. I told him about Gilbert, about the flat, and lastly about

81

my brief call at Denman's Hill. Nothing I said seemed to surprise Frankie in the least and I was beginning to wonder how much I really knew about life in Inner London, when Frankie beckoned me forward across the table. I'd been talking about Gilbert's bruise and the fight he'd evidently had with Witcher. Frankie was very theatrical. I could feel his breath on my ear.

'Kev and his candles,' he said. 'That was probably what triggered it.'

I remembered the line of candles on Kevin Witcher's Welsh dresser.

'How come?' I queried.

'Easy. Kev loves candles. The bigger the better, them scented sort preferably. It's a real treat, really lovely, really nice, but you've got to want it. He likes to light them afterwards and then he plays funny music – you know, classical stuff. Requiems. All sorts. Brilliant, if you're in the mood.'

I was lost. Frankie could see it in my eyes and it made him laugh, though not unkindly. I decided to start with the obvious.

'You see a lot of Kevin?'

'Most weeks, yeah.'

'You know he's had some kind of accident?'

'Of course, that's why he's been off work so long.'

He started to tell me about Witcher's job. It seemed he was a civil servant in Whitehall.

'But this accident,' I kept saying. 'What happened?'

Frankie was enjoying himself now, refusing to give me a straight answer. He'd sussed where I was coming from, what it was I really wanted to know, and he was determined to string the conversation out until either my patience gave out or we were both blind drunk. After six, at Frankie's insistence, I'd switched to shorts – vodka and coke, no ice – and now I sat back, sprawled in the chair, listening to Frankie's plans to launch himself into the world of film-making. This bit of the conversation was my own fault. I'd let slip what I did for a living, knowing at once it was a mistake. Frankie was bursting with ideas. He had access to a word processor. All he needed was a name, and an address, and he knew, he just *knew* that he'd be heading for the big time. The people he'd met. The stories he could tell. The strokes some guys would pull to get inside those amazing leather loons.

At last, gone nine, I managed to pin him down. The pub was a blur of bodies around us. The sheer volume of noise made ordinary conversation impossible.

'Kevin Witcher's arm,' I shouted. 'Who broke it?'

Frankie was blowing kisses at someone behind me. I grabbed his hand, hauling him towards me, repeating the question. Frankie frowned, the way you do when you've forgotten a detail or two.

'That bloke,' he said. 'The one you mentioned.'

'Gilbert?'

'Yeah, him.'

'*Gilbert* broke his arm?'

'Yeah,' he nodded vigorously. 'And the rest, too.'

We were listening to heavy metal now. I couldn't hear a thing.

'What rest?' I yelled.

Frankie's hands began to pat various parts of his body. I pulled him closer, my ear practically in his mouth.

'Plus his ribs,' he was saying, 'and his kidneys. And a couple of teeth. Kev told me about the X-rays. Real make-over. Geezer must have known what he was about.'

'*Gilbert*?' I shouted again.

'Yeah.'

'Gilbert beat him up?'

'Yeah.'

I collapsed back in my chair. I'm probably slow on the uptake but there wasn't enough vodka in the world to blanket the implications of what this boy was telling me. Gilbert, if I was to believe him, wasn't just mad but violent too. So violent, he'd put the previous occupant of 31 Napier Road in hospital.

A question occurred to me. Frankie was on his feet, swaying with the music, his arm round a blond youth with a pony tail. I beckoned him down. My time was nearly up.

'Why?' I mouthed.

'Why what?'

'Why did Gilbert do it?'

Frankie gazed at me for a moment and I saw the faraway look in his eye. Then he blinked.

'Kevin can be a dickhead,' he grinned. 'Candles aren't everyone's cup of tea.'

Candles? I woke up on Sunday morning with another blinding headache, half convinced I was back in Bournemouth. That last year, I'd lived in a bedsit about half a mile from the university. It was seedy in the extreme but I was passionately in love with a lecturer from the College of Art and Design and our snatched nights together blinded me to the damp-stained wallpaper and ever-dripping taps. He was married, of course, and it all ended in tears but there were Sunday mornings exactly like this when we'd wake up to find the duvet puddled with sunshine, and our mouths tasting of ashes, and we'd prove beyond doubt that no hangover on earth could survive a head-shattering orgasm and an hour or so of cosy oblivion afterwards.

That option, alas, was no longer on offer and by the time I'd found my dressing gown and inspected my pale face in the bathroom mirror I realised that one of the feelings I was trying to keep at bay was loneliness. The pub that night had been full of people who knew each other, laughed a lot, got pissed together. Why was I always too busy to have any of that?

The ding-dong of the front door chimes came an hour or so later. Three Nurofens and a pot of coffee had taken the edge off the headache but the rather bleak feeling that came with it was definitely in for the day. I opened the door to find Brendan standing in the sunshine. He was wearing a pair of shorts and a T-shirt. We were a week or so into early spring, but even so he was making a very brave fashion statement indeed.

'Borrowed it for the weekend. Thought you'd do the honours.'

He jerked a thumb over his shoulder. His Mercedes stood at the kerbside. Lashed to a brand new roofrack was a sailboard. I began to laugh.

'You want to go windsurfing? In February?'

'Yep. And I want you to teach me.'

'Today?'

'This morning.'

'Where?'

'Place called Jaywick,' he nodded at the Mercedes. 'An hour and a bit.'

It took me about a second and a half to say yes. I had a loose arrangement with a firm of locksmiths for a get-together after lunch but to be frank the thought of spending my precious Sunday trying to decide between a five-lever Chubb and whatever else they might recommend was infinitely depressing. Brendan was right. The sunshine was glorious. The day was still young. Real life could wait.

Jaywick was out on the Essex coast, a huddle of wooden chalets and rickety bungalows sheltering behind a long stretch of seawall. It was far too early in the year for visitors and we bumped along the empty, pot-holed roads, following signs for the beach. There was something so abandoned about the place, so makeshift and temporary, that it actually seemed attractive. Behind the broken, boarded-up windows, any number of people could be spinning out their lives, and I felt an enormous temptation to stop, and knock on a few doors, and inquire further. What did people do here? How on earth did they get by?

I tried to share these thoughts with Brendan but he was too busy being technical about the wind. He'd been on to the weather people that very morning, and according to the forecast we could expect a force 3-4 south-westerly, backing to north-west during the day. I'd spent most of the journey down trying to explain the importance of wind direction but Brendan isn't a natural listener and I don't think he'd picked very much of it up. In this respect, it had become very obvious, very quickly, that Brendan and windsurfing were made for each other. It would, he implied, be like more or less everything else in his life. In other words, a doddle.

The board, at least, was more or less OK, a Mistral Malibu, comfortably long, lots of flotation. When you start windsurfing, you need something solid to take your weight and the Malibu would certainly do that. Only later, when you've cracked it, can you start poncing around on those skimpy little short boards you see in the pages of the lifestyle mags.

We got changed in the lee of a row of beach huts. The wind felt stiffer than a 4 to me, and it was cold down by the water, but Brendan was undaunted. He'd borrowed a wetsuit from the owner of the Malibu and he stripped down to his bathers before struggling into it. Given his lifestyle, he had a nice body, surprisingly well-muscled, and his chest was dusted with freckles and little whorls of reddish hair.

He offered his back to me and I did up his zip while he peered out at the sheet of slate-grey water before us. He'd chosen Jaywick for his baptism on the recommendation of a friend of a friend. A reef of newly-dumped rocks formed a natural lagoon and the conditions were said to be ideal for novice work. Looking at the vicious little lop whipped up by the wind, I was far from convinced but the water in the lee of the rocks was much calmer and this is where we started.

The flip side of over-confidence is impatience, and within an hour Brendan had given up. Most people teach in stages, a slow, methodical process that should get you out on the water, enjoying yourself, within a couple of days. Stage one involves something called The Uphaul, getting your balance on the board, heaving the mast and sail out of the water, and then transferring your weight and your grip so that the thing begins to move. It isn't as easy as it sounds, and clambering back on the board after your umpteenth header can be knackering, as well as bad for morale. In Brendan's case, it was the latter that was the real problem, and the more irritated he became, the less care he took to get the details right.

It was, almost inevitably, my fault, an almost identical repetition of certain situations we'd been through at work.

'Why won't this fucking thing stay still?'

'Because you're not holding it right.'

'I did exactly what you said.'

'No, you didn't.'

'OK, you bloody do it.'

87

I did. I'd brought my winter competition wetsuit up to London in the vague hope that I might – one day – use it, and I backed the board into the shallows before angling the sail across the wind and launching into a perfect beach start. I hauled in as much as I dared, testing my weight against the wind, and once I was sure about the limits of the rig I took the board out into the rougher water, tracking back and forth across the lagoon.

The wind, as forecast, was beginning to shift and stiffen a little, and within minutes the last residues of my headache had gone completely and I was back in an element I understood far more thoroughly than either London or television. Out where the finger of rock curled to a point, the tide was ebbing fast and it was here that I was really able to put Brendan's board through the whole repertoire, gybing and counter-gybing, exultant that the skills I'd worked so hard to master hadn't left me.

Once or twice, showing off, I planed back towards the beach, risking extravagant carve-gybes, wondering whether to bother stopping to make adjustments to the sail. The battens hadn't been rigged properly, my own fault for not checking, but I was only looking at a tiny percentage improvement and while I was enjoying myself so much, it hardly seemed worth the effort. What was especially pleasing was the camera that had appeared in Brendan's hands. He was sitting on the beach, huddled in my tracksuit top, steadying the long telephoto lens on his knees. I was beginning to wonder whether he hadn't engineered the whole expedition to grab the odd snap when I heard the jet skis.

There were two of them, identical youths on board, crop-haired, rubber-suited, mad. They must have launched further along the beach. They came roaring into the lagoon in line abreast, clearly intent on mischief.

I was on a broad reach at this point, flat out across the wind, and they parted to let me through then hauled the jet skis round with wild whoops of glee, the water fountaining behind them. I braced to hit the twin wakes, and I felt the board lift beneath my feet, light as a feather. Stable again, I gybed hard, meaning to head back towards the beach. I'd no taste for games like this. With the lagoon to myself, the sail had been perfect. That was the memory I wanted to keep.

Back on a broad reach, shorebound this time, I picked up speed. The first jet ski came from my right, narrowly missing me. The second one I didn't even see. The impact must have knocked me out because I was face down in the water when consciousness returned, my lungs beginning to fill with water. Dimly, I felt a pair of hands hauling me out. I tried to cough. Nothing happened. Someone was hitting me on the back. Hard. Then a voice I didn't recognise, a flat, ugly, London accent. In situations like these, oddly enough, you recognise fear. Not mine. His.

'Get her out, mate, get her out, she's fucking drowning.'

More hands. More shouting. Then the scrape of sand beneath my feet. I was being dragged up the beach. I could hear a third voice, Brendan's. Soon, I knew, I'd start to choke.

'You,' I heard him snarl. 'Don't just stand there. Fuck off and get an ambulance.'

'Steady mate.'

'Just do what I say.'

I felt myself being half-lifted, half-rolled, then a hand at my jaw and a voice in my ear. It sounded so warm, so close.

'You're OK, Jules, you're gonna be OK.'

A mouth over mine, warm air in my lungs, the strangest sensation. I started to groan, then I turned my

head to one side, nauseous, the water frothing out of me.
I began to convulse, coughing and coughing. I felt strong
hands beneath my armpits, hauling me upright, ducking
my head.

'Is this the way you do it? Or have I got it wrong
again?'

It was Brendan's voice. He was making a joke. I
grinned feebly back. I was going to survive. I knew it.

We drove back in the late afternoon. I'd dissuaded the
ambulancemen from taking me to Colchester hospital
for a check-up but I was grateful for the brandies
Brendan had forced on me at a pub on Clacton seafront.
Sitting in the car, watching the A12 race past, I felt
sleepy and a bit sore but above all grateful. Brendan may
have flunked the windsurfing but when it had come to
saving my life he'd done just fine. He'd got me to dry
land. He'd sorted out the bastards on the jet skis. And
then, with a competence and authority I'd never
suspected, he'd done the full resus number.

We'd stopped at a roundabout. A question had been
intriguing me all day.

'So where's the wife?' I murmured.

Brendan aimed the Mercedes at a gap in the oncoming
traffic.

'Haven't a clue,' he said at last. 'I left her on Friday.'

That, of course, was ambiguous. It could have meant
anything and though I was grateful and – yes, a bit
surprised – my gratitude didn't extend to anything as
extravagant as the invitation to stay the night that
Brendan clearly felt he'd earned. Instead, I offered to
cook him a meal, wandering dozily round the kitchen,

throwing together a spaghetti bolognaise while he drove down to the off-licence in Lordship Lane for a couple of celebratory bottles of Rioja.

While he was away, I eyed the camera on the kitchen table. It was a top-of-the-range Minolta, one of the reasons he wasn't keen on leaving it in the car, and looking at it I thought again about the jet skis. What had happened out there on the lagoon already seemed like history. I'd never been that close to drowning before but I marvelled at the way my subconscious seemed to have tucked the incident away. Only six hours later, it seemed ghostlike and slightly unreal, like something I'd read about in the paper. Had that really been me on the beach? Half dead, gasping for air?

Brendan, when he came back, sensibly laid the subject to rest. He'd taken a couple of shots of the guys on the jet skis and he'd gone up the road and got the number of the 4-wheel they'd been driving. Neither had volunteered a name but the photos of the incident should be pretty conclusive and he planned to send the file to the local police. They'd doubtless be in touch, and they'd probably want a statement from both of us. When he decanted the Rioja and raised his glass the toast was to windsurfing. Mine, not his.

'You were sensational,' he said. 'Like something out of a movie.'

'What were you expecting?'

'I've no idea. I'd never really thought about it. Windsurfing?' he shrugged. 'Piece of piss. You just get on and off you go. Like riding a bike.'

'Really?'

'Yeah.' He nodded ruefully. 'Some fucking bike.'

He had the grace to laugh. Overhead, I could hear Gilbert softly running through a series of scales on his flute, and I thought briefly about my conversation with

Frankie in the Queen's. But that, like drowning, seemed to belong to another life. For now, all I wanted was to be warm, and cosy, and talked to.

Brendan was telling me about what had happened with Sandra. Apparently they'd had an enormous row because Brendan, for once, had answered back. The way he described it, this was a new development in their relationship, the result of advice from his therapist. She'd told him he needed to get back on terms with himself. He needed to stand tall, fight fire with fire. This is exactly what he'd done and Sandra had responded exactly the way his therapist had warned, by moving the goalposts.

The argument had begun over the loading of the dishwasher. Brendan, in Sandra's view, was far too cavalier. Brendan had duly raised the stakes and within minutes, inflamed, the issue was whether or not the marriage deserved to survive. In Sandra's view, it most certainly did, but emphatically on her terms. Brendan's line was a little more radical.

'I told her to stuff it. I said I'd had enough.'

'Enough of what?'

'Enough of everything. Enough of her going on all the time. She's a fascist, Jules, an absolute nightmare to live with.' He nodded. 'And she's obsessed, too.'

'By what?'

'Money. How we can save it. Why we need more of it. How we can chisel out an extra quid or two. Jesus, it's not like we're broke, Jules, believe me.'

'I do.'

'Quite.' He nodded. 'You should try it some day.'

'Wealth?'

'Marriage.'

'No, thanks.'

He looked at me over the rim of his glass. He'd never

been the slightest bit interested in the small print of my love life but now was obviously the time to start. I tried to let the invitation pass, but he wasn't having it.

'How about you?'

I shrugged. A mouthful or two of Rioja had begun to detach my brain from the rest of me. I heard myself talking about university, about my lecturer friend, and about where – in my wildest moments – I'd thought the relationship might lead. I didn't spare him any of the details, a candour I put down to delayed shock.

By the time I'd finished, most of the first bottle had gone. Brendan was standing by the stove, stirring the bolognaise.

'You ever see him again?'

'Never.'

'Never tempted?'

'Of course. But that's not the point. The point is he ratted, bottled, call it whatever you like. It was there for the taking, what we had, what we'd built, but when it came to the crunch he preferred to go back to his wife. In my book you get one chance, and one chance only. We blew it.'

'We?'

'Yes, him and me. Had we been stronger, both of us, it would have happened, I know it would.'

'So how did you feel when he went?'

'Awful. I felt awful.'

I looked at him, wondering whether to add the bit about the malt whisky and the sleeping tablets, but I knew I had to draw the line somewhere. He was still my boss, for God's sake. Why should he give office space to someone who'd seriously toyed with ending it all?

Brendan slopped a little more wine into the bolognaise sauce.

'Did you blame yourself?'

'Mostly. He was the one who would have suffered.'

'How come?'

'By losing his wife and kids, by taking that great leap in the dark.' I bit my lip, hearing Harvey's voice. Even the night he left me, he made a beautiful job of it. 'He understood language,' I told Brendan. 'He understood how powerful it can be. He abused it, like he abused everything else, but he was a hard man to say no to.'

'I can tell.' Brendan was looking pensive. 'Did you love him?'

'Very much.'

'And do you still love him?'

I thought about the question. Brendan was playing therapist now but I was too drunk, and too tired to care.

'I love the idea of him,' I ventured at last. 'I love some of the times we had. I love what I thought we could become. But Harvey?' I shrugged. 'Probably not.'

Brendan was impressed. He'd even stopped stirring the sauce.

'That's fucking honest, if I may say so.'

'Thank you.'

'Not at all.' Brendan frowned. 'This Harvey, has he ever tried to get in touch?'

'Yes, lots of times.'

'Recently?'

'No, not since I've moved up here.'

'Why not?'

'He can't. He hasn't got the address. Or the phone number.'

'But what would happen if he did? Say he phoned? Say he suggested a drink? How would you cope with that?'

'I've no idea,' I said wearily. 'It's been a long time.'

'But you might say yes?'

94

'I doubt it.'

'Why?'

I frowned, trying to concentrate, trying to find the phrase that would bring this conversation to an end. Finally, I realised that the truth was all too simple.

'I don't want to get hurt any more.' I closed my eyes. 'So maybe I'll just stick to windsurfing.'

I heard Brendan's soft laugh.

'You think *that's* safe?'

'Safer.' I yawned. 'Definitely.'

Brendan left after we'd eaten. He didn't push his luck about staying the night and for that I was grateful. The moment I lay down in bed I slipped into a long, dreamless sleep and by the time I awoke it was ten o'clock in the morning. Hours late for work, I ran for the bus.

Mid-afternoon, my phone rang. It was Brendan. He sounded warm and cheerful, nothing like as hectic as usual. After he'd checked that I was OK, he said he'd forgotten his camera. He'd left it on the side in the kitchen. Could I bring it into work tomorrow?

I did what he asked. Two days later, we had lunch together at a bistro in Upper Street. He showed no signs of wanting to talk about his marriage and I didn't inquire further. After we'd resolved most of the morning's crises on *Members Only*, he produced one of those photographic print envelopes you get from Boots.

'Take a look.'

I began to open the envelope. His face gave nothing away. I emptied the prints onto the table. Every one of them was black. No beach. No windsurfer. No jet skis. No Julie. Just black.

I looked up.

'What happened?'

'I dunno.'

I frowned, examining one of the prints.

'Was it the camera?'

'No, I've checked it, ran another film through. Everything's fine.'

I thought of the lunatics on the jet skis, off the hook now. Might they have interfered somehow? Opened the camera? Exposed the film?

'Definitely not. I put the camera back in my bag. They never went near it.' He slipped the prints back into the envelope. 'I've phoned the labs. They had a guy look into it. They sent this across.'

From his pocket he produced the little canister that had once contained the roll of film. I picked it up. Kodak Gold. 24 exposure. Brendan reached out, revolving the canister until I could see the other side. He tapped the ASA rating.

'100,' he said.

'So?'

'I loaded 200.'

'You're sure?'

'Positive. The weather's too grim this time of year for 100. I never use it, never take the risk.'

'So what are you saying? They developed the wrong film?'

'Yeah,' he nodded. 'Though they say that's impossible. They swear they've been through the whole batch. Every fucking one.'

'So what else could it be?'

There was a long silence. The guys at the next table were awaiting Brendan's reply with some interest.

He leaned forward, lowering his voice.

'It was at your flat all day,' he said. 'Before you brought it in.'

'That's right.'

'In the kitchen?'

'Yes.'

'Does anyone . . .' he shrugged, '. . . have a key at all?'

Gilbert opened his door to my first knock. One way or another I was determined to get into his flat. He looked down at me, filling the space between the door and the jamb. Behind him, the hall was in darkness.

'I was wondering whether I could borrow your phone,' I said. 'Mine's on the blink.'

'Mine, too,' he said at once. 'Must be the line outside. Have you phoned the engineering people?'

I shook my head, amazed at how quickly he'd parried my first thrust. Of course I hadn't phoned the bloody engineers.

'Do you think I might try though?'

I stepped forward to push past him. He didn't move an inch.

'No,' he said simply.

I stared at him, trying to read the expression on his face, that pale mask that so seldom slipped. Had he been expecting me? This unannounced visit? This pathetic little pretext?

'You could try the phone box at the end of the road,' he was saying. 'They seem to work these days.'

'Of course.'

I turned to go, knowing that the mission was hopeless, but then my anger got the better of me. He was still standing in the half-opened doorway, still gazing down at me, expressionless, unfathomable.

'You've been in my flat again,' I said. 'And you've been playing around with a camera. I know you have. There's no point denying it.'

A smile ghosted across his face, barely perceptible, and I realised he liked seeing me angry. For some reason, God knows why, it turned him on.

'You're admitting it? You've got the film?'

The smile had gone now. He didn't move a muscle.

'Where is it?'

'It's not here.'

'But you had it?'

He didn't answer. I put the question again, telling him I'd go to the police, reminding him he risked arrest, telling him I was sick of it all. I'd tried very hard to be friends. I'd tried to understand him. I'd put up with all his silly games, his funny ways, because – despite everything – I still trusted him, still thought of him as a good person. But now it had gone beyond a joke. Now it was time for me to stop playing Ms Nice and change the locks and then put the flat on the market. I was serious. I'd had enough. I'd tried and I'd tried and I'd failed. Whatever relationship we'd had was gone. It was time to move out.

Gilbert followed every word, his head bowed, listening intently, the kind of concentration you bring to a conversation in a foreign language. I've done it myself in French street markets. You're determined to get every last detail. You want to be sure you understand.

Gilbert understood. I could tell by the way his head came up at the end, by the wild flicker of anxiety in his eyes.

'Well?' I said finally.

I could see him trying to reach for an answer but fail to put it into words. At last, he shook his head twice, very deliberate movements, exactly the way he'd nodded at me the night he'd stood at the foot of my bed in the darkness. Then he backed into his flat and closed the door.

Two days later, testing the deadlock on my new Chubb five-lever, I heard the softest footfall outside my front door. I waited for several minutes, not daring to move. When Gilbert's footsteps resumed in the flat above my head, back and forth, I at last opened the door. A big brown envelope lay on the hall carpet. It had my name on it. I recognised the handwriting from the shopping lists Gilbert still left out.

I opened the envelope in the kitchen. There were twenty-four blow-ups inside, big colour prints. All of them were impressive but two or three were truly outstanding, wonderful studies of the Malibu at full blast, the water feathering back from the board, yours truly horizontal, perfectly balanced, blonde hair streaming out in the wind. I held the prints up one by one, then looked for a note. At the bottom of the envelope, carefully folded, was a carbon copy of the order form Gilbert must have completed. I glanced at the details. In the box marked 'Number of Sets', he'd scribbled '2'.

I looked at the prints again, spread across the kitchen table. Including the copy of the order form was deliberate, it had to be. It meant that Gilbert had let himself into the flat, and found the camera, and swopped the film for a roll of his own. The latter he would have exposed – hence the black – but Brendan's roll he'd taken to be developed. The resulting pictures told the story of our day out at Jaywick, and he'd helped himself to a share of that extraordinary afternoon.

I picked slowly through the prints until I came to the ones with the jet skis. Brendan hadn't captured the moment of collision but there were before and after shots and it was slightly eerie to pore over a photograph of two burly youths in wetsuits bent over a shape in the water, knowing that the object of their curiosity was me.

I got up, reaching for the envelope, struck by another thought. How had Gilbert realised the significance of the camera? Why had he swopped the films? I sat down at the table again. A couple of months ago, like most girls my age, I'd had nothing more challenging to think about than a broken heart and zero job prospects. Now, I seemed to spend most of my waking hours trying to get inside the mind of a man who – at best – was seriously disturbed.

I looked up, peering at the ceiling, wondering just how Gilbert had known about the camera in the first place. The ceiling had been the first bit of the kitchen I'd decorated and as far as I could see the emulsion was intact. I cleared a space on the table and clambered up for a closer look. My new Habitat lampshade hung on a long flex from a central fitting. I moved it to one side, meaning to inspect the bit where the fitting met the ceiling itself, and as I did so I became aware of a small, irregular-shaped hole, about the size of a five-pence coin. The hole hadn't been there when I decorated, of that I was certain, and when I looked harder I saw that there was something inside it, catching the light. I bent for a chair, meaning to get closer still, but then I stopped, quite motionless, realising what it was that I'd just discovered.

An eye. Watching me.

Two

Tottenham Green police station is part of the complex of civic offices just north of Seven Sisters tube station. The taxi dropped me across the road. It was pouring with rain and I was dripping wet by the time I got inside.

The waiting area was nearly full. There was a counter at one end and the walls were plastered with posters. The one above the remaining empty seat featured a gloved hand reaching through a pane of broken glass. '*Beware of Uninvited Guests*', it read. '*Check Your Doors and Windows*'.

I waited nearly forty minutes for my turn at the counter, watching a succession of distraught locals tangling with the police bureaucracy. The one who took the longest was a bent old lady who'd lost her cat to a youth with an air rifle, and by the time she'd finished the desk officer had been joined by a younger man. This younger guy was in uniform as well and he beckoned me forward to the counter. I'm guessing but I'd say he was my age. He was big. He had broad shoulders, and short blond hair, and the coldest eyes I'd ever seen. All he needed at weekends, I remember thinking, was a big fat jet ski.

I'd half-rehearsed what I was going to say but the words came out in the wrong order.

'I've got a problem,' I told him. 'It's . . . I can't . . .' I looked wildly round. The waiting room was filling up again, and two youths nearby were watching me with interest. One of them had a newly stitched wound under his left eye.

'You want to come round the back?'

The young policeman was indicating a gap in the counter. I stepped through. A door led to the main part of the police station. At the end of a corridor, beside a drinks dispenser, he showed me into a small bare room with a table and three chairs.

I sat down. My Berghaus was dry now but my jeans were still soaking.

'You want to take that thing off?' He was nodding at the anorak. I was cold. I shook my head. None of this felt right.

The young guy searched round for a pad. The drawer in the desk made a hollow metallic clang as he pushed it shut.

'So what can we do you for?'

He was looking at me. I thought I detected a smile but I could easily have been wrong. I gave him my name and told him where I lived. Then I explained about Gilbert. Trying to be fair meant that the account took much longer than I'd intended. At the end of it, he got up and left the room. Outside, in the corridor, I could hear him feeding coins into the Automat. His face reappeared round the door.

'Sugar?'

I nodded. I was looking at his pad. Apart from my name and address he hadn't made a single note. He returned with the teas. He had huge hands and there was a tattoo of an eagle on one forearm. After he'd sat down, he toyed with his pen, watching me.

'You're saying you lent this guy your key?'

'Yes.'

'Wasn't very clever, was it?'

'I . . . we were friends. I'd no idea. Not then.'

'But six weeks? Isn't that a bit . . .' he tapped the pen softly on the edge of the table, '. . . swift?'

'Not really.'

'Are you always like that?'

'Like what?'

'So trusting?'

I reached for the tea. In truth, it was a question I'd often asked myself, but coming from this hard-eyed young man it sounded infinitely more menacing. Maybe he had a point. Maybe it was crazy taking people at face value.

Crazy?

'I think he's the mad one,' I said defensively. 'Don't you?'

'I'm not sure. I can think of saner things than lending a stranger my flat keys.'

'He wasn't a stranger. Not then.'

'So you say.'

'I mean it. There was nothing, no clues, nothing. It just seemed normal.'

'Sleeping in your bed?'

'Before. I meant before.'

'I know, I heard you.' He was fingering the empty pad. 'Look at it his way. He's living on top of you. It's all nice and cosy. You're letting him shop for you, run the odd errand, whatever. That's how relationships start, isn't it?'

'Of course.'

'So . . .' he shrugged, '. . . why the surprise?'

I stared at him, not quite believing what I'd heard. I'd come, with the greatest reluctance, to seek a little protection, a little redress, a little comfort. There were laws here that I thought could help me, anti-harassment laws, anti-stalker laws. Yet here I was, the tables turned, bringing accusations on myself. I'd been too forward. I'd led him on. Poor Gilbert.

'What about keeping the keys, though? What about

the cats? What about breaking in that night? Scaring me shitless?'

A smile this time, definitely.

'You've got evidence?'

'Evidence of what?'

'That it happened?'

For the second time in a minute, I thought I had trouble with my ears. Then my disbelief gave way to something a bit earthier.

'For God's sake,' I snapped. 'I'm not making this stuff up. The guy's crazy. He walks round and round, day and night. He makes holes in my ceiling. He watches me, listens to my conversations, keeps tabs on my friends. He's obsessed. It's bloody obvious.'

'Friends?'

'Yes, people who come round, visitors . . .' I loosened my jacket, exasperated, '. . . friends.'

'They've seen anything? These friends?'

His hand was hovering over the pad now, the pen uncapped. I thought about the question. Brendan? The odd mate from work? The occasional pal from university days? Had they had dealings, first hand, with Gilbert? Could they support my story?

'No,' I said uncertainly. 'It's just me really.'

'But what about the night you mentioned? The night he came down?'

'I was by myself, if that's what you're asking.'

'No one for company?'

'Absolutely not.'

'Maybe that's the answer then. Maybe you need protection.' He looked at me, newly thoughtful. 'It can be a problem, living alone, someone like you.'

He let the thought hang between us. I was beginning to feel uncomfortable and angry again, too. What right had this man to lecture me on the way I chose to live?

On how daft I was to rely on my own company? I'd come, after all, with a story to tell. If it hadn't, so far, produced the response I'd anticipated, then maybe that was my fault.

'He's violent, too,' I said. 'And I can prove it.'

'How?'

I told him what I knew about Witcher, the previous tenant, and how Gilbert had beaten him up. After I'd spelled Witcher's name, and given him the address on Denman's Hill, I waited for him to finish scribbling on the pad.

'You're telling me this Witcher bloke's gay?'

'Yes, apparently.'

'And he told you what happened? Getting beaten up? All that stuff?'

'No, he wouldn't.'

'Then how do you know it's true?'

I mentioned Frankie. The ballpoint slowed, then stopped.

'This guy Witcher didn't report the incident?'

'I don't think so.'

'He ended up in hospital and didn't say anything? Didn't contact us?'

'I don't know . . . I . . .'

The policeman stood up and left the room. Minutes later, he was back again.

'You're right,' he said briefly. 'His name's not on file.' He began to circle the room, hands in his pockets. I heard him stop behind me. 'This Frankie. You say he's gay, too?'

'Very.'

'And he has something going with Witcher?'

'Yes, that's the impression I got.'

'Pity.' He stepped into view and made himself comfortable on a corner of the desk. 'Straight, he might have been some use to us. The way it is, the evidence is tainted.'

'Because he's gay?'

'Because he's got something going with Witcher. The other fella, your fella . . .' He shrugged. 'Who's to say Frankie didn't do it? Where's the proof?'

I nodded, saying nothing, interested only in where this interview might lead. All this clever speculation left me cold. I wanted hard, practical things. I wanted someone up there, someone in a uniform to search Gilbert's flat, someone to find the other set of photos, someone to concentrate my poor mad neighbour's mind.

'Tell me what you're going to do,' I said bleakly. 'Only this is getting beyond a joke.'

He was on his feet again. He began to talk about some CID detective, a woman on the station called Gaynor who specialised in cases like these. She was back on shift tomorrow. I'd be interviewed again. She'd tell me the score. She knew everything worth knowing about stalkers.

Stalkers? I thought hard about the word. Even now it was difficult to associate Gilbert with the guys I'd read about in the papers.

My friend with the notepad was back behind the desk and for a moment or two I toyed with sharing this thought with him but he didn't give me the chance.

'What about tonight?' he said. 'Have you got somewhere to go?'

'Yes,' I lied at once. 'Why?'

'Just asking.' He checked the phone number I'd given him and then pocketed the notepad. 'Someone'll be in touch tomorrow.'

Outside the police station, it had stopped raining. I

stood at the kerbside, trying to decide what to do. This area of north London is generally hopeless for cabs and in the end I set off on foot. I'd been in the police station for nearly two hours but it was still barely nine o'clock.

I was in the High Road when I saw him. He was on the other side of the road, keeping pace with me, that distinctive walk, head bowed, shoulders slightly sagging. The moment I stopped and looked across the road he ducked into the doorway of a video store, his back turned. There were half a dozen or so people inside the store. I could see them through the metal grilles on the big plate glass windows. They gave me courage.

I crossed the road and tapped Gilbert on the shoulder. The back of his jacket was soaked. He must have been standing in the rain for ages. He turned round. His eyes seemed red and inflamed and I swear he'd been crying. Again.

'You know where I've been. You must do.'

He nodded, then wiped his nose with the back of his hand.

'You said you would,' he muttered.

'This is serious, Gilbert. I've been in there for over an hour, talking to them. I've told them everything. They know what you've been doing.'

He nodded again.

'It'll be OK,' he said hopelessly.

'It won't be OK, Gilbert. It won't be OK until you leave me alone; until you let me get on with my own life. Do you understand that?'

'Of course.'

'You'll leave me alone?'

'I've never touched you.'

'You have. You're doing it all the time, not physically maybe, but in other ways. That's not right, Gilbert, and it's against the law too.' I must have been more forceful

109

than I'd intended because Gilbert backed into the shop. I followed him, determined not to surrender the advantage. One or two heads turned, curious. 'The law,' I repeated. 'You're breaking the law.'

Trapped against a rack of Action Movies, Gilbert shook his head.

'Laws don't matter,' he said hotly. 'I'm here to protect you against all that.'

'*Protect* me?' I stared at him. Gilbert tried to push past me but I had him cornered. Close to, he smelled of damp and neglect. For one overpowering moment, I wanted to give him a good scrub and a bowl of something filling, and tuck him up in bed. Then I remembered the kitchen ceiling again. That same eye. Watching me.

'I'm not who you think I am,' I told him. 'I'm normal, and boring, just like everyone else. So let's just forget it.'

'Forget what?'

'Me. What's happened. Let's just go back to normal, back to the way we were before.' I smiled with what little hope I could muster. 'Yes?'

Gilbert gazed down at me for a while, not answering, then I felt his hand gripping my upper arm. To my surprise, he was immensely strong. By the time we were outside, he was hurting me.

'Let go,' I said.

He was walking fast. I had to half-run beside him. He was beginning to pant, little choking gasps. Couples strolling towards us made space in the middle of the pavement. No one intervened. They must have thought it was personal. If so, they were right.

'Let go,' I said again.

Gilbert was beginning to slow. We were close to a pedestrian crossing. He was mumbling to himself now, some phrase or other, over and over, punctuated by the rasp of his breathing. When I spotted a break in the traffic, I wrenched my arm free and bolted across the road. Safe on the other side, I ran as fast as I could. Beside the subway to Seven Sisters tube station, still trembling, I stopped and looked back. Gilbert had disappeared.

Brendan was inspecting the bruises on my upper arm, an almost perfect set of fingertips, purpled and angry.

'How did you know where to find me?'

'There was an address on that Boots envelope. The one you showed me at lunch the other day.'

'And you memorised it?'

'More or less.'

'Why?'

'Because I'm nosy.'

His new flat was a rented place, a spacious split-level basement in a pleasant Dalston square. All I'd seen on the Boots envelope was the name of the square, De Beauvoir. The flat itself I'd found by trial and error, circling the square until I'd spotted the Mercedes, then ringing the bell chimes until I found the right door. Seeing me standing there hadn't surprised him in the least. He was cooking, he'd said, and there was plenty for two.

Now, we were standing in the bathroom. Brendan filled the washbasin with ice-cold water, then bathed my upper arm. For the second time in less than a week, his expertise surprised me.

'How did it happen?' he asked at last.

I began to explain about Gilbert. Half an hour later, we were finishing the story in his lounge, me sprawled across his enormous sofa, Brendan sitting on the floor, his back propped against an armchair. Not once, to my astonishment, had he interrupted, a restraint I put down to a couple of enormous tumblers of Glenlivet.

'You think he's mad?'

'Yes.'

'And does he frighten you?'

'Yes,' I nodded. 'He does.'

'Because he's obsessed?'

'Because he's unpredictable. I don't think he can help himself. I don't want to see him locked up but I'm not sure there's an alternative.'

'But who locks him up?'

'God knows. The police? The Social Services? I've no idea. But he'd be better off locked up. I mean it.'

Brendan pulled a face and got to his feet. Out in the kitchen I could hear him opening and closing the oven door. When he came back, he had a sweater loosely knotted around his shoulders. He held out a hand. I took it and he hauled me to my feet.

'Where are we going?'

'Your place.'

I shook my head. The last thing I needed was Brendan trying to settle my account, another little outburst of violence to even the score. His earlier suggestion sounded nicer. I thought I could handle supper and a bottle of wine.

Brendan was grinning. Sometimes, I'd noticed, he could be truly intuitive.

'Don't worry,' he said. 'I just want to see those photies.'

Napier Road was in darkness when we got there, no sign of life from upstairs. I let Brendan into the flat and led him through to the kitchen. The photos were where I'd left them, littered over the table, and while I shuffled them into the envelope and let the cats out, Brendan did what I'd done, standing on the table and peering upwards. There's not a lot you can say about holes in the ceiling and we were back in the hall before Brendan voiced the obvious question.

'Do you want to stay here?'

'No.'

'You want to come back with me?'

'Please,' I looked at him. 'Is that OK?'

We took the short cut across to Dalston, Brendan threading the Mercedes through a warren of side streets. Somewhere in Stoke Newington, he reached out, turning down the volume on the CD.

'So what will you do?'

'I don't know.'

I was looking out of the window. Every passing shadow might have been Gilbert. I'd already told Brendan about going to the police. Now I mentioned the specialist detective, Gaynor. With luck, she was due to make contact next day.

'Then what?'

'I don't know,' I said again.

'Will they arrest him? Give him a warning?'

'I've no idea.'

'Say it's a warning, say they slap his wrists. If he's as crazy as he sounds, that'll make fuck-all difference. They might as well not bother.'

'Thanks.'

We exchanged looks. I genuinely think it was the first time he realised I was scared. Saying it, earlier, had been one thing. Now, in the car, he could see it for himself. His hand found mine and gave it a little squeeze. When he tried to withdraw it, I wouldn't let him.

Brendan turned out to be an inspired cook. We tucked into a wonderful Couscous Royale, blessed with a bottle and a half of Moroccan red. Although the flat was rented, Brendan had added one or two bits and pieces of his own, and while he was out in the kitchen, putting the finishing touches to a lavish fruit salad, I wandered around the lounge, trying to guess which fragments of his former life he'd managed to rescue from the bitch-queen.

One obvious souvenir was a glorious photograph of a bunch of guys standing knee-deep in snow beside a half-completed igloo. None of them had shaved for weeks and their beards were matted with ice and I was still trying to decide which one was Brendan when I felt him touch my arm. He told me that the photo had come from a documentary shoot in the Canadian Arctic. He'd been tasked to report on the devastating impact of welfare hand-outs on the luckless Eskimos and the assignment had gone way over schedule. Stranded in the back of beyond, Brendan had realised too late that he'd made the wrong film. The Eskimos weren't, in reality, the helpless, drunken castaways he'd been led to believe. On the contrary, they were still tough, still resourceful, still proud. Listening to him talk like this, I said that the Arctic seemed a long way from smart-arse metropolitan quiz shows and politicians on the make. He shrugged, telling me it was a long time ago, and I returned to the photo, not the least put off.

'So which one's you?'

'Third from the left,' he said. 'The good-looking bastard.'

We ate the fruit salad on the sofa while Brendan told me a little more about his days in documentary. It turned out that he'd done stuff all over the world, and he obviously had the awards to prove it, but to my shame I hadn't seen a single film of the dozens he mentioned. When I asked him whether he had dupes on cassette, he said yes but that bit of the conversation went no further and he certainly made no effort to offer me a look at any of them. There'd be no point, he said, because the memories he treasured weren't of the movies themselves but of their making – the locations he'd scouted, the people he'd met, the trials he'd endured trying to capture reality with a bolshie film crew and the usual logistic nightmares. These were problems I could talk about first-hand – my beloved council estate overlooking Southampton Water – and it was gone midnight before it occurred to either of us that there was still half a bowl of fruit salad to finish.

I was still spooning up the juice when Brendan produced the malt whisky again. The measures were as huge as ever, though by this time I was past caring.

'To sanity.' He grinned, raising his glass. 'Whatever the fuck that might be.'

He settled beside me on the sofa. We'd touched on his marriage throughout the evening, rueful asides, the odd dig at Sandra, but he'd shown no appetite for the full post-mortem which was just as well because I was in no mood to play the pathologist. What was beyond dispute was the fact that he'd left her, and that – just now – was quite enough for me.

'You're much too trusting,' he said suddenly. 'You know that?'

This, alas, was yesterday's news. My art college lecturer had told me more or less the same thing. Often.

'I know,' I admitted. 'I'm made that way.'

'It's not a criticism. You should just be careful, that's all.'

'Is that a warning? Should I take it personally?'

Brendan laughed softly. He'd propped the windsurfing blow-ups against the wall, like individual frames from a movie, and he was looking at them through half-closed eyes. I'm not as objective as I should be but they were really impressive, no question. He'd caught exactly the essence of the sport – its exhilaration, its raw excitement – and that isn't easy. To have been part of that – not just doing it, but having the moments frozen forever – was doubly wonderful and I told him so. He smiled, accepting the compliment, and then he put his tumbler on the carpet beside the sofa.

'It was a privilege,' he said softly, 'and I'd like to say thank you.'

I was still wearing the jeans I show up to work in. They have a buttoned fly. I felt his fingers tugging softly at the clasp on the belt and I reached out for him, cupping his face. He kissed the palms of my hands, one after the other, nuzzling the soft little pad inside the thumb, then he slipped off the sofa, kneeling before me on the carpet. I tensed a moment, not quite at ease, not quite decided, then I felt the gentlest pressure as he pushed me back.

'Hey,' he murmured. 'Relax.'

My jeans peeled off. Then he was running his tongue up the insides of my thighs. I wear very skimpy briefs. After a while I felt him nuzzling me, the lightest, deftest touch through the thin cotton. I was wet, and he knew it. I wanted him. Properly. My hands again, reaching out. His kisses again, telling me to wait, to be patient. The insides of my thighs, at the very top, have always been a very special place. Harvey, my ill-starred Bournemouth lover, once boasted that he could make me come just by looking at them. He never did, of course, but some nights – playing – he'd count to ten, like the anaesthetist, and if he'd done everything else right I'd never make it past five. Harvey was good, no question, but Brendan, I was beginning to suspect, was in a different league entirely. Palme d'Or. Cannes Film Festival. Standing ovation.

My briefs, don't ask me how, had gone. Scissors?

Smoke and mirrors? I didn't care. My legs spread, his fingers parted me, wider and wider. I felt myself swelling, and then my back began to arch, and I called out for him, all of him, but all I got was the lightest flick of his tongue, dancing and dancing, perfect control, perfect timing, and then a deep, deep surge, the big, big waves, my little board at sea again, abandoned, gleeful, utterly helpless.

Not long afterwards, he did it again. And then again. I've never come so often, or so easily, in my life. He didn't want anything back, the favour returned. He didn't try and fuck me. He didn't even kiss me. He was simply happy, as he put it, to say thank you.

'For what?'

'You don't know?'

'No.'

He gazed at me, his face moist and shiny.

'I love you,' he said simply.

Later, he insisted on making a bed up for me on the sofa. When I asked about the outside door, he said he'd locked and bolted it. After he'd tip-toed away, I sank beneath the blankets and dreamed about my father. He was home on leave from the Navy. He took myself and my brother sailing in a dinghy on Chichester Harbour. Afterwards, we went to a pub in Bosham and played skittles with those small chicken pies you can buy at Sainsburys. None of my pies made it to the end of the alley but it didn't seem to matter in the slightest. It was a lovely dream and I awoke at dawn with my father still chuckling about how useless I was at skittles. I lay in the darkness for a while, savouring the dream, and then I got up and picked my way across the darkened lounge until I made it to the kitchen. In the light from the kitchen, I found the door to the hall. Brendan's bedroom was at the end. He was asleep when I slipped under the duvet but it wasn't hard to arouse him. He tasted wonderful and we did it again, an hour or so later, together this time.

Brendan took me to work next morning in the Mercedes. Doubleact wasn't the kind of place where anything stayed a secret for very long but even so I was surprised by his indifference to office gossip. In the car, he'd told me I should move in with him. Before he took the stairs to the third floor, he kissed me on the lips and told me he loved me. The phrase would have been relayed to the bitch-queen within minutes. I expect she looked it up in the dictionary.

After lunch, with Brendan's blessing, I returned to Napier Road. I'd left my number at the police station, and at two o'clock, as promised, the phone rang. I was expecting a woman's voice, Gaynor, but it was the young guy I'd met the previous evening. This time he took the trouble of introducing himself. PC Hegarty. Or Dave, for short.

'Someone'll be round in an hour or so,' he told me. 'You'll be in?'

I was still explaining how busy I was at work when he cut the conversation short. Someone would be calling by, he repeated. Then he hung up.

He was outside the house twenty minutes later. I watched him getting out of the little white Panda car and straightening his jacket before he locked the door. There was no sign of Gaynor.

I invited him into the kitchen. I'd already put a chair on the table beneath the hole in the ceiling but he was far too tall to need it. He peered up.

'When did it happen?'

'Last night. I told you.'

'That's when you first noticed it. I asked you when it might have happened. When he might have made the hole.'

It was a daft question, impossible to answer, and he must have realised that from the expression on my face because he changed the subject at once. I'd left the kettle on the gas stove.

'Are you offering me coffee then?'

His bluntness touched a nerve. Already, after last night with Brendan, I'd half-decided not to pursue Gilbert through the police and the only point of returning to the flat was the prospect of meeting Gaynor. If she had experience of this kind of thing, I was more than happy to take advice. What I wasn't going to do was encourage the likes of Dave Hegarty. One obsessive was quite enough for me.

'I've run out of instant,' I said.

'Tea?'

'That, too.'

He didn't bother to disguise the fact that he didn't believe me. He began to inspect the ceiling again.

'There's no proof, of course,' he said. 'No real evidence that he did it. It could be anything, loose plaster, cracks around the light fitting. These kinds of places . . .' he gestured dismissively around, '. . . they're falling apart.'

'You're telling me he didn't do it?'

'I'm telling you it's unproven. In the hands of a good brief, you'd be laughed out of court. Assuming it even got that far.'

'*Laughed?*' This was a new departure. To date, I hadn't found Gilbert remotely comic.

'Yeah,' Hegarty nodded. 'It's a game, love. I've seen it a million times, rock solid case, absolutely sincere, torn to pieces. You've got a problem? Fine, I believe you. But you need evidence, witnesses, corroboration. Without that, it's his word against yours.'

I thought at once of the people in the video shop, the couples in the street outside. They'd been there. They must have seen Gilbert marching me off. But how would I find them? Where on earth would I start?

Hegarty produced a baton. With a flick of his wrist, he extended it full length. I had the impression he practised this a lot. He reached up, poking at the hole. A big piece of plaster broke off, shattering on the seat of the chair immediately below. The hole was now three or four times its previous size.

Hegarty seemed unperturbed.

'See what I mean? Crap plaster. Crap workmanship.'

I was still looking at the hole. At this rate, Gilbert wouldn't have to use the door to get into my flat. He could shimmy down on a rope. I began to have second thoughts about the tea. Maybe it would save my kitchen from further damage.

I filled the kettle and switched it on. Hegarty had returned the baton to his belt and stepped out into the hall.

'Mind if I look round?'

I didn't say a word. Seconds later, I could hear him moving around next door. Next door was my bedroom. By the time he came back, the tea was brewing in the pot. I'd recovered the chair from the table and swept up the plaster. Hegarty sat down.

'Is he in, do you know?'

I said I wasn't sure. I'd been out in the back garden looking for the cats and I'd heard or seen nothing of him but that didn't mean he wasn't up there.

'Take a look then, shall we?'

I followed Hegarty out into the hall and up the stairs. The back of his neck was mapped with acne scars. On the top landing I stood to one side while he rapped on the door. Even if Gilbert was in, I knew there was no chance of him making an appearance for our benefit. He'd have seen the police car outside. He'd probably been listening to our conversation down there in the kitchen. Why on earth would he want to take part in this pantomime?

After the second knock, Hegarty turned ponderously away. I had some faint notion that he might have kicked the door down, or drilled out the lock, but this obviously wasn't to be.

Back in the kitchen, he spooned sugar into his tea.

'Diver, are you? Keen on the old watersports?'

'Windsurfing.'

'Ah,' he nodded. 'I clocked the wetsuit. Funny that, I thought.'

'Funny?'

'Keeping it in the bedroom.' He smiled a private smile, 'Good fun, is it?'

I was still thinking about the wetsuit, hanging on the back of my bedroom door. I wasn't at all sure I wanted to continue this conversation. I changed the subject, asking about Gilbert again. What were the police proposing to do? And why wasn't Gaynor on the case?

'Flu.' Hegarty smothered a yawn. 'I'm double-shifting to cover her. She's back next week. I'll pass on the file.'

I thanked him, all gratitude, remembering our conversation in the interview room at the police station. Judging by what little he'd bothered to write down, Gaynor would be inheriting one of the thinner files.

'What can she do? What's the procedure?'

'She'll do what I've done. She'll come round, ask you a few questions, try and raise chummy upstairs. Normally, she'd talk to the Social Services people, too, but I've done that already.'

'And?'

'They've never heard of him. Mind you,' he frowned, 'we've only got the name and address to go on. The address is obviously kosher, but the name? You tell me.'

'You think it's not Phillips?'

'I don't know, and you don't, either. Anyone can invent a name. Names mean nothing. Two a penny, names.'

I tried to work out whether this was a bid to impress me, another piece of macho street lore, and decided it wasn't. It must be strange, I thought, having to operate in a world where nothing was certain, nothing was beyond doubt.

'Phillips is pretty common, too,' he was saying. 'Must be thousands of them. If you wanted to disappear, Phillips is exactly the kind of name you'd choose. You with me?'

I said I was, then I brought the conversation back to Gaynor. Say something else happened? Say I suddenly needed help?

'She may give you a bleeper. Little hand-held thing.'

'What would that do?'

'Bring us running.' He favoured me with a rare smile. 'Lucky thing.'

After Hegarty had gone, I sat down and forced myself to think. The instinct was to rush back to work and plunge into that deep, deep pool of manic phone calls and impossible deadlines, the best anaesthetic I'd yet found for the very real pain that living beneath Gilbert had become. But immersing myself in Doubleact was simply postponing the moment when I'd have to make a decision and last night had brought matters to a head. Thanks to Gilbert, I knew I was facing at least the possibility of violence. But thanks to Brendan, I now had a very agreeable alternative. He wanted me to move in with him. He wanted to turn last night into real life.

I sat through another cup of tea, weighing the pros and cons, trying to imagine what lay the other side of either decision. Might last night have equally frightened Gilbert? Might he now, at last, behave himself? And might it, therefore, be wiser to hang onto my hard-won independence? On the other hand, might Brendan turn out to be the man I'd always, deep down, been wanting? Someone strong, and warm, and funny? Someone who'd know how to unlock me? Someone genuine who really cared?

I piled the questions up, did my best to sort them out, then returned the cup to the kitchen sink. Being me, like being more or less everyone else on the planet, you can only take so much of all this rational shit. Then you just get on and do it.

I met Sandra by the photocopier at Doubleact that same afternoon. Sandra has a hard disk instead of a memory. She forgets nothing. She told me she needed to ball-park the spend on the last four programmes in the series. We'd done that three days ago.

Sandra's office was on the same floor as Brendan's. I sat across the desk from her. When she got really angry she had a habit of compressing her lips so her mouth became a thin white line. Just now, it was practically invisible.

The nonsense about budget estimates was, as I'd thought, a pretext.

'He's a dickhead,' she raved. 'He's self-obsessed; he's weak; he lies all the time; and he puts it around wherever he thinks he can get a free ride. There are no free rides, Julie. I'm just telling you, that's all. Just telling you.'

I thought hard of something to say. Thank you seemed appropriate.

'Another thing. You'll find he's very persuasive. You'll think he cares. You'll think he can't possibly have said all those wonderful things to anyone else. And just when he's got you where he really wants you, he'll bugger off again. It's too early for that yet, way too early, but just have a think about the rest of what I've said.' She glared at me, demanding a reaction. 'Well?'

I was wondering, by now, just how much she knew about us both. In truth, it only amounted to a couple of hours of the most sensational oral sex ever but even that was enough to have lit a very big fire indeed, so maybe she had a point. Either way, she definitely wanted him back, and the harder she tried to disguise it, the more obvious it became. Given last night, I can't say I blamed her and it crossed my mind that the marriage might have been a lot stronger than Brendan had so far admitted.

'We're friends,' I said. 'It's got nothing to do with you breaking up.'

'It's not? So how come you know about it?'

'Everyone knows about it.'

'But you know more about it, huh? You know lots and lots about it, huh? Because he's told you, am I right?'

In this mood, Sandra was a force of nature, like wind off a rock face, gusting Force Zillion. I spun on my rope, hanging on like mad.

'He's told me practically nothing,' I said wearily. 'And in case you're wondering, I haven't asked, either.'

'Why not?' Sandra was outraged.

'Because it's none of my business.'

'So what is your business? Is my husband your business?'

I didn't answer. Then I told her about the wind-surfing. The day on the coast had been his idea, not mine. Me? I was cheap tuition, nothing more. Sandra followed this aside with an interest I sensed was unfeigned.

'So how did he do?'

'He was terrible. Completely clueless.'

She threw back her head and barked with laughter and for a second or two there was an expression on her face that I recognised as affection. Not just the oral sex, I thought. Not just the wild nights. She loves him. She really does.

She was slumped in the chair now, her long fingers entwined around a pencil. She was a tall, angular, raw-boned woman. The set of her face told you everything, barely caging the passions inside.

'He's crazy about you,' she announced wistfully. 'You know that, don't you? He's been crazy about you since the day you turned up. Live with a man long enough, and you can read it in his face. He wanted you and now he's got you. I should have been a weather forecaster. I'm never bloody wrong.'

'But you think it will pass,' I pointed out. 'So what's the problem?'

'Him. He is. Brendan's the problem. That's what I'm trying to tell you, Julie. That's why I asked you up here. You think it's wonderful. I can see it. He's your boss. He's the older man. All that experience. All those stories. He's so funny. He's so wise. He's so accom-plished, so good at everything.' She paused, shaking her head. 'But it's not what you think it is. It just isn't.'

'I don't think anything. It's not like that.'

'Then what is it like?'

'I don't know.' I was looking hard at the Egon Shiele print on her wall. 'You're right, he's said things, lots of over-the-top things, but I'm not sure I take them seriously.'

'Not yet you don't.'

'Maybe not ever. I just don't know.'

'But you'll try, won't you?' She nodded, winding herself up again. 'Bet your sweet fanny you'll try. That's his gift, you see, that's his special talent. He becomes the proposition you can't resist. You think he's flaky, he'll prove you wrong. You think he's coked out of his head most of the time, he's suddenly Mr Clean. You think he's sold out, he'll come on strong with all that documentary shit. Am I right, Julie? Am I getting warm?'

It was my turn to listen hard. This was a Brendan I recognised. This was the man who'd saved my life, cooked me a wonderful meal, and crowned it with an unforgettable desert. Fruit salad would never taste the same again.

'Well?' She was watching me, amused.

'I don't know,' I repeated.

'But you'll damn sure find out?'

I looked her in the eye, realising all too late that there was a great deal more to this woman than I'd ever suspected. Not just the bitch-queen. Not just the manic phone calls from the third floor. But a human being. Hurting.

'I'm sorry,' I said, getting to my feet, 'But it's not my problem.'

Sandra shook her head, part sorrow, part anger.

'Not yet it isn't,' she said, tossing the pencil onto the desk then turning away.

I moved in with Brendan that night. At first it was a strictly temporary arrangement, a form of camping-out that we both accepted as a kind of foreplay. We had to get to know each other. We had to bend to each other's funny little ways. Quickly, though, we acquired a routine that itself became a cement that hardened the relationship, turning it into something semi-permanent.

Every morning, we got up even earlier than usual, driving the five miles up to Tottenham Green for me to attend to the cats. Ideally, of course, the cats should have come with me – just like my cardboard boxes full of CDs and favourite paperbacks – but Brendan turned out to be allergic to cats so a change of address for Pinot and Noir was out of the question. Instead, I fed them every morning and evening, leaving them out during the day. As the weeks went by, I became aware that they were growing more and more wild but we were still months away from Nikki's return and when I thought about the question at all, I told myself that there was plenty of time to coax them back to domesticity.

Quite when that would happen, I didn't know. Whatever Sandra had said, life with Brendan was undeniably sweet. The manic, gaunt-faced forty-year-old I'd met back in January quickly faded from view. In his place, I found myself living with a warm, funny, surprisingly practical man who had a rare talent for finding the middle ground between domestic routine and the wild, off-the-wall pantomime that was life at Doubleact.

Often, during the week, we stayed in, hopelessly content, endlessly talking, forever comparing professional notes. Simply by listening, I learned a great deal about the hard practicalities of what I really wanted to do, about how difficult it was to resist the contagion of the marketplace, though the more I learned, the steadier became my resolve to give documentaries a try. This, in turn, caught Brendan's interest and he became, I think, genuinely fascinated by what he called my blind eye.

It was all of a piece, he said, with the other bits of me that he loved. My energy. My gutsiness. My crude belief in the benefits of physical exercise. The latter had taken us to a nearby park at weekends. I'd bought Brendan a tracksuit for his birthday, and a decent pair of Reeboks, and after a month of regular outings we were up to six miles at a reasonable pace with no stops. It was the first time for years that Brendan had risked serious exercise and the flood of endorphines afterwards entranced him. It was, he confided, infinitely better than cocaine, and infinitely cheaper, too.

It was after these outings that the sex was best of all and after a leisurely shower we'd bury the rest of the afternoon beneath the duvet. He was a brilliant lover and the times we shared slowly pulled me clear of Gilbert's shadow. I thought about him less and less. Emotionally, and in real life, he became practically invisible, a person of no account. Mornings and evenings, in our trips to Napier Road, we never saw him, or even heard him. The only sign that he was still in residence was the occasional movement in the window upstairs as fingers plucked at the ever-closed curtains.

After a while, as the weeks went by, I began to think of selling Napier Road. So far I'd held off, not quite believing how good things could be with Brendan, but the closer we became the more obvious it was that neither of us would have any need for my little cul-de-sac. Brendan really was the person who'd rescued me. Not just once – out on the coast – but again now, by listening, and understanding, and taking me away from a situation – Gilbert – that had got totally out of control. Even better, he'd managed to work this magic without once giving me the feeling that I'd become any less independent. I was still Julie Emerson. I was still my own person. And I still had a great career ahead of me.

Members Only, by now, was nearly at the end of its transmission run but Brendan had made it clear that there was work for me at Doubleact for as long as I wanted it, a decision which – curiously – Sandra hadn't questioned. After the confrontation in her office, she'd never raised the issue of Brendan again and both of us were extremely careful to fence off our working relationship from the wreckage of her private life. At the time I can remember thinking that this restraint of hers was truly remarkable though I suspect I put it down to my own professionalism. I was, without doubt, bloody good at my job, and even my lover's estranged wife had to admit it.

I phoned the estate agent in late May. Because I was lazy, I simply chose the people I'd bought the place from in the first place. The woman I'd dealt with had left but I made an appointment to meet a young guy called Mark.

We walked round the flat together, Mark taking notes. I'd done my best to hoover through and I'd even bought some flowers but it smelled damp and neglected and a dull, cloudy day did less than justice to my beautifully sanded floorboards. I hadn't done anything to the kitchen ceiling, either, though I'm not sure Mark noticed. At the end of the inspection, we agreed to try it at £55,000, a price which would net me a tidy profit. Mark said he had a couple of prospects already lined up and he'd be round with the first lot tomorrow. I said that sounded fine and gave him the spare key.

I got the call from Mark the following afternoon. I was at the office, tackling the paperwork after the last recording of *Members Only*. Brendan had pushed out the boat for the end-of-series party and I felt terrible.

'There's a problem,' Mark said. 'I don't really want to talk about it on the phone. Can you come over?'

We met outside the flat. Mark was looking, if anything, embarrassed. He was a local lad, extremely efficient, but I'm not sure that his three months on the job had prepared him for the news he was about to break.

'It's them cats,' he said. 'Or one of them, anyway.'

I followed him inside. I'd last seen both cats a couple of days earlier. Since then Pinot had disappeared but I hadn't been unduly concerned because he'd always been the wanderer. Wherever he got to, he unfailingly came back. Until now.

Mark led me through to the kitchen. Noir, the other cat, was waiting beside the door. Mark opened the fridge. The fridge of course, was empty. Or had been. Now, curled on the middle shelf, was Pinot. I stared at him. He seemed to be asleep. I looked at Mark.

'He's thawing,' he said. 'I couldn't think of any other place.'

Mark had arrived earlier in the day with the first lot of prospective buyers, a young Australian couple. He'd let them into the shared hall, only to find the cat lying on the carpet outside my front door. The cat hadn't moved. The woman had touched him first. Pinot had been frozen solid. He was very dead.

'Shit.' I was thinking of Nikki. 'Shit, shit.'

'They went.'

'Who did?'

'The people I was showing round. Didn't want to know. Especially the woman. She was spooked.'

'I'm not surprised.'

I took a step back and risked a little look at the ceiling. For a moment, I swear I saw the glint of a watching eye, though I may have imagined it.

'How come?' Mark was asking. 'I don't understand it.'

'Me neither.'

He looked at me, unconvinced. What hadn't I told him? What was going on here?

'It was like a message,' he said. 'People don't put cats in freezers, just leave them there, then plonk them outside someone else's front door.' He paused. 'It *is* your cat, isn't it?'

'It's a friend's,' I said. 'She's away for a while. She'll be mortified.'

'But why . . .' he gestured at the fridge, '. . . would anyone want to do that? It's mad, isn't it? Crazy?'

I mustered a weak smile and agreed with him. It had to be Gilbert, had to be. There was no other suspect half as crazy as he was. I shivered. The shadow had fallen over me again. And it had taken less than three minutes.

'Have you had any other interest?'

'Yeah, two or three calls. It's a competitive price.'

'And you'll bring these people round?'

'Yeah, just as long as . . .' he turned away, closing the fridge door, '. . . there's nothing funny going on.'

With the greatest reluctance, that afternoon, I phoned Tottenham Green police station. The news that PC Dave Hegarty had gone on leave was a huge relief. I asked, instead, for Gaynor. When she came to the phone, she said she'd never heard of me.

We met that night at half past six. We'd had a long chat on the phone and by the time she got to Napier Road, she'd had time to get her thoughts in some kind of order. Face to face, she turned out to be a slim, pretty woman a couple of years older than me. She had watchful eyes and a flat North London accent. She could easily have been Mark's sister.

We sat in the kitchen over a pot of tea. I'd shown her the cat in the fridge, and the hole in the ceiling, and I'd filled in one or two of the bits I hadn't mentioned on the phone. When she asked me why it had taken me so long to get in touch again after reporting Gilbert in the first place, I told her a little about Brendan. I'd been living with him, I said, and that had sorted things for a while. But now Gilbert was back in my life. With a vengeance.

'The law's all changed,' she said. 'You probably realise that.'

I nodded. Back at the end of last year, there'd been a lot of publicity about a reform of the law with regard to stalking. According to Gaynor, there were two new criminal offences. The first involved violence, but to commit the lesser offence, in the words of the legislation, it was enough to cause harassment. I thought of the night Gilbert appeared at my bedside, the shape in the darkness looking down at me. Harassment seemed a pretty weak word to describe the moment when I turned on the light and saw him standing there.

Gaynor was studying her notes. Unlike Dave Hegarty, she appeared to believe me. She was also, to my immense relief, extremely straightforward. No dramas. No funny games. Just a ready grasp of the practicalities of the situation.

'What do you want to do?' she asked at last. 'Frighten him?'

'Warn him off.'

'Same thing, isn't it? He's not actually pursuing you, not following you, not from what you say.' Her eyes returned to the notepad. 'Apart from that night you came to the station.'

'That's right.'

'So it's not like you're under physical threat.'

'No, not any more.'

'An irritation then? Is that it?'

'Yes.'

Gaynor nodded and I sensed at once that I'd made a mistake, permitting her to play it down like this.

'He can still be pretty scary,' I said, 'Breaking into my flat the way he did.'

'He didn't break in. Not technically.'

'But he did. He did when he came into the bedroom, and again when he took the cats, and again that time he stole the film from the camera. That makes him a burglar, doesn't it?'

Gaynor poured herself another cup of tea.

'To get him for breaking and entering, we have to prove intent. Because you lent him the keys, we can't do that.'

'But I'd got the keys back. He must have taken copies.'

'Doesn't matter. You've given him access to the flat. His fingerprints will be everywhere. As evidence, they'd mean nothing.'

'What about the film?'

'You told me he got the stuff developed.'

'He did.'

'And then gave you the prints.'

'Yes.'

'So where's the offence?'

I had no answer. Gaynor was infinitely nicer than her uniformed chum but the message seemed to be the same. By lending Gilbert the keys, I'd effectively destroyed any case I might later want to bring against him, regardless of what he'd done. I went back to the new stalking laws. Surely they might stand between me and the lunatic upstairs?

'You need two specific incidents. We have to prove harassment on two separate occasions.'

'I can do that. I've told you.'

'And will he admit it?'

'God knows. But say he does? What then?'

Gaynor asked whether I minded her smoking. I fetched an ashtray, still waiting for an answer. She produced a packet of Silk Cut.

'We can arrest him.' She lit the cigarette. 'We can haul him off down the nick. He'll be interviewed. The allegation will be put to him. And if he admits it, shows remorse . . .' she tilted her head towards the ceiling, '. . . the paperwork goes off upstairs and a couple of weeks later he'll be down the nick again.'

'What for?'

'A caution. That means a bollocking from the uniformed inspector.'

'And that's it? No court case? No fine? Nothing?'

'Not unless he's got any previous.'

'You think he might have?'

'No. I looked this afternoon. After you gave me his name on the phone.'

I sat back, deflated. Then I remembered a line of Hegarty's.

'It might be a fake name,' I pointed out, 'Phillips.'

'Of course,' Gaynor smiled at me. 'Do you have another one?'

'No, but . . .' I shrugged, feeling more than usually stupid. How come I hadn't thought this thing through? How come I had such primitive faith in the forces of law and order?

Gaynor was looking at the ceiling again.

'I've been thinking about that.' She indicated the jagged hole beside the light fitting. 'We could be looking at criminal damage.'

'We could?'

'Yes, and criminal damage is an arrestable offence. Once I've nicked him I can go in and look for whatever he's used to make the hole in the first place.'

'You mean search his flat?'

'Yes. And finding what we're after might take a while. If you know what I mean.'

I didn't, and minutes later, beside the front door, I said so. Gaynor was pocketing her Silk Cut. She put a hand on my arm.

'We need to frighten him,' she reminded me quietly. 'We need to warn him off. We could try other ways but this one's best, believe you me.'

'But how do we do that?'

'We've just done it.'

'We have?'

'Yes,' she smiled, and stepped into the evening sunshine. 'You're telling me he wasn't up there listening?'

Brendan, as usual, was on the phone when I got back to his flat. I slipped a frozen pitta bread into the microwave and dug out the bowl of hummus I'd made at the weekend. I was ladling the stuff over a little nest of lettuce leaves inside the pitta bread when I felt Brendan's hands encircling my breasts. Brendan had very distinctive ways of saying hello. This was one of them.

I offered him half the pitta, wondering where to start with Gaynor, but Brendan was already off on a gig of his own.

'What are you doing tomorrow?' he asked me.

I thought of my desk at Doubleact. What nobody ever tells you about television is the mountain of paperwork.

The series might be over but the truly boring bit was yet to come.

'Clearing up,' I said, 'and then more clearing up.'

'Fancy a trip?'

'Where to?'

I looked round at him, waiting for an answer, but half my pitta bread had already disappeared and it was pretty obvious that we were in for another of Brendan's gourmet nights. No chance of getting fat, I thought, following him towards the bedroom.

We were over at Napier Road by half past six next morning. It took me a couple of minutes to find my passport, and then we were off to Heathrow. I was still none the wiser about where we were going but Terminal Four was a bloody good start. The first seven destinations on the Departures board were all in other continents.

Brendan picked up a couple of BA tickets at a desk near the door. When he put them on the counter while he hunted for his credit card I had a chance to sneak a look. I'd never been to New York before and the grin on my face must have told him so.

'It's a thank you,' he said as we joined the queue at gate seventeen, 'for changing my life.'

That line was typical of Brendan, completely over the top, and it does me no favours to say that I loved it. By the time we'd left the west coast of Ireland behind, I'd forgotten entirely about Gilbert, and Napier Road, and poor Mark's attempts to sell the place, preferring to wallow in the comforts of Club World. We were onto our fourth glass of champagne. Sunshine was pouring through the window beside me. Best of all, I was heading for the city of my dreams, cocooned in a little bubble of mid-atlantic luxury, and there was – it seemed – a yet bigger treat awaiting me on the other side. Quite what it might be, Brendan wouldn't say but I was certain that it had something to do with work. One of Brendan's many gifts was the ability to mesh pleasure with more or less every other aspect of his busy, busy life. He very seldom did anything without at least half a dozen ulterior motives.

And I was right, of course. We touched down at JFK in the early afternoon and took a yellow cab downtown. The Triboro Bridge gave me my first grandstand view of Manhattan and I was still on mental overload when we booked into the Sherry Netherlands Hotel. Our suite was way up on the sixteenth floor. From the window, I could see right along Central Park West towards the gothic battlements of the Dakota Building. The Dakota Building was where John Lennon had met his death. For little me, the video-queen from the Bournemouth (Hons) Media production course, this was truly the biz.

Brendan had ordered coffee and club sandwiches. When the guy from room service arrived, there were four cups on the tray. Brendan was on the phone, talking to the office back in London. God knows who was still there.

'Due any minute,' I heard him say. 'Can't wait.'

Can't wait for what? I was still trying to prise the odd clue from Brendan when there was another knock on the door. Brendan was across the room in seconds. When our visitor came in, something told me that he and Brendan hadn't met before. Not, at least, in person.

'Meet Everett,' he gestured grandly at his new chum. 'Everett, meet Jules.'

Everett was a tall, fit-looking American in his early thirties. He had a strong handshake and a big smile that never quite got as far as his eyes. His eyes were the lightest blue.

We sat down around the low coffee table, Everett

unbuttoning his jacket. It already felt like a business meeting. I handed round the sandwiches. Everett declined.

'Forgive me,' Brendan had his hand on Everett's arm. 'You mind if I put Jules here in the picture?'

'She doesn't know?'

'It's a surprise.'

'Sure.' Everett looked briefly amused. 'Go ahead.'

Brendan shot me the look I always got when there was a pressie in the offing. Then he began to talk about what I first assumed was a programme idea but the deeper he got into it, the more I realised that he was way, way past what we TV folks call 'development'. The big juicy bone that Brendan was depositing at my feet was a pilot for a series, fully worked out and – more important still – fully funded.

The notion, in essence, was simple. It took a bunch of kids from one of the rougher big city council estates and put them under the care of an ex-SAS instructor for a month. While he worked the special forces magic, a similar bunch of kids, this time American, were jumping through the same kind of hoops with an ex-Green Beret. This brush with the world's supermen would exactly answer society's conclusion that problem kids today were – in Brendan's phrase – 'under-challenged'.

At the end of the month, with plenty of training footage in the can, the two teams would meet on the Brecon Beacons for an elaborate game of Paintball. One of the two teams would be entrusted with a casket. They had two days and a night to carry the casket forty miles over gruelling terrain. The other team were tasked to stop them. Inside the casket, for real, was £10,000, to be spent by the winning kids on sports facilities for their home estate.

It was, Brendan assured me, a wonderful concept. The

British version would be followed by an American sequel. The latter, with the blessing of the Pentagon, would be staged at Fort Bragg, home of the Green Berets. If the two pilot shows went well, Doubleact were looking at a series order for another twelve. A big ITV company had already lined up a major sponsor. Working title, for the pilots at least, was *Home Run*.

Brendan broke off to demolish the rest of his club sandwich. I was still wrestling with the small print of his latest wheeze.

'What are the Green Berets?'

Brendan gestured at Everett. The American threw me a casual half-salute, one sinewy hand brushing his right temple.

'At your service, ma'am.'

'You're a Green Beret?'

'Always. I'm technically on the reserve list now, but it makes no difference.'

'But what are they? What do they do?'

'Special Forces, ma'am. Uncle Sam's shock troops. Infil. Exfil. Sabotage. Intelligence gathering. You want *à la carte*? The whole damn menu?'

I laughed. He was bright, this man. I liked him.

'You had a hand in this idea? Cooking it up?'

'Sort of, but it's Brendan's baby really. Him and Gary.'

'Gary?'

Brendan reached for the phone again. I was looking at the fourth cup.

'Gary's our SAS lead,' Brendan explained. 'He's an old tart really but at least he looks the part.'

'And he's due here?'

'Any time.'

Gary arrived several minutes later. Apparently he'd been waiting in the lobby downstairs. Brendan ribbed him about this and I found myself wondering why. Maybe he expected something more dramatic, like Gary arriving through the window on the end of a rope.

I listened while Gary and Everett exchanged notes. It was evident at once that they'd just spent several days together. Compared to the American, Gary was a scruff: long, greasy hair, flat, slightly lop-sided face, bitten nails, scuffed trainers, but the two of them shared the kind of nerveless, laid-back rapport you often find amongst top windsurfers. They'd been there. They'd done it. Not very much got under their skins.

Eventually, I established that the germ of the idea had come from Gary. A fan of *Members Only*, he'd lifted the phone and asked to speak to Brendan, whose name – inevitably – was always last on the credits roll.

'Bold,' I murmured.

Gary had cornered the club sandwiches.

'Yeah,' he said through a mouthful of tuna mayonnaise, 'but it was Brendan who ran with it. My idea was shit. I hadn't got much further than hide and seek on Pen-y-Fan.'

'Pen-y-what?'

'It's a hill on the Beacons. Bloody vertical. Goes on forever, real bastard of a climb.' He wiped his chin. 'The rest was down to Brendan, like I say. He was the one who dreamed up all the stuff about the kids. That's the key, isn't it? That's what unlocks the dosh.'

I found myself looking at Brendan with something close to respect. He'd spent a lot of the last two months telling me about his documentary days but I'd come away with the conviction that this was a chapter of his life that was firmly over. Market forces had turned him into a businessman, a machine – as the office joke had it

– for turning bad coffee into worse quiz shows. When I inquired what had possessed him to flirt once again with a social conscience, he looked wounded.

'You don't think it's any good? The concept?'

'I think it's great.'

'And you're serious? You don't know where it comes from?'

'No.' I shook my head. 'I haven't got a clue.'

He looked wonderingly at the other two and then told them about my precious undergraduate video. It was, he said, the best piece of student film-making he'd ever seen. It had sat on a shelf in his office for months and months while he watched me soil myself with *Members Only*. One day, he'd sworn, he'd figure out just how to marry the two disciplines, how to combine what he called my very special documentary talents with the demands of the commercial marketplace. The trip hadn't been easy, but over the last month or two, in the course of several million phone calls, the three of them had come up with something pretty workmanlike and now the rest – the really important bit – was down to me.

I glanced over my shoulder, impressed by this little speech, wondering just who he could possibly be talking about. Only when I heard their laughter did I realise he was serious.

'You want me to produce this thing?'

'Sure.' He reached for a stray prawn. 'And direct it, too.'

Much later, we took a cab to a Cajun restaurant called Baby Jakes on First Avenue. Everett had been a regular at the place for years. A waiter showed us to a table at the back and we were halfway through fried catfish and salmon fajitas before I was quite certain that this wasn't another of Brendan's elaborate gestures. He really was making me responsible for the UK end of the shoot. And I really would be in charge.

I'd squeezed his hand in the back of the cab. Now, under the table, I did it again. He was talking about production schedules. It sounded nearly as exciting as sex.

'We shoot in the hills in November,' he said. 'All the prelim training stuff during the summer.'

'November?' I began to argue about the light, about short days, about the weather.

'Shit weather,' Brendan agreed. 'But that's all part of the story. The network's bought challenge, the sponsors too. That's what's fired them up. We're going to give these kids a fucking great mountain to climb, and November's part of that mountain. It's about confrontation. It's about self-esteem. It's about . . .' he nodded, ' . . . manhood.'

I'd seen Brendan in these moods before, bless him. He was a genius at pitching an idea, at marshalling little squads of cliché and sending them into battle. The fact that he so obviously believed in whatever he was trying to sell simply added to his appeal, and that night in the restaurant was a perfect example of Brendan losing his grip on the real world. Within minutes, at this rate, *Home Run* would have solved the nation's crime problem. The series would doubtless end with a guest appearance from a grateful Home Secretary and knighthoods all round.

I tried to bring him back to earth. Half a year in television had taught me that *Home Run*, like anything else, would only be as good as the facilities we threw at it.

'Talk to me about helicopters,' I said.

Helicopters are a good test when you're talking high-performance ideas. At £700 an hour, even one would make a hefty dent in any Doubleact budget I'd ever seen.

'Two,' Brendan said at once. 'Minimum.'

'For how long?'

'As long as it takes.'

The others were nodding. They could afford to. They wouldn't be the ones running the figures past Sandra. I looked inquiringly at Brendan a moment, then decided to let it pass. The evening was too lovely an experience to muddy with the harder questions.

'And ground level?' I asked instead. 'What do we do there?'

'Handheld mini-cams with video uplinks.' Brendan was helping himself to the fifth bottle of wine. 'You'll have recorders on the choppers.'

'How many cameramen?'

'None.'

I paused, wondering whether I'd heard him properly. *No* cameramen? Was he serious?

'How come?'

'The kids shoot their own pics.'

'The *kids*?'

Brendan nodded vigorously.

'All part of the game,' he said. 'All part of the challenge.'

'So who teaches them?'

'We do.'

It was Gary this time. I couldn't help noticing how little he'd drunk. Even Everett, Mr Clean-Cut, was at least a bottle ahead.

'While you're training them to survive? Is that what you're saying? You'll turn them into cameramen as well as everything else?'

'Yeah,' Gary looked me in the eye. 'That's exactly what we'll do.'

I ducked my head, not wanting to take the exchange any further, but Everett pressed the point.

'I guess you'll be wanting them raw, these pictures,' he said. 'I don't know about English kids but the guys over here are pretty familiar with camcorders and stuff. I guess that generation grew up on camera.'

'Raw?' I queried softly.

'Everett means alive, as-it-happens, in-your-face.' Brendan was pitching again, this time to me. 'I see using the kids themselves as a positive advantage. What we don't need here is art, polish, four-man crews, wide-shots, close-ups, GVs, all that horseshit. These kids are out on the edge, out in the wild. That's where we've put them. That's what we've done to them, that's what *society*'s done to them. The pictures need to reflect that. SIY does it for us, Jules.'

'SIY?'

'Shoot it Yourself.' He beamed at me over the table, encouraging me to laugh. I did, of course, but for the first time I felt just a twinge of anxiety. My three years at Bournemouth may not have qualified me for Holly-wood but it had certainly bred a healthy respect for the basics of film-making. Those basics included most of the list he'd just dismissed and I knew that without them we were in danger of ending up with a soup of meaningless close-ups. The helicopters would help, of course, but there's a limit to what you can do from five hundred feet.

Gary was still watching me. Disguising himself as a tramp had certain advantages. One was a dangerous temptation not to take him too seriously.

'Where have we gone wrong?' he asked me. 'What haven't we sorted? No bullshit.'

I tried to flannel but I could sense at once that the issue wouldn't go away. Gary had flattened me with a direct question and the least I owed him was an honest stab at an answer.

'I think it's a great idea,' I said slowly, 'but I think there are problems.'

'There are always problems. That's what makes television fun.'

There was no avoiding Brendan. I gave him the grateful nod he was after.

'Of course,' I said. 'And nothing's insoluble.'

'But?'

I looked at Gary again. The restaurant went in for red candles wedged in empty wine bottles, hopelessly sixties, and the dancing shadows spilled across his face, emphasising its strange contours.

'Take the kids,' I said. 'I assume we're looking for the hard cases, the loners, the real misfits. Yes?'

'Yeah,' Gary nodded. 'For sure.'

'Then getting them onside won't be easy. Not in a month.'

I paused, only too aware of just how little I knew about these kids. We'd met them on the estate in Southampton, dozens of them, but that didn't make me an expert.

'You'll have all summer,' Brendan was saying. 'That should be long enough.'

'I thought you said a month?'

'It works out to be a month, all in.'

'It's not one long chunk?'

'No, it's bits and pieces, has to be.'

'Why?'

'That's the way the schedule works.'

'Whose schedule?'

'Ours. And Gary's.' He glanced across at Gary. Gary nodded, still watching me.

'That makes it worse. A month solid, no distractions,

145

no fucking about, you might have a chance.' I shrugged. 'What you're saying now sounds like Scout meetings. Every Wednesday night. Weather permitting.'

Gary was grinning. In some strange way, I sensed I'd answered his question.

'No problem,' he said.

'With the kids?'

'No, love.' The grin widened, then his hand closed over mine. 'With you.'

Back at the hotel, I realised how exhausted I was. Twenty-seven hours on my feet, most of them fuelled by alcohol, had taken their toll. I sank into the enormous bed, letting Brendan enfold me. In the cab, coming back from the restaurant, he'd told me what an impact I'd made on the other two, and how certain they both were that the pilots would be a smasheroo. The UK end of the series would be shot on the Beacons but if the formula worked (the merest detail) then there was no limit to the geographical reach of subsequent series. He told me there were tourist boards across the world just aching for the screen exposure of *Home Rum*, and Brendan was still rhapsodising about the places we could recce together when I drifted off to sleep.

I awoke before dawn. I could hear the wail of a siren from the street below. I made my way to the bathroom in time to throw up. I was sick twice more after that and I dimly remember wondering just how much I'd allowed myself to drink at the restaurant before returning on tip-toe to bed.

Twenty-four hours later, still nauseous, I was back at my desk in London, trying to decipher a scribbled message from the girl who'd been standing in for me. 'Phone Mark,' it said. 'Urgent.'

This time, Mark's preferred rendezvous was the office where he worked. I'd borrowed Brendan's Mercedes to drive across to Napier Road to feed the cat, and I left it on a double yellow line on the Seven Sisters Road while I ran inside to find Mark. He offered me coffee but I said I was in a hurry. The moment I'd seen his face, I knew I was back in the real world.

'What's happened?'

Mark had the form ready on his desk. He picked it up, shielding it from me while he told me about his latest visit to my flat. He'd gone round yesterday, only to find the prospective buyer standing on the pavement outside surrounded by broken tiles. The tiles, he said, must have come off the roof. It hadn't been the best advert for what the details were calling 'a solid, well constructed turn-of-the-century property'.

'You're telling me it was deliberate?'

'Has to be.'

I nodded, wondering whether this little act of vandalism might qualify as harassment. If so, it might be time to lift the phone to Gaynor.

Mark had his eye on Brendan's Mercedes. He obviously thought it belonged to me.

'So what about the buyers?' I asked him.

'I blamed it on the weather.'

'Has it been windy?'

'No.'

'So did they believe you?'

'What do you think?'

Mark at last gave me the form. It came from the Law Society. Across the top it read 'Seller's Property Information'. When I looked blank, Mark opened it, indicating Section Two. Section Two was headed Disputes. Four separate questions invited my thoughts about my neighbour. Question 2.3 read, 'Have you made any complaint to any neighbour about what the neighbour has or hasn't done?'

'If we get a buyer,' Mark said pointedly, 'you'll have to fill that bit up. If you don't, you can get sued.' He nodded. 'It happens a lot.'

I read the Disputes section again, beginning to understand. It was a matter of record that I'd been less than happy with Gilbert. In fact I'd been to the police about him. Twice. The two lines provided for the answer to question 2.3 were quite enough, therefore, to see off any potential buyer. After the cat, the tiles, I thought grimly. And after the tiles, this innocent little form with its nice blue logo.

I checked the car. No parking warden. No ticket.

'You might as well be honest,' Mark said. 'What's the score with the bloke upstairs?'

I fought the urge to lie. What would be the point?

'He's a bit odd,' I admitted.

'You've had problems?'

'One or two.'

'That cat? You think he might have . . .' Mark was looking at me.

I nodded glumly. I'd buried Pinot in the one corner of the back garden that Gilbert's windows didn't overlook. God knows how I was going to explain any of this to Nikki but it gave me a dogged satisfaction to deny Gilbert the sight of the grave.

'So what happens next?' I asked. 'Are you giving up?'

'Course not. Just wondered if you could have a word, that's all.'

'Who with?'

'This geezer upstairs. Tell him he's out of order. Tell him whatever you like. But get him to back off, eh?'

I folded the Law Society form and slipped it into my pocket. The notion of facing Gilbert, of having a quiet word – so logical, so obvious – brought a smile to my face. Mark was shepherding me towards the door.

'And another thing you might try is getting in touch with the freeholder. Geezer starts chucking tiles around, that's gotta be against the lease, hasn't it?' He smiled at me, opening the door. 'Just a thought.'

Gilbert had the paintbrush out, minutes later, when I drove up Napier Road to feed the cat. The sight of him stooped in the porch made me pull the car to a halt several houses short of the end of the cul-de-sac. I'd felt sick all day on and off, and the nausea suddenly gusted upwards, making me swallow hard. I didn't want to confront him. It was difficult just getting out of the car.

I was at the front gate before he turned round. He was wearing an old denim smock, scabbed with paint. His eyes were shadowed with the kind of deep exhaustion my father had before the stroke took his life.

I gestured at the brush. There were big splashes of paint all over the doorstep.

'Why mauve?' I said.

'I happen to like it.'

'But why didn't you mention it? I live here too.'

'Do you?'

He stared down at me. On some days, like today, I'd noticed an air of defeat about him, or perhaps bewilderment. Here was a man, I thought, who'd set out on a journey but kept losing the map.

I fingered the catch on the gate, flicking it back and forth, giving away my nervousness.

'What about the tiles?' I said, changing the subject.

'What tiles?'

'The tiles you've been knocking off the roof? This morning?' I looked down at the pavement. There was no sign of any tiles so I stepped back into the road, studying the roof. As far as I could see it was intact. By the time I got back to the porch, Gilbert was painting again. The conversation was becoming surreal. Nothing new, I thought bitterly, as far as Gilbert was concerned.

'You killed my cat,' I said heatedly. 'You'll deny it but I know it was you. That was a terrible thing to do. Terrible. I thought you liked cats.'

'I love cats.'

He didn't stop painting. Big mauve stripes, up and down.

'So why kill it?'

'I didn't kill it.'

He broke off and looked round. The paint was dripping onto his jeans. I didn't bother to point it out. Instead I told him about Gaynor. Gaynor was a policewoman, a detective. One phone call from me and she'd be round. If she didn't get an answer at his door, she'd be summoning help. One way or another, she'd get inside the flat. There'd be traces in the freezer. Bound to be.

'Traces of what?'

'Pinot. The cat.'

'Of course.'

'You're admitting it?'

'Yes, absolutely, of course I am.'

I frowned, not knowing quite where to go next. Insanity, I thought, is a tricky thing to argue with.

'You killed my cat,' I said slowly. 'And then you put him in your freezer.'

Gilbert was looking down the road. The sight of the Mercedes seemed to send a physical shiver down his thin frame.

'He was in the road,' he muttered. 'I found him in the road.'

'Dead?'

'Yes. I brought him back. I put him in the freezer. I wanted you to have him.'

I tried to remember the state of the cat. To be honest, I hadn't taken a proper look before I'd buried him. There was just a chance, I supposed, that Gilbert was telling the truth but I rather doubted it. A passing car, at the end of a cul-de-sac, sounded like yet another of his fantasies.

'How can I be sure?' I asked.

'Sure of what?'

'Sure about what you're telling me. Anything could have happened.'

'Of course,' Gilbert recharged his brush. 'But then you wouldn't know, would you?'

'Why not?'

He paused a moment, turning his back to me, then he jabbed viciously at the door, a heavy mauve daub that began to run at once.

'Why not?' he echoed softly. 'Because you're never here.'

I went to the doctor two days later. I hadn't bothered to sign on at a practice and in the end I took Brendan's advice and went along to the local health centre. A harassed middle-aged lady GP listened to my symptoms and mused aloud about stomach upsets. There was always a bug of some description around and this week's gave you diarrhoea and vomiting. She typed a message into her computer and the printer alongside produced a prescription. As an afterthought, as I was leaving the consulting room, she asked me if I'd missed any periods. As it happened, I had. Twice.

'Is that unusual? With you?'

'Not especially. It's happened before.'

'Might you be pregnant? Have you thought of that?'

I hadn't. Apart from that first time, I'd taken careful

precautions. The doctor nodded, tapping her pencil on her teeth, listening. The practice nurse occupied a room down the corridor. I had the test result within an hour. It was positive.

I spent most of that evening with a friend in a pub off Upper Street around the corner from the office. I hadn't seen Michelle for nearly a year which, oddly enough, made her the perfect confidante. We'd been good friends on the course down in Bournemouth and she'd been one of the few third-years to share my passion for documentary. One of the reasons she'd phoned was to tap me for contacts. Where could she write that she hadn't tried already? Did I have any particular names? How was I getting on?

Against my instincts, I spared her the news about *Home Run*, partly because it seemed unnecessarily tactless – compounding her frustration – and partly because I didn't altogether believe the thing would ever fly. Television is full of false starts, and though I knew Brendan was totally sincere in handing me my big, big, big challenge, there was still a zillion miles to go before we could start spending serious money. Big money is the acid test in television. Once you're past your first £25,000, it's stick back, wheels up, and away. To date, though, thanks to some extremely creative accounting and a judicious dip or two into other Doubleact budgets, we were barely into four figures.

But as far as Michelle was concerned, *Members Only* was fame enough, and I spent a good part of the evening sharing some of the raunchier gossip. Nearly all of it featured politicians, some of them extremely prominent. Her father, whom I happened to know, took the *Telegraph* daily and lived in the never-never world of squeaky-clean Tory politicians. Once Michelle got home and rang him with the news, he was clearly in for a shock.

Later, past ten o'clock, we got into the personal bits. How was I doing? Had I found anyone interesting? Was I making out? I'd braced myself for these questions all evening, not because I wasn't happy – I most certainly was – but because my session with the practice nurse had affected me so deeply. Already, in the most fundamental way, I felt there were two of us. I was no expert on prenatal development, but I was absolutely positive that the read-out from the test she'd given me represented a face, and a body, and a pair of the most exquisite little hands. I was no longer alone. For as long as I could possibly imagine I'd always have someone who'd need to rely on me, someone who'd be my friend.

Given that Brendan was the father, and that I'd fallen in love with him, all this probably sounds daft, even insulting. With Brendan to love me, why would I feel alone? To that question, I had no answer. Neither, as it turned out, did Michelle.

'What's he like? Brendan?'

Good question. I told her as much as I knew. I told her that he was older than me, and very bright, and a bit manic. I told her that he'd been dotty about me from the start, and had courted me like mad, but had never really been a pain about it. Since I'd moved in, we'd got to know each other well, really well, and the more of him I saw, the more I knew he was for me. I went easy on the bit about Brendan's special talents but Michelle and I had been pretty frank with each other in our Bournemouth days and I think she guessed that the sex was wonderful. I also admitted, when she asked, that he was married.

'Do you trust him?'

Better question still. I said I did.

'Why?'

'Because he's never let me down. Not once. Because he's kind, really kind. Because he says we're important, the most important thing of all, and I believe him.'

'Does he make you laugh?'

'Yes.'

'On purpose?'

'Yes, and in other ways, too. He can be funny because he tries so hard, and funny because he thinks he's fooled you, but you can see through him, right through him. He could come back as double glazing. He's completely transparent. I tell him that sometimes.' I grinned. 'He keeps the warmth in, too. Do you know what I mean?'

Michelle looked briefly troubled and I knew I'd touched a nerve. Living with Brendan had taught me just how rare it is to find a relationship like ours and telling other people about it sometimes isn't kind. Maybe I should have stuck to *Home Run* after all, I thought. Who wants to hear about other people falling in love?

I got us both another drink. Michelle was still looking gloomy.

'It's not all roses,' I told her. 'Don't think that.'

She brightened up at once.

'It's not?'

'No.' I sat down. 'I'm pregnant.'

She stared at me and I could tell at once that it was the last thing she'd expected to hear. Canny, street-wise Julie Emerson? The Viking goddess of the windsurf set? *Pregnant*?

'How come?'

I told her how I thought it must have happened. Blaming it on drink was the oldest excuse in the book but I genuinely couldn't think of another. Since that first night, and the morning after, I'd been back on the pill so

Brendan's malt whisky had a great deal to answer for.

'How has he taken it?'

'He doesn't know.'

I explained about my visit to the GP. We were talking hot news, I said, and I'd yet to decide whether or not to share it with Brendan.

'What's stopping you?'

'I don't know.' I stared at my glass of Pils. 'I'm a bit confused.'

'You think it might change things?'

'I doubt it but . . .' I pulled a face, '. . . I suppose it might.'

'And you don't want that to happen?'

'No, of course not.'

'So why don't you . . .' Michelle made a loose, circular motion with her hand.

'Get rid of it?'

'Yes.'

'I couldn't.'

'You *couldn't*? Why not?'

'Because . . .' I frowned, concentrating hard, '. . . it's not mine to get rid of.'

'Of course it is.'

'No, it's not.'

'Whose is it then? Brendan's?'

'No.'

'*Not* Brendan's?'

'No, it's his, of course it is. But it's not, if you see what I mean.'

Michelle was looking bewildered. Surprise had given way to disbelief. Then blank incomprehension.

'It's a baby,' I said at last. 'It's alive. It exists. I can't just get rid of it . . .' I touched my glass to hers, '. . . can I?'

*

As it happens, I couldn't tell Brendan my little bit of news, not at once anyway, because he chose the whole of the next fortnight to go away. Co-production deals had taken him off to Australia and the postcards began arriving within days, dozens of variations on a theme of mile-long beaches, curling waves, and hunky surfers daubed in pink sunblock. In a way, this absence of his was a blessing. Not only did it give me a breathing space to get things sorted out in my head but it also offered a chance to nail down some dates. So far I only had the confirmation that I was pregnant. Now I wanted the entire script.

I returned to the GP. She was still waiting for my notes to come up from Petersfield but in the meantime I gave her a brisk summary of my form to date. No major diseases. No broken bones. And a level of fitness that was, by media standards, pretty impressive. The GP concluded her examination with some wary questions about what she termed my 'situation'. In this, she covered pretty much the same ground as Michelle, with one exception.

'You still have a flat of your own?'

'Yes.'

'And you'll be keeping it?'

I gave the question some thought. Given half a chance, I'd sell the place tomorrow but Gilbert had just added two enormous eyes, in white gloss, to the front door and his message to would-be buyers had become all too effective. Mark was still telling me to hassle the freeholder, something I hadn't had time to do, but even if I got some kind of result I could tell that Mark was close to giving up on the place. His last prospect, plus half the street, had been given the full Mozart treatment on CD, some concerto or other, at something close to a million decibels.

'For a while,' I said carefully, 'I'll probably hang on to it.'

'That might be wise. Could you cope alone there? You and the baby?'

The question made me blink a bit. Most GPs take extraordinary care to keep their distance from patients' private lives, but this one sounded just like my mother.

'Of course we'd cope,' I said brightly. 'But I'm sure it won't come to that.'

Even now, nearly a year later, I can see that doctor's face. I was on my feet, the consultation over, her questions answered, and as I backed towards the door I remember her glancing up from her desk, pen in hand. She looked weary, like they all do, but there was something else in her expression as well, an odd mixture of amusement and sympathy. She sat in this room every day. She probably saw hundreds of young women like me. And there was a part of her, way down, that felt sorry for us.

I worked harder than ever during the next couple of weeks, mainly trying to nurse my other baby, *Home Run*. The dates that came through on the pregnancy ringed the week of 17 December, 1997, a deadline that gave me barely any leeway at all for post-production after the November shoot. There'd be pictures to edit, sound tracks to lay, and a fine cut to agree before we'd be ready for the final dub. This process was complex enough but the fact that we were dealing with a pilot made it doubly so. This first programme would be a template for everything that followed, and if we got anything wrong then the fault would be magnified over subsequent shows. We'd therefore be in for weeks of anguished debate over the off-line, wrangles over what was to come out, what should survive. Would I really be able to fight my corner, the way a real producer should, when any day I might become a mother?

The prospects for both babies were, to be frank, worrying and I knew there was no point pretending otherwise. But arguing for a change in the production schedule would inevitably risk declaring my hand. Was Brendan really ready to confront life as a threesome? When he'd only just made room for me?

Until Brendan came back I couldn't begin to resolve this issue so I got on with the nuts and bolts business of actually producing the thing. First call, of course, was for the kids themselves and I spent an infinitely depressing week in the company of various Inner London social workers, touring the dodgier council estates. Each of them was testament to different kinds of failure and the more kids I met, the more sullen and wary they seemed to become.

Before he'd plunged into the arms of Qantas, Brendan had stressed how important it was to end up with the right ethnic mix, and Gary and I argued for hours on the telephone about exactly how many blacks, browns, yellows and greens we should be adding to the pool of contenders. Put this way, the process sounds a bit like cooking and it was only after Gary came up to town for a longish session in the pub that we settled on a recipe that satisfied us both. In all, the team would number twelve. Half should be white. Of the rest, at least four should be West Indian, Bengali, Chinese or Malay. The other two places were up for grabs, depending on the talent available.

It was after we'd met in the pub, incidentally, that Gary announced he'd missed the last train. He lived in the outskirts of Ross-on-Wye, a house he'd bought when he was still with the SAS at Hereford, and the chances of making it back after half past nine were zilch. We'd had a nice time at the pub, laughing at the small print of what we were up to, and I was delighted to offer him the key to Napier Road when he inquired about a bed for the night. I scribbled the address on a scrap of paper and gave it to him before he ducked into the taxi.

'Make yourself at home,' I told him. 'Use whatever you want.'

That night I lay awake waiting for Brendan to phone from Australia, wondering whether Gilbert might confuse Gary with me. The thought of my crazy neighbour appearing at Gary's bedside in the small hours was too yummy to resist, and despite the absence of a call from Sydney, I drifted off to sleep with a smile on my face. Gary would probably throttle him. That would make Mark's day.

Gary appeared at the office next morning. When I asked him whether he'd slept OK, he looked surprised.

'Yeah,' he said. 'Any reason why not?'

It was at this point that Sandra, of all people, disappeared. We'd had a couple of preliminary meetings about *Home Run*, trying to block out cash flow on the basis of the pledges Brendan had wrung from the sponsor. Both meetings, to my relief, had been business-like, even civilised, and Sandra had listened to my critique of the original idea with something close to sympathy.

Like me, she was wary of underestimating the challenge of trying to motivate the kids, and she also agreed that Brendan was shortchanging us over location facil-ities for the shoot itself. Leaving the pictures to the kids was the kind of after-lunch decision that simply wouldn't survive contact with reality. The principle was sound enough – whole programmes had been built around it – but in this case the pressures were far too heavy for us to expect the kids to produce half-decent pictures as well. Wouldn't they have enough on their plates simply trying to survive? My despairing question drew an understanding nod from Sandra, and when I went back to Brendan's original decision, the word 'macho' brought a smile to her lips.

Our third meeting, the most important, was scheduled for the Thursday of that last week Brendan was away. I was beginning to miss him a very great deal and I'd planned to take the rest of the afternoon off. He was crazy about early jazz classics – artists like Charlie Parker and Miles Davis – and there was a brilliant second-hand record store off the Essex Road. With luck, and a bit of time, I might just find Brendan the vinyl of his dreams.

When I got to Sandra's office I found the door open. She and Brendan shared a secretary-cum-PA called Andi. Andi was sitting behind Sandra's desk, looking bemused.

'She's gone,' she said blankly. 'Just went.'

'Where?'

'Wouldn't say.'

She showed me Sandra's scribbled note. Something had come up. She'd had to drop everything and run. With luck, she should be back by Monday. If not, she'd try and phone.

I met Andi's eyes over the note. Sandra was Double-act's equivalent of gravity. She held us together. She kept our feet on the ground. Buggering off like that – no apologies, no explanation – just wasn't her style.

'What do you think?' I said. 'Sex or shopping?'

Andi grinned back. My role in Sandra's private life

had been an open secret since the morning I'd turned up in Brendan's Mercedes.

'You tell me.' She put her feet on the desk. 'You're the expert.'

With Sandra out of town, my afternoon off started rather earlier than I'd expected. I spent an hour in the record store, going through box after box of ancient LPs, and I was about to settle on a Charlie Parker classic called *Inglewood Jam* when another album, *Montparnasse*, caught my eye. Unlike the rest of the stuff in the box, it was in almost mint condition. Across the top, beneath the title, ran a shout-line announcing 'A Major New Talent', while below, occupying most of the cover, was a grainy black and white photo of the soloist featured on the album. He was sitting on a stool on some kind of dais. His head was cocked to one side and the single spotlight threw the shadow of the flute across his face. He was playing with great concentration, his eyes half-closed. I looked at the fingers, the long body, the stoop of the shoulders, and then at the face again, making sure. There was no doubt about it, absolutely none. I was looking at a younger Gilbert.

I turned the album over. It had been published in 1968. The artist's name was Gilles Phillippe. I caught myself smiling at this simple sleight of hand, Gilbert's thin disguise. At the counter, I paid for both records, taking a taxi back to Brendan's flat. In the taxi, I read the sleeve notes. They struck me as pure invention, the equivalent of the nonsense they put beside the centrefold in men's magazines. Gilles Phillippe was billed as a bohemian ex-student from the Montparnasse of the album's title. In his spare time, he wrote poetry. He had plans to become an actor. With luck, he said, he might one day make it into feature films, and work under some of his favourite *nouvelle vague* directors.

I put the record on Brendan's turntable. The music was beautiful, more recognisably Gilbert than even his face on the cover, and I lay full-length on the sofa, remembering the way it had been those first few weeks at Napier Road, hearing this stuff filtering down from the flat above. Most of it was lyrical, haunting, as hopelessly exposed as the man himself, and by the time I got to the end of Side One I was beginning to question the way I'd felt about him these last few months.

He was odd, without a doubt. He did some very strange things indeed. But there was a line in there somewhere connecting all these dots and the deeper I got into the music, the more convinced I became that I'd not only misjudged him but that – in some undefined way – I'd probably let him down. The last conversation we'd had, just days ago on the doorstep, came flooding back. He hadn't after all killed Pinot. He'd never harm a cat. On the contrary, he'd carried the poor animal back, and stored it as best he could, and waited for my return. I was never there any more. I left the place empty, cold, untended. The cats had to fend for themselves and one of them hadn't made it. Abandoning Napier Road like that was a betrayal. That's what he'd really been saying.

Next day, at the office, I made time to phone the publishing company listed on the back of the album. Inevitably, the company no longer existed but half a dozen more calls took me to a clerk in the Performing Rights Society for whom Palisade Music seemed to ring a bell. He sounded elderly and slightly startled by anyone wanting to waste their time on such an inquiry.

'It was a vanity operation,' he said. 'There were dozens of them around at the time.'

He told me the way the deal had worked. Ambitious musicians with little hope of a recording contract could, for a hefty fee, pay to have their talents immortalised on vinyl. He interspersed the key words – talents, immortalised, vinyl – with a series of throaty chuckles, and the way he did it convinced me he'd had a hand in the action. When I suggested exactly this he denied it but the longer we talked the less guarded he became and by the end of the conversation he was being extremely frank.

'Most of it was dreadful,' he said. 'Absolute bilge.'

'Can you remember any names at all?'

'No.'

'Gilles Phillippe?'

'Who?'

I spelled the name. He said he'd never heard of him, just like no one had ever heard of the rest of them. We went back to Palisade. They'd been, he said, the most blatant scam of all. Laying down eight tracks – say forty minutes of recorded music – would cost well over a grand. At today's prices, for *Montparnasse*, Gilbert would have wasted at least £10,000.

I scribbled the sum down. It sounded a great deal of money for a penniless young student from some draughty Left Bank atelier.

'You mean Paris?'

'Yes.'

'Who told you that?'

'It was in the sleeve notes.'

My contact chuckled again. The sleeve notes, as I'd suspected, formed part of the deal. The fee you paid covered the packaging as well as the music. Ditto the so-called distribution. For more money than most people could ever afford, Palisade promised to make you a star.

'And did it work? Ever?'

'You're joking. Most of the stuff never saw the inside of a shop. The artist was entitled to thirty presentation LPs. Often, the company never pressed more than that. The profit was all front-end.'

'So there was no distribution? Is that what you're saying?'

'Exactly.'

'And the artists?'

'Got their thirty LPs.'

I thanked him and hung up, reviewing my scribbled notes. Poor Gilbert, I thought. In the shape of *Montparnasse*, they'd sold him an expensive fantasy. He'd paid his money, and played his music, and had his photograph taken. Weeks later, instead of fame, or recognition, or even the odd letter, he'd been left with a box of LPs and the grim frustrations of scouring the record stores for an album that would never be on sale. How many other bids had he made for the big time? How much more money could he afford to chuck away? No wonder he'd ended up in Napier Road. Decorating the front door with those huge white eyes.

Brendan was due back the next day on the morning Qantas flight. I was literally on the point of leaving for the airport when the phone rang. It was Brendan.

'I'm still in Sydney,' he said. 'There's been a fuck-up.'

'How come?'

'God knows, but I'm here for the weekend. I'll fax the office on Monday. How's tricks?'

I told him I missed him. At length it dawned on me that he wanted to know about *Home Run*.

'It's fine,' I said. 'Everything's fine. Why?'

'I've got some interest. Bunch of guys up in Queensland. They're talking big money, major investment.'

'I thought it was all covered?'

'It is, but you know what they say. While the pot's bubbling, keep the bastard fed.'

I'd returned the Mercedes key to the hook beneath the

mirror. I hadn't a clue what he was talking about. He sounded slightly manic, a voice I hadn't heard for a month or two. The jazz LP I'd bought him as a coming-home present was lying beside the telephone. I'd spent nearly half an hour getting the bow on top just right.

'When do you think then?' I asked him.

'Next week. Definitely.'

There was a long silence. For one awful moment I thought we'd end up talking about the weather then, in a whisper, he told me he loved me.

'Say it again,' I caught sight of myself in the hall mirror. 'Please.'

There was a muffled cough at the other end. Then the line seemed to go dead and I was still staring at the mirror when the operator came on. She was extremely businesslike. She sounded, if anything, slightly oriental.

'Your call is finished,' she announced. 'Will you please hang up.'

I went earlier than usual to Napier Road to feed the cat. I took Gilbert's record with me, hiding it in a fold of the *Guardian* as I let myself in. As far as I could see the house was intact though when I stooped to retrieve the envelope with my name on it from the mat inside the door I found out why. The note came from Mark. He'd had a word with his boss and they'd both agreed that I should contact the landlord. He was the guy to put the squeeze on our friend upstairs. Once he'd quietened down, my flat could go back on the market. Until then, he thought it best to hold off. No more ambushed would-be buyers. No more awkward doorstep scenes.

I let myself into my flat. Despite the heat wave that had settled on London, it felt as cold and damp as ever. I made a fuss of Noir and opened the tin of cat food I'd bought him. He watched from the kitchen door. He looked neglected, reproachful, and I picked him up again, holding him tight. Upstairs, I could hear Gilbert moving around and I took the cat through to the front room where I'd left the LP. The stylus on my turntable really needed a new needle but I put the record on regardless, turning up the volume as the first track started.

The cat had fled back to the kitchen by now and I stood in the window, feeling the warmth of the sunshine through my grandmother's net curtains, listening to the music. Until I'd heard Gilbert play, I'd never really understood the word 'plangent'. It means mournful, resonant, resounding, the kind of music that strikes chords way down keep inside you, and *Montparnasse* was full of it.

Upstairs, the footsteps had come to a halt. The music was loud enough for Gilbert to hear and when we got into the second track I heard him moving about again. Then, magically, came the sound of a second flute, same theme, same haunting musical figures, echoing the LP. At first, he was perfectly in time, then – like the jazz musician he'd undoubtedly become – he began to improvise, gliding up and down the scale, changing key, stretching the melody this way and that. Track 3, 'Souvenirs de Printemps', was lighter in mood, and overhead came a new sound, footsteps again, heavier, quicker, a tempo that urgently shadowed the music. Still standing in the window, I tried to visualise what was going on up there, what on earth Gilbert was doing, then I heard a little yelp, the kind we girls used to make at primary school in music and movement lessons, and I finally realised what he was up to. Gilbert, my nightmare pal, my loony neighbour, was dancing.

After Side One, I retreated to the kitchen to see how

the cat was getting on. Gilbert must have come downstairs very quietly because I didn't hear his footsteps in
the hall, or even the sound of the front door opening, but
he'd definitely been out there because there were
splashes of fresh paint on the step when I left. The paint
was white gloss and it wasn't until I turned round to
close the door that I understood what he'd been doing.
Beneath the two big eyes, straddling the letter box,
Gilbert had added a big, fat, happy mouth. Our little
house once again had a smile on its face.

Back at Brendan's flat that night I got a phone call from
Gaynor. I'd given her the number and she'd called to
check I was OK. It was a nice thought and I told her so.

'Yeah,' she sounded unconvinced. 'You sure though?'

'Sure of what?'

She told me she'd been talking to one of the community beat lads. She'd asked him to keep an eye on Napier
Road and he'd come back only yesterday with a tale
about eyes on the front door.

'Are you still trying to sell the place?'

'Yes. Sort of.'

'And he's messing you around again?'

I thought about the question. In essence, of course,
she was right. Gilbert was making it as hard as he
possibly could for me to find a buyer. But there was a
logic in there somewhere, no matter how crazy, and one
way or another I was determined to understand it.

'I'm going to find the freeholder,' I told Gaynor, 'and
sort it out that way.'

'Are you sure? Only we could have him for harassment . . .'

For a second or two I gave the proposition serious
thought. Then I heard the music again, and the clumsy,

artless thump of Gilbert dancing around upstairs, and I knew there was no way. He didn't deserve to be arrested, cautioned, bollocked. If anything, it would probably make him worse. Another betrayal. More evidence of the world turning its back.

'Thanks,' I told Gaynor. 'But I still think I'll sort it with whoever owns the freehold.'

It was a month and a half before I got the chance. Brendan returned on the Wednesday of the following week, physically exhausted but bursting with ideas. It was lovely to see him and we had a glorious morning in bed before the umpteenth call on the mobile tugged him back to the office. The bedroom at De Beauvoir Square opened out onto a terrace at the back of the house. The garden faced south and we'd had the French doors open since dawn, flooding the room with sunshine.

I lay in bed, wrapped in a single sheet, watching him get dressed. He seemed to have lost weight. He looked thinner, and very pale.

'So tell me,' I said, 'about these Queensland people.'

Brendan mentioned a couple of names, production companies I'd never heard of. It seemed they were big players in Infotainment, a category of programming into which *Home Run* would evidently fit. Brendan had pitched them the concept in separate meetings and they'd both come back the next day.

'They liked it?'

'Bigtime, they liked it.'

'So what happened?'

'We're in an auction situation, one against the other.' He threw me a grin. 'Whatever happens, we're definitely looking at a co-production.'

'I thought we already had a co-production?'

'I mean three ways.'

He'd done a little research. Australia, it turned out, had a modest special forces outfit. They tended to avoid the limelight but lately there'd been threats of budget cutbacks.

'Meaning?'

'They want publicity. Of the right kind, of course.'

He'd talked to some people in the Ministry of Defence in Canberra. The notion of hoisting dead-end kids onto prime-time TV had caught their imagination. A deal was more than possible. How did I feel about producing *Home Run* down under?

I said it sounded lovely. I was trying to coax him back to bed. Without the sheet, the breeze through the French windows felt cool against my body. Brendan was trying to decide between a denim outfit and a beautiful shirt in a cotton print I'd bought him a couple of weeks back. I rolled over, stretching out a hand for him. He sat on the side of the bed for a moment, rubbing his face, preoccupied.

'One thing I forgot to mention,' he said, 'but I'm sure it won't be a problem.'

'What's that?'

'We'll have to bring the production schedule forward, a couple of weeks at least. Otherwise the shoot times don't work out.'

I gazed up at him, wondering what I'd done to deserve such a perfect morning. First Brendan, back in one piece. Then this abrupt change of birthplan for *Home Run*. Bringing the location forward to – say – September would be the answer to my prayers. Not only would we be shooting in sensible weather but I'd have ample post-production time to get the thing into some kind of shape before the real baby arrived.

'What do you think? Can do?' Brendan was looking

anxious. Obviously he'd made promises only I could fulfil.

I lay back, taking his hand again and guiding it downwards. En route, as warm as ever, it strayed across my belly. Was now the time? Should I tell him our news? Break it gently? Make his day?

I reached up, cupping his face in my hands.

'I love you,' I told him. 'And everything'll be just fine.'

Advancing the shoot, though, gave Gary and me a pretty savage deadline. It was already June. By September, we needed to have the kids sorted, a month's worth of training in the can, and all the production assets in place for the Brecon Beacons shoot. So far we'd drawn a blank on the kids and the Brecon Beacons, as far as I was concerned, was no more than a name on the map. And that, of course, was only the UK end of the shoot. What about the US operation? The fabled Green Berets? Fort Bragg? All that?

I'd been in touch, off and on, with Everett, and with the PBS station in Washington DC that Brendan had roped in as co-producers. To date they'd been making good progress – better, certainly, than us – and when I phoned again Everett had some good news.

'Found the kids,' he told me, 'and you won't believe how good they are.'

He'd started by looking in Washington, assuming that a *Home Run* team from the capital city would give the show the right profile. If anything, though, Washington had been too far gone. Most of the problem kids were up to their eyes in hard drugs and he'd had to widen the trawl first to Baltimore, and then south to Richmond, and finally out to the coast. Norfolk, Virginia, he said, was perfect. There was a big naval base, a sprawl of inner city projects, and a suburb called Portsmouth where he'd found exactly what the show needed.

'Like?'

'Like the right kind of kids. Bright. Sassy. On-line.'

'Poor?'

'Poor?' He echoed the word. 'You want to talk poor? Serious poor?'

He ran through the statistics, the bare minima on which these families had to survive. By themselves, the figures meant very little – I hadn't a clue how many groceries $93 worth of food stamps would buy for a week – but I could tell by his voice that he was excited and that was enough for me. What I'd seen of Everett in New York I'd liked a great deal. I could trust this man. He had integrity, and the way he was talking about the kids proved it. Big Duane. Skinny Calvin. And a little dynamo known as The Mouth who, he'd bet serious money, would nail the Brits to the wall.

I was scribbling notes to myself while he talked. Mention of Portsmouth had triggered one or two thoughts of my own. Maybe Everett was showing us the way. Maybe we were heading up a blind alley by restricting ourselves to London. Why not look elsewhere? Why not, for that matter, try our own Portsmouth?

The call to Everett over, I phoned Gary. He was on the payroll now, waiting at home in Ross-on-Wye until I came up with a masterplan.

'What about Portsmouth?' I suggested. 'Why don't we look there?'

I explained about Everett. He'd already settled on Portsmouth, Virginia. Twinning the two cities would be clever. I knew our own Portsmouth from my Petersfield days and I was certain it had exactly the right profile.

'It's big,' I told Gary. 'And it's poor. And it's full of

high-rise council estates. It's bloody rough, too. How about it?'

Gary and I met next morning at Portsmouth and South-sea station. The heat wave was over and a thin drizzle cloaked the surrounding tower blocks. They looked grim and forbidding, gaunt echoes of my undergraduate video, and the group of crop-haired truants loitering by the taxi rank broadened my grin. The place was perfect. I knew it already.

I'd arranged to meet a women from Social Services. Later, we'd be talking to the city council PR people. Before we got on the train for London I wanted Pompey – as the locals call it – in the bag.

Our Social Services contact turned out to be a rangy Essex University graduate called Sarah. She was very bright and – I sensed – very ambitious. She had lots of front-line experience with problem kids and I think my pitch on the phone must have fired her up because she took us at once to an area near the naval dockyard. Portsea, she told us, had always been a slum, home for the poorest families and the toughest kids. Lately, the local authority had been spending a fortune tarting up the acres of council housing and even in the rain the place looked half-decent, but there wasn't a budget big enough to wipe the poverty off the faces of the kids we met.

They looked, in a word, excluded. They seemed to come from another planet, another age. Their trainers were old. The bottoms of their jeans were frayed. They looked shabby, and neglected, and – best of all – deeply pissed off. Sarah had bribed half a dozen of them into joining us for lunch at a community centre. They sat around the table, silent at first but increasingly vocal once we'd established what we were about. It was Gary, naturally, who set the pace. He told them a bit about his days in the SAS, and described one or two of the operations he'd been on, operating behind enemy lines in the Falklands, stalking suspected terrorists in Belfast, and finally gearing up for a high-altitude parachute drop behind Iraqi lines after the invasion of Kuwait. It was the latter adventure that really broke the ice. One of the kids had been reading *Bravo Two Zero*, the Andy McNab book, and the realisation that Gary came from the same mould was quite enough for him.

'Fucking well hard,' he told his mates, with an approving nod.

That single comment seemed to do the trick. The rest of the lunch hour they spent trying to find ways they could use Gary to sort out the hated Scummers, rival football fans from Southampton, the next city west along the coast. When I pointed out that the *Home Run* opposition would be coming from across the Atlantic they took no notice, and by two o'clock the Scummers' fate was sealed. Gary would get them some Semtex. And then they'd blow the bastards away.

Gary and I were still laughing when we turned up at the council offices to meet the PR people. Sarah was still with us and she briefed them on progress to date. Portsea seemed to have taken our fancy. She thought there'd be no shortage of volunteers. The training period would take place during the summer holidays and she didn't foresee any problems with parental consents. Most of the kids, in any case, would be over sixteen and if there were any younger than that then she suspected that their mothers would be only too pleased to get them off their hands. The PR people, both ex-journalists, obviously thought it was Christmas. An hour's prime-time TV exposure had fallen into the city's lap and we set off on another tour, this time with a view to showing us the nicer bits.

As I've said, I already knew Portsmouth but I wasn't prepared for the way the city had changed since I'd last had a proper look round. Over the last couple of years, thanks to a string of commemorative occasions, Pompey had put itself well and truly on the map. The world's media had descended for the fortieth anniversary of D-Day, and weeks later the city had hosted a stage of the Tour de France. A brand new university had supplanted the old Poly and the naval dockyard now boasted the finest collection of historical ships in the world. Everywhere we looked, there were fabulous pictures to brighten the documentary bits of *Home Run* and what was especially pleasing were the historical links with the States. Emigrants had sailed from Portsmouth, back in the nineteenth century, and elements of the US fleet – Virginia-based – still made regular visits.

On the train going back to London, Gary and I settled down with a half-bottle of Scotch and a milk jug full of water from the buffet car. I knew the day had been a knockout but I wanted to be sure.

'You're OK about the kids?' I asked him.

'They're great. As great as we'll get. Vicious little bastards. Absolutely bloody perfect.'

'So how do we crack the training?'

This was a problem. Brendan was still banging on about lifting the odd day here and there, stitching together a month's induction, but Gary – even more than me – knew that was crazy. What he had to build was a sense of *esprit*, a sense of belonging, and to do that he had to prise our kids out of Pompey and take them somewhere wild and remote where they could test themselves – individually and collectively – against some pretty heavy physical odds.

'Anywhere in mind?'

'Skye,' Gary grunted. 'The Cuillins.'

The Western Isles, it turned out, had long been Gary's favourite playground. He'd holidayed there as a kid and returned years later with a bunch of mates to tackle some of the more formidable peaks. The Cuillin range offered some of the toughest rockfaces in Europe and, over his third glass of Scotch, Gary confided that his first experience of one of them – a monster called Am Basteir – had literally shaped the rest of his life. After Am Basteir, he said, he'd been addicted to physical risk. Thus his decision to join the army. And thus, a little later, the months and months of savage training that had finally taken him into the SAS. The way he put it, that nod of quiet satisfaction, was the closest I'd yet come to pinning down exactly what it was that lay at the heart of *Home Run*. By taking these kids, and pitting them against themselves, we'd be showing thousands of others just what might be possible.

I tackled Brendan about the training schedule that same night. We hadn't seen each other for days. I told him about Portsea, and about our conversation over cold pizza in the community centre. He didn't like what he heard.

'Why Portsmouth? Why not here? London?'

I told him about Everett. That simply compounded the problem.

'He's not using Washington kids?'

'No, I just told you. He's out on the coast. Portsmouth, Virginia. Suburb of Norfolk. And he's thrilled about it.'

'But we agreed capital cities.'

'No, we didn't.'

'Excuse me, I think we did.'

We were sitting in a restaurant round the corner from

the office, a Greek place that served excellent moussaka. Brendan had barely touched his. I poured him another glass of retsina.

'Portsmouth's fine,' I assured him. 'And Gary's happy, too. It'll work. I know it'll work.'

I could see Brendan wasn't convinced. I decided to go back to the training issue but there were problems there too.

'Skye's out of the question.' He dismissed it with a shake of his head. 'Too bloody far. Too bloody expensive.'

'*Expensive*?' I was beginning to get angry. 'I thought you'd lined up all this backing? I thought we had money coming out of our ears?'

'Pledges,' he said. 'We have pledges. It's not cash. Not yet.'

'Then borrow,' I said. 'Isn't that what banks are for?'

Brendan caught the taunt in my voice and I could tell at once that he didn't like it. Money was his department. I belonged in the Creatives cage. I reached for his hand, giving it a little squeeze. No point screwing the boss and not using the leverage.

'Say we make it three weeks.'

'Where?'

'Skye.'

'No.'

'Where else then?'

'Fuck knows. Salisbury Plain. Isle of Wight. Somewhere handy. Somewhere cheaper.'

He withdrew his hand and emptied his glass at a single gulp. To do that with retsina you've got to be seriously drunk or seriously upset. Brendan wasn't drunk.

'What's the matter?'

He looked away, shaking his head.

'Nothing.'

'Tell me.'

'It's nothing.'

'Please.'

He summoned a chilly smile and then signalled the waiter for the bill. I looked at the remains of his moussaka. Dessert would have been nice.

'Is there a real problem?' I tried to sound as sympathetic as I could.

'With what?'

'The money. The budget.'

I should have anticipated his reaction. Asking Brendan a question like that after banging on for the last couple of minutes was like questioning his manhood. He got to his feet and pushed the chair back. He scribbled a signature on the Access chit and then headed for the door. I didn't move. Through the window, I could see him wrestling furiously with the car keys. Seconds later, the Mercedes had gone.

I caught up with him at home in De Beauvoir Square. He was lying full-length on the sofa, his eyes closed, listening to the record I'd bought him when he returned that time from Australia. I circled the living room, turning off lights, then I settled on the carpet beside the half-empty bottle of Glenlivet, my back against the sofa. His hand found mine.

'He's brilliant,' he murmured. 'You have to admit it.'

I listened to Charlie Parker for a while. Saxophones had never turned me on but now wasn't the time to admit it.

'I never told you why I bought it.' I glanced up at him. 'I bought it to say thank you.'

'For what?'

'For you,' I kissed his hand. 'And for *Home Run*.'

'Fuck *Home Run*.'

'For you, then.'

He held my hand tight. We listened to the music. Finally he got up on one elbow. I could smell the whisky on his breath.

'I mean it about *Home Run*,' he said. 'It's not important. It shouldn't . . .' he made a loose, flapping motion with his hand, '. . . come between us.'

'I agree.'

I smiled up at him. I was going to get Skye after all. I knew it. Tonight, tomorrow, next week, Brendan was going to say yes.

'Let's forget it.' I said, 'We can talk about it some other time.'

He gazed down at me, saying nothing, and I fought the temptation to join him on the sofa. That could come later. And doubtless would.

'I love you,' he said at last. 'It's important you know that.'

'I do.'

'And believe it.'

'I do.'

He nodded, as if the question had somehow been directed at himself, then began to trace the outlines of my face with a single moistened finger, the way kids make a pattern in the condensation on cold glass. It was something he occasionally did in bed, after we'd made love. I trapped his finger in my mouth, and sucked it softly.

'I'm dead serious,' he said. 'I sometimes don't think I tell you often enough, you know. Maybe I let other things get in the way.' He frowned. 'They won't, will they?'

'What?'

'Get in the way?'

I wondered exactly what he was talking about, what

he meant. There was an odd expression on his face, almost supplicatory, and for a second or two it reminded me overwhelmingly of Gilbert. Same need, I thought. Same strange sense of lostness, almost despair.

It was my turn to talk about priorities.

'*Home Run*'s important,' I said gently. 'But it isn't this.'

'What?'

'Us. It isn't us.'

He nodded.

'It isn't,' he said. 'And it mustn't ever be.'

'No.'

'You promise?'

'Of course.'

'Thank Christ for that.'

He lay back on the sofa, his eyes closing again, and for a second or two I had an overwhelming urge to tell him about the baby. Then I wondered whether the news might tip him over again, destroying this closeness between us, and the moment passed. After we'd gone to bed, he said he was sorry about the restaurant, what had happened, the way he'd lost his cool. Three days later, Gary, myself, and Sarah from Portsmouth Social Services were toiling up the southern approaches to Am Basteir.

The recce was a blast. We were on Skye for barely four days yet at the end of it I felt like I'd been shaken inside out, like an old rag doll, then made whole again. That far north, in late June, it hardly got dark at all and we scrambled up peak after peak listening to Gary explaining the way it would be for the kids he'd select.

From his own old maps and notebooks, he'd compiled a list of climbs, ranking them in order of difficulty. At the start of the month, he'd concentrate on basic fitness, getting them up to speed, getting them used to the 6.00 a.m. starts, and cold showers, and all the other delights of life under canvas. With Brendan's blessing, he'd hired three mates for the month – all ex-SAS – and between them they'd monitor each boy's progress. Only when they were all, in Gary's phrase, 'run in' would they start on the climbs. By day ten, with luck, they'd be into serious ropework and the final week should see them tackling the peaks that would ask the really hard questions.

In all of this, the emphasis would be on teamwork, and the better I got to know Gary, the more obvious the logic of Skye became. Taming a beast like Am Basteir demanded a level of trust and mutual reliance that literally put your life in the hands of the next guy down the rope. That was the only way Gary wanted it. That was the only way, he said, that his lads would slot the Yanks when it came to the shoot-out on the Brecon Beacons.

On the plane back to Heathrow, we talked about the kids using cameras. I'd be taking a professional crew up to Skye to shoot the training sequences but Gary – as practical as ever – suggested we give two or three of the kids little camcorders. That way, under the kind of physical pressures they'd have to cope with during the game itself, they'd have a chance to grab their own pictures. If the results were as terrible as we expected, then Brendan, bless him, would have to let me solve the coverage problem some other way.

Back in London, over the next week, I kept in daily touch with Gary while he sorted out eighteen lads from Portsea. The six extras he'd decided to recruit in case of accidents or homesickness. The latter sounded highly unlikely but as Sarah pointed out, delinquency was often the other face of acute insecurity, and we'd be foolish to accept some of these kids' toughness at face value.

Between them, our little band had amassed three A4 pages of major and minor convictions. They'd taken to calling themselves 'The G-Force', a quiet compliment to Gary, whom they clearly worshipped. Star of the G-Force was Dean, who at seventeen had five convictions for removing motor cars without their owners' consent. His favourite had been a Golf GTI belonging to a local solicitor's wife. He'd left it upside down in a field of growing wheat after rolling the car at 95 m.p.h. Questioned afterwards, he'd blamed the accident on the police. Had they not pursued him with quite so much vigour, the car – he said – would still be in one piece.

By now, it was mid-July. Two and a half months of non-stop work had left me totally exhausted and I knew the time was coming when I had to take a break. I was doing my best to eat sensibly, and lay off the alcohol, but every article I had time to read about pregnancy seemed to stress how much the experience took out of you. Rest, of course, was the answer, but it was difficult to slip away. The programme seeds we'd planted back in May were beginning to blossom and someone had to be there, day after day, tending our little plot.

Best of all were the kids. Everett's reports from Virginia were never less than optimistic and Gary, quite out of character, was positively gleeful about the progress of the G-Force. He was getting them together on a regular basis down in Portsmouth, prior to the trip to Skye, and they were basking in the attention that *Home Run* had attracted from the local media. An early location day in Portsea had given me footage of the lives our kids would be shedding, and these sequences – one could sense already – would provide the benchmarks against which we could measure the flesh and blood effects of *Home Run*. In human terms, the thing was working beautifully and that, to me, was the hinge on the door we were trying so hard to push open.

I tried the image on Sandra. We were into the third week of July. In a couple of days, their summer term over, the kids would be heading north. After a great deal of thought, I'd decided to request a freelance director for the initial shoot on Skye. That way, with the minimum of fuss, I could have a week off.

Sandra sat behind her desk while I finished my health check on the dodgier parts of the budget. Brendan had flown to Los Angeles in pursuit of yet another co-production deal, some other series this time. When I'd finished, Sandra fired up the computer and scrolled through the spend to date. I was quite right. We had money to spare for a good freelance director.

She peered at me over the desk. The last month or two she'd taken to wearing glasses, the kind of severe half-moons you expect to see perched on the nose of your local bank manager. They suited her wonderfully.

'But I don't understand,' she said. 'Why don't you *want* to do it? Why don't you find the time? It's your first shoot, for God's sake. It's not like you to miss a chance like that.'

I pointed out that we'd already had a day and a half down in Portsea. I'd directed on that occasion and I was more than pleased with the results.

'Then why not now? Why not Skye?'

I told her I was exhausted. It was the truth but it sounded pathetic.

She was beginning to look interested. My bust was even bigger than usual, another departure from the norm.

'I thought you were super-fit?' She frowned. 'All those exercises? All that running?'

I wondered how she knew about the running. I'd never told her, and no one else in the office knew either.

I shrugged.

'It must be the weather,' I said feebly. 'And it's been non-stop since January.'

'The weather?'

'No, the work. But the weather doesn't help.' I gestured at the line of wilting plants on her window sill. 'It's just so airless up here. London's pure exhaust. It gets to you in the end.'

Sandra was clearly unconvinced. Finally, she stood up, smoothing the creases in her dress. She was thinner than I'd ever seen her, a collection of acute angles hung together by a tension you could practically feel.

'You're pregnant,' she said abruptly. 'I can tell.'

I felt myself colour. I didn't even deny it. She sat down again, reaching behind her for the little fridge she kept stocked with Tango. She produced two cans, pushing one across the desk.

'When is it due?'

I heard myself telling her. It was like being in a dream. She could have been my mother, so powerful, so all-knowing.

'Is it Brendan's?'

'Yes.'

'Have you told him?'

'No.'

'Don't you think you ought to?'

Brendan, I was fairly certain, had sussed it already. Partly because of the weight I'd put on, and partly because of the very obvious absence of my periods. At the start, I'd toyed with trying to fake periods but the thought of walking around with a bone-dry Tampax inside me was so repellent that I'd never got round to it.

Sandra was still waiting for an answer. I told her I didn't know.

'But you are having it?'

'Yes, I'm afraid so.'

'I see.'

I looked away, hearing the can open with an angry little fizz. She'd be talking about marriage next, though that was the last thing on my wish list. I'd already seen what marriage had done to Brendan. A coke habit and psychotherapy I could do without.

I heard her sipping at the can. When I looked back, she was staring thoughtfully at the screen.

'What about the programme?' she asked.

'The programme's fine. I can manage.'

'No you can't. You're asking for a director.'

'That's different. That's just the once.'

'So what happens for the rest of the shoot?'

'I'll do it.'

'Including Brecon?'

'Of course.'

She took off her glasses and gave them a polish. According to Brendan, she'd never had a child of her own and I wondered just what difference that made. Was she jealous? Or just pissed off that I was wasting precious budget on something as flippant as a week's leave?

'Next week the kids are just bedding down,' I pointed out. 'The director I have in mind's first class. Boys prefer men around. I'm adding value here. Everyone wins.'

'That's hardly the point, dear. The point is, you're supposed to be coping. You're supposed to be in there, controlling the bloody thing. That's why we pay you. That's what a producer *does*.'

I stared at her. It was a clear threat, the shot across my bows I'd been expecting for months. The phoney war was over. My being pregnant had opened hostilities.

'OK,' I shrugged. 'I'll cancel the director and go back to plan A.'

'What do you mean?'

'I mean I'll direct it myself. Go up to Skye.' I gave her a smile. 'Take control.'

'You can't,' she said sharply. 'You're exhausted.'

'I'm not.'

'Yes you are. You just told me.'

'I was lying. I'm fine. It's no problem. I can handle it.'

'And the baby?'

'We'll handle it together.'

The answer hurt her. I could see it. She almost winced. For a long time, she stared at the Tango can. It was hot in the office and little beads of condensation had formed around the outside.

'I still love him, you know. And I miss him, too.' She glanced up. 'Should I be telling you that?'

I said I didn't know. It sounded as pathetic as telling her I was knackered. I was looking for an excuse to leave now, though in retrospect I suspect I didn't need one. What followed did neither of us any favours.

She put the can to her lips, swallowing barely a mouthful.

'He's talented, isn't he? Clever?'

'How do you mean?'

'How do you think I mean?' She stared at me, then motioned crudely at her lap. 'Good with it. Skilful. Too good really.'

I gave her a weak smile, more to invite her to shut up than anything else. Deliberately or otherwise, she ploughed on.

'Does he spoil you?' she asked. 'Have you done the honey yet? The yoghurt? The bananas? All that?'

As it happens, we had, though I wasn't going to give her the satisfaction of confirming it.

'I haven't a clue what you're talking about,' I said primly.

'You're lying,' she said hotly. 'Jesus, look at you, sex on legs.' She paused. 'Ever wonder why he goes away so much? Why he's forever late back? Why it has to be Australia, or New York, or Los Angeles? Ever think of all those hotel rooms? Those opportunities? Those big, empty beds?' She tipped the can of Tango towards me in a mock toast. 'The man's insatiable,' she said softly. 'Here's to baby.'

I'd had enough. I'd long ago abandoned the moral high ground and I had precious little to lose except my job and whatever shreds of a relationship I still shared with this twisted woman.

I stood up, looking her in the eye.

'If you're telling me he gets bored, I'm sure you're right. The trick is to keep him happy, keep him satisfied. Maybe you should have tried a bit harder. Taramasalata's good, by the way. Much better than honey.'

I reached forward, putting my unopened Tango can beside hers. Then I left.

My friend Nikki returned from South Africa that same week. The night after I'd broken the news about Pinot, I took her out for a consolatory meal. We both got very drunk, ending up back at De Beauvoir Square. I'd promised her a puppy. In fact I think I'd promised her dozens.

She circled the flat, colliding with various bits of

furniture. I'd been describing my run-in with Sandra. The digs about Brendan had got under my skin. Bitch.

'You have to trust him,' Nikki kept saying. 'You have no option.'

'I do trust him. I trust him with my life. That's the bloody problem.'

'What?'

'My life. He's got it, all of it. I gave it to him.'

'You did?'

'Yes.'

'You're stupid.'

'That's what Sandra said. In so many words.'

'She's his wife. She's bound to say that.'

'I know. But you said it too.'

'When?'

'Just now.'

The conversation went round and round, dizzier and dizzier, getting us nowhere. The fact that I'd got so hopelessly drunk made me even more frustrated.

'How can I know?' I wailed. 'How can I know for sure? Shit, maybe she's right. She should know. Cow.'

'She's inventing it. She's winding you up.'

'You think so?'

'Definitely. Come here.'

She gave me a big, wet kiss and we staggered off to bed. Next morning, early for once, Brendan turned up from the airport. I was still in the flat. Nikki had left in a taxi. My head hurt and I was feeling extremely insecure.

I sat Brendan down and made him a bacon sandwich. Twelve hours on the plane from LA had left him in an even worse state than me. I hosed tomato ketchup all over the bacon, sealing the sandwich with a kiss. The smell of it made me want to throw up.

'Here,' I said, giving it to him. 'Real food. Make you feel better.'

Brendan nibbled at the edges of the sandwich before pushing it away. Whenever I looked at him I couldn't help thinking of all those yawning hotel beds. King sized. Newly folded down.

'Tired?'

'Not really.'

'Don't fancy . . . ?'

I put my hand over his and felt him flinch. He'd never done that before. I plugged the kettle in, meaning to make some fresh coffee. When I turned round, he was examining the gas bill. *Gas* bill? Was I that irresistible?

I circled him warily. Whatever happened next was completely out of my hands. One way or another I had to get to him before the bitch-queen did. Better me breaking the news than Sandra.

'I'm pregnant,' I told him. 'I'm going to have a baby.'

Brendan was peering at the bottom of the bill. *If you use more than ten trillion BTUs, you qualify for a discount.*

'You what?'

'I'm going to have a baby.'

He looked up at last. Under the neon strip light, his skin was the colour of putty. Too much indoors, I told myself. Too many hotel bedrooms.

'When?'

'December.'

'But when did it happen?'

'March.' I smiled wearily. 'You probably remember.'

'But you told me . . .' he frowned, still holding the bill.

'I was wrong.' I did my best to keep smiling. 'But it's great news, isn't it?'

We had our crisis meeting two and a half weeks later. It

happened to be the 12th August. I remember that because Nikki had a disgusting boyfriend who went shooting in Scotland and he sent her a dead pheasant care of Interbird or something and she phoned me up and told me. I was about to go into Brendan's office and she wished me luck.

Sandra was already there, and so was the company accountant, a grey-faced man from somewhere in the City. His visits to Doubleact, mercifully rare, always spelled big trouble. I joined the three of them at Brendan's little conference table. They were drinking iced water. Another bad sign.

Brendan launched off. He hadn't been away since Los Angeles but I'd seen very little of him. Night after night he'd come crawling in the wrong side of midnight, never hungry, never thirsty, never wanting anything except a deep and dreamless sleep. These days he seemed to live in a fog of near-permanent exhaustion, shrouded against the outside world. I'd tried so many times to get through, it had almost become a joke.

The file on the table in front of him had the letters CHR in big black Pentel on the front. He opened it and I recognised the letterhead of one of our American partners on the top sheet of correspondence.

'An opportunity has come our way . . .' he glanced round. 'This may be the biggest break we'll ever get.'

I tried to focus on my empty notepad, wondering why on earth I'd been invited. With *Home Run*, I had quite enough on my plate. Was he expecting me to shoulder something else as well?

Brendan was talking about some agent or other on the West Coast. The agent had secured some big name agreements. In principle, stars of the order of Brad Pitt and Tom Cruise were prepared to talk to us. Not only talk but maybe, just maybe, contract.

'For what?' the accountant inquired.

I shot him a grateful look. Someone, at least, still lived in the real world.

A frown briefly clouded Brendan's face. Then he glanced sideways at me.

'*Celebrity Home Run,*' he said.

At first, I didn't think I'd heard him properly. Neither did the accountant.

'*Celebrity Home Run,*' Brendan repeated. 'We're having to adapt the format. Our sponsors insist. So do the networks.'

'How?' I asked at once. 'How do we adapt the format?'

Brendan steadied himself for a moment and I began to understand why the last couple of weeks had been so conversation-free. He must have known, I thought. He must have known since Los Angeles.

'There's been a little unease,' he began, 'about elements in the mix, chiefly the documentary thing. It's a great concept, kids from the ghettos, but the worry – understandably – is there. The people out on the Coast are anxious about the thing getting too preachy.'

'*Preachy?*' I said hotly. 'What does "preachy" mean?'

'It means they're unhappy about having the show issue-based. They're saying it's a people medium, not an issue-medium. And they're right, of course. That's exactly what it is.'

I was thinking about Gary's gang from Portsea. Dean. Gimble. Crater-face. Jason.

'We've got people,' I said. 'In spades.'

'No,' Brendan shook his head. 'We've got a bunch of C2/Ds from the wrong side of the tracks. We've got a social issue here and we've bolted on a game show to give it a bit of zip. The game show's no problem. They love the game show, the shoot-out, the Brecon Beacons, all that special forces shit: they think that's great.'

'I bet they do.'

'Sure.' Brendan leaned forward. 'And that's where guys like Brad figure. They're queuing up. They're after part of the action. They want to be *in* it.'

'With the kids?'

'Instead of the kids.'

'You're dreaming. Brad *Pitt*?'

'Sure.' Brendan wasn't looking at me any more. 'The way it works, they'll each pick their own teams. An American star, an English star. They'll go for fellow actors, more faces, more names, more profile.' I watched him smile at Sandra. 'The networks are creaming themselves.'

I pushed my chair back, meaning to get up and leave. Then I had second thoughts.

'Just say I believe you? What about Gary? And Everett?'

'They think it's great, too.'

'They do?'

'Of course.' Brendan was pouring himself a glass of water. 'It wouldn't work without them.'

'And they're happy? Just to . . .' I made a hopeless, despairing gesture, '. . . swop boats like that? Midstream?'

'Of course,' Brendan said again. 'Wouldn't you? Brad Pitt? Hughie Grant? Ken Branagh?'

I said nothing. Shock had robbed me of the power of thought. Then the details came seeping back, the small print of the last three impossible months, the little battles we'd fought and won, the kids we'd found, the lives we'd change, the stories we'd lay before an audience of millions. All that was gone? Just tossed aside? Because of some fantasy about Brad Pitt?

'We're on a learning curve here,' Brendan said briskly. 'That's what development's about. Some things work, some don't. Lame horses you leave for the Indians.'

I couldn't stop thinking about Portsea.

'The kids would have worked. You know they would.'

'Brad Pitt works better.'

'Who says?'

'The West Coast says. The sponsors. The networks. Everyone.'

'And you? What do you think?'

The question was deeply personal, a challenge, and everyone knew it. Brendan frowned, sipped a little more water, then reminded us all that we were running a business. Sentiment was fine, but it was money that talked. He glanced up at me. I was absolutely welcome to stay on board, stay in charge, in fact Doubleact expected it. On the other hand, if I found the change of direction too traumatic, there were other options open to me.

By this time I was on my feet.

'These kids have nothing,' I said. 'The Brad Pitts of this world have millions. Where's the justice in that?'

'Justice?' Brendan looked briefly pained. 'Is that an issue here?'

'Yes, it is. Don't you think so?'

Brendan wouldn't answer. The accountant looked at his notes. Sandra was smiling. At length, Brendan closed his file. Those initials again. CHR.

I bent to the table, my mouth close to Brendan's ear. In a moment or two, I'd be gone. But not before I'd told him what I really felt.

'*Celebrity Home Run,*' I said softly, 'is a pile of shit.'

*

Brendan and I parted the following evening. I hadn't been to work that day. I spent most of the morning sorting out the things I wanted to take away and by the time I'd finished I was exhausted. I slept most of the afternoon, though by the time Brendan came in I was back in the kitchen, making myself a peanut butter sandwich.

He'd seen my cases by the door. I could tell from his face that he wasn't the least bit surprised.

'It's best,' I said simply. 'You don't want me here.'

'I do. Don't think that.'

'You don't. Otherwise it would all be different.'

'I'm sorry about yesterday. It's out of my hands.'

'It's not, but that's not the point. It's not the programme. Not the fucking Americans. Not Brad Pitt. It's us.'

'What do you mean?'

For the first time in weeks, I'd got through, made a connection, triggered something in his brain. He looked, if anything, frightened.

'Something's happened,' I said softly. 'You won't tell me what, which is why I've never asked. But that's enough to tell me it's over.'

'What's enough?'

'The fact that you won't talk to me. The fact that you don't trust me. The fact that you can't be bothered any more. I don't want that. Not now. Not ever.'

'It'll change,' he said half-heartedly. 'I promise.'

I carried on with the peanut butter sandwich. He was watching me, still apprehensive.

'What about the baby?' he asked at last.

'What about it?'

'You really want to keep it? Only . . .' He touched the pocket where he kept his cheque book. It was an obscene gesture and I ignored it.

'The baby's due in December,' I said. 'That makes me nearly six months pregnant. Six months is dangerous, even if I wanted an abortion.' I gave him a cold smile. 'Don't you think you've done enough damage?'

I watched him swallowing.

'So you're keeping it?'

'Yes.'

'How will you cope? For money?'

'Christ knows. There'll be a way.'

He looked far from convinced. He asked me where I intended to live. I didn't answer.

'Tell me where,' he repeated. 'I need an address.'

'Why?'

'Because . . .' he shrugged, looking hopeless, robbed of an answer.

I'd nearly finished the sandwich. Afterwards, I washed up my plate and asked him to call me a cab. When the cab came, he helped me load my things into the back. Only after he'd returned to the flat and shut the door did I tell the cabbie the address.

'Tottenham Green, please.' I collapsed back against the seat. 'Napier Road.'

Three

The next few days, to be frank, passed me by. Robbed of my routine – my early starts, my endless phone calls, my snatched meals – I surrendered to the waves of exhaustion that had been threatening to engulf me for weeks. I slept late, only getting up to make tea and a slice or two of toast. The moment I felt tired again, I retreated back to bed, happy to close my bedroom curtains against the world. Living with Brendan, commuting to the office through rush hour traffic, I'd forgotten how quiet Napier Road could be. With Nikki back from South Africa, I didn't even have the cat to break the silence.

Slowly, I began to surface. Some of the numbness wore off, replaced by a deep anger. The word that preoccupied me more and more was betrayal. I thought about the programme promises we'd made, to each other first of all, and then to an ever-widening circle of people who'd been silly enough to believe us. The kids, of course, and their parents, and the local authority contacts in Portsmouth, and then individuals like the woman from the probation service who'd been so knocked out by the idea that she'd threatened to put Gary up for the MBE. These were people who knew what it was like at the bottom of the pile, who cared about the damage we were inflicting on our children and on each other. What, I asked myself, would Brad Pitt do for them? Except thicken the soup of glitz and violence that television already dished up by the bucketful?

I pursued these questions around the flat, brooding on the way that Brendan had throttled my boisterous little infant. He'd done it because something else had taken his fancy. He'd done it because, in the end, he couldn't resist the lure of the big money. That wasn't especially wicked. It wasn't even, on reflection, a surprise. It was just weak, and predictable, and utterly gutless. For once, we'd happened on something truly original. We'd worked our bollocks off trying to get the programme into shape and we'd had a fighting chance of playing to a huge audience. It would have been popular, and decent, and good fun. Now, like so much else, it was just wrapping.

Towards the end of the week, mid-August now, Gary turned up. I hadn't bothered to phone either him or Everett, mainly because I couldn't bear to believe that they, too, had been part of the betrayal. We sat in the kitchen. Gary looked fit and bronzed and weather-beaten.

'How was Skye?' I asked him.

He told me the training had been abandoned after the first week. Brendan had phoned through on the mobile and ordered them all back south. It had, said Gary, been a kind of blessing.

'A *blessing*?'

'Yeah. Most of the kids couldn't hack it.'

'What do you mean?'

'They were completely off the pace. Half of them couldn't wait to get back on the train.'

I toyed glumly with my coffee. This didn't begin to fit my script. I wanted to hear about heartbreak, disillusion, dashed hopes. Not a bunch of adolescents pining for McDonald's.

'Are you serious? You were *glad* it was called off?'

'Not me, love. Them.'

'But you'd have seen it through, surely?'

'Of course.'

Gary was rolling a cigarette. He licked the gummed seam then looked up.

'They'd have cracked it in the end, one way or another, but it wouldn't have been easy. Not as easy as we thought, anyway.'

'That was you. You thought it would be easy. Me? I thought it would be bloody impossible. Or nearly, anyway.'

'Yeah, well, you were right.'

'But that was the point, wasn't it? Challenge? Up against the odds? All that?'

Gary lit the cigarette. Smoke curled up towards the wreckage of my ceiling.

'I don't blame you,' he conceded after a while. 'I'd be pissed off, too.'

'But you're not?' I pointed out. 'You're not pissed off.'

'Who says?'

'Brendan. He told me that you and Everett agreed the change of plan.' I pushed a saucer towards him for the toppling ash. 'True?'

'Sort of,' he nodded.

'Why?'

Gary didn't answer. Finally, he pulled an envelope from his pocket and put it on the table. It had my name on it. I recognised Brendan's handwriting.

'What's that?'

'I get the impression it's money.'

I didn't pick the envelope up. Gary had known about me and Brendan and had obviously realised that the thing was over. We talked about it for a minute or two but I could sense his embarrassment and quickly took the conversation back to the kids. The fact that he'd fallen in with Brendan's change of plan still hurt. I nodded at the envelope, still lying on the table.

'Is that your answer?' I asked him. 'You did it for money? Said yes for money? Quiet life? Cash in hand?'

'They're paying the bills,' he pointed out. 'They're giving the orders.'

'But Gary, the orders are crap.'

'That's not my problem, love. I've worked with dickheads all my life. The man says jump, you jump.'

This was a side of Gary I'd never seen before. I was amazed, not just by his compliance but by his honesty in admitting it. If he shrugged once more I'd begin to believe he really didn't care.

The envelope still lay between us. Gary was keen to change the subject.

'It's from Brendan,' he said. 'He asked me to bring it round because he thought you wouldn't let him in.'

'He's right. I wouldn't.'

'You want me to tell him that?'

'Yes,' I nodded, 'please.'

Gary left soon afterwards. Only when we were in the hall did he stoop to peck me on the cheek.

'It's a fucking shame,' he muttered. 'We had a few laughs, didn't we?'

'We did.'

'Yeah.' He opened the front door, looking out at the street. 'Still, can't be helped, eh?'

Back in the kitchen, depressed as hell, I opened Brendan's envelope. Gary had been right about the money. Inside, stapled to a note, was a cheque for £5,000. When I read the note it wasn't at all clear what the money was for but the payee was definitely me and I suppose it helped a bit to know that finding some kind of work wasn't quite as pressing as I'd thought. If I was careful with the money I'd managed to save, £5,000 would last me well into the autumn. Once I'd got my little boat trimmed out again, maybe I could make some sensible decisions.

I took Brendan's note through to the front room. The fact that I was beginning to miss him I was determined to put down to force of habit but hearing his voice behind the scribbled phrases didn't help at all. He said that he was sorry for everything that had happened. He admitted that he'd been keeping things from me but said there were good reasons why. One day, maybe, there'd be a chance to explain properly and then I might understand. In the meantime I was to take very great care and try not to think the worst of him. At the end of the note, typically, he'd signed off with a flourish. There were some winds, he'd written, that were too strong even for me.

I read the note for a third time, beginning to realise that he wasn't talking about *Home Run*. This laboured apology, this plea in mitigation, was to do with us. He'd been keeping secrets. He'd tried to weather some kind of crisis. And he'd failed. I folded the note and returned it to the envelope, trying to resist the temptation to get out my magnifying glass, and crawl all over the last few months we'd shared, looking for clues to what had really happened.

When it came down to the pair of us – flesh on flesh – I was pretty certain I hadn't been fooling myself. I'd been through enough affairs to distinguish between make-believe and the real thing, and I knew that those times together had touched us both in the deepest places. Apart from anything else, in this one respect he'd find me bloody hard to replace and if there was anything of the real Brendan in the warm, generous man I'd made love to, then he was in for some very lonely nights indeed. This knowledge was far from comforting, chiefly because it applied equally to me. You simply can't give so much of yourself away, pile your chips so recklessly on a single square, and then just shrug it off when the run of the dice turns against you. Life, thank Christ, isn't like that. We'd loved each other. And we'd lost it. And that was a very great shame.

Still in a daze, I heard Gilbert clattering downstairs and out through the front door. Since I'd been back, I'd scarcely been aware of him at all – no flute, no prowling up and down all night – but now there was no avoiding the man. Not only was there a spring in his step, but he was whistling, something I'd never known him do before. I turned in the chair, looking over my shoulder, watching him lope off down the street. His head was up and the slouch had gone. Maybe it's the weather, I thought. Or maybe he's turned some personal corner. Whatever the reason, I was glad for both of us. One crisis was quite enough.

Andi from work phoned an hour or so later. She'd been wanting to get in touch but she'd lost my number and when she'd gone into the computer for the personal details we were all obliged to register, she'd found that mine had been deleted.

'You're a non-person,' she giggled. 'Lucky thing.'

We chatted for a while. Once she'd sussed that I wasn't suicidal, conversation was easy, the usual swamp of office gossip. As soon as I decently could, I steered her round to Brendan.

'How is he?' I inquired.

'He's OK. Manic as ever.'

I could hear how guarded she'd suddenly become and for one awful moment it occurred to me that he might have shacked up with someone else.

'What's he up to?'

'The usual. Chasing sponsors, sweet-talking the networks, you know, smoothing his way around.'

'I didn't mean that.'

'Ah . . . '

There was a long silence. I pointed out that I'd more or less got over it. The worst had come and gone. Nothing she said could possibly make any difference.

'OK.' I could visualise Andi nodding. 'So are you ready for this?'

'Yes.'

'He's gone back to his wife.'

'*Sandra*?'

'The very same.'

'Moved back in?'

'As we speak.'

For some reason, God knows why, it was the last thing I expected. I'd been living in a world of hotel bedrooms, expense account meals, and limitless free Moët, an agonising fantasy scored for some outrageous bimbo with legs the length of my body and talents to match. Instead, my ex-lover had chosen to return to the dungeon and shackle himself to the bitch-queen. Poor Brendan. Poor, sad man.

'Why?' I heard myself saying.

'That's what we're all asking.'

'And Sandra?'

'She probably knows, at least I imagine she does. Maybe she's got something on him, maybe he *likes* getting beaten up.'

My mind was racing ahead. Brendan was probably back with the shrink by now, pouring his heart out. Either that, or he'd be into heavy drugs again – though a moment's thought told me there wasn't enough cocaine in the world to buffer the likes of Brendan from his wife. They were totally different animals, different species even. In a zoo, Sandra would have an enclosure all of her own.

'That's incredible,' I said at last. 'I'm not sure I believe it.'

'It's true. Definitely. I had to get him on the phone this morning. She wanted a price on the new set for *Members Only*.'

'Where was he?'

'At home.'

Home was De Beauvoir Square. That's where he'd lived. That's the place we'd made our own. Sandra lived north, a lordly pile Brendan had once shown me from the car.

'You mean Highgate?'

'Yeah, the family pad. He's been back there a couple of days now. Doesn't come in until late morning.'

'And she phones him?'

'All the time.' She giggled again. 'I'm sure she's doing it for our benefit really. She's making a point. It's all kissy-kissy. You should hear it. Yuk.'

I tried to imagine Sandra getting herself around the simplest endearments. Even saying please was a skill she'd never mastered.

'I don't get it,' I said. 'I just don't get it.'

'Neither does he, probably, fool that he is. Tell me, Jules . . . '

'What?'

'Why do men always fuck it up?'

Why indeed? I took Brendan's cheque to the bank that afternoon and spent longer than I should have done filling in the deposit slip. The conversation with Andi had roped me to the memories of the spring and early summer and I hauled myself back over those blissful months, testing every knot, every memory, looking once again for clues. Where had I gone wrong? What had I missed?

Walking back to Napier Road, I took a detour through the park off Lordship Lane. After the recent heatwave, the grass was parched and brown and I settled myself on a bench, feeling fat and bewildered, replaying a phone call in my head. The phone call had come from Brendan in Australia. When he'd rung to tell me he'd been delayed, there'd been no explanation, no small talk, none of his usual gush, and the moment I'd risked a little intimacy he'd rung off. At the time I'd thought that was strange, wholly out of character, but only now did I remember that Sandra, too, had gone missing. The weekend Brendan hadn't come home was the weekend she'd so abruptly disappeared. Who was to say she hadn't left the country? What was to stop them meeting abroad? At some agreed location?

The harder I thought about the coincidence, the more convinced I became that something must have happened. It was after the Australian trip that Brendan had started to duck and dive again, to cloak our relationship in a thin tissue of evasions. We were both maniacally busy and it had taken me a while to realise how distant he was becoming. But tracing it backwards, I had absolutely no doubts that his Australian trip had been the start of it all.

Next to the sandpit was a phone box. I dialled Andi at Doubleact. Two little black girls were trying to build a fairy castle. When Andi answered, I told her what I thought was the date of the mystery weekend. She'd have access to payments made that month. What might the computer tell her? I hung on while she dived into the accounts file. A minute or two later, she was back.

'You're right,' she announced breathlessly. 'We were invoiced for a return ticket to Singapore.'

'In whose name?'

'Sandra's.'

'Did she book anything else?'

'Yes.'

'What?'

'Three nights at the Hyatt Regency.'

'Single or double?'

'Double.'

I thanked her and hung up, remembering the voice of the operator the morning Brendan had phoned to tell me he'd been delayed. She'd sounded oriental. Of that, now, I was quite certain. I leaned back against the door, looking across at the sandpit. The fairy castle had collapsed.

I returned home to find a huge bouquet of fresh flowers on the hall carpet at the foot of my door. Beside it, nicely wrapped, was a present of some kind. Shamefully, I thought at once of Brendan but there was no way he could have let himself in unless, of course, Gilbert had opened the door to him. I glanced up the stairs. Gilbert's door, for once, was open. He was standing just inside.

'For you,' he called cheerfully.

I picked the flowers up. Just smelling them reminded me that there was a life out there beyond the events of the last week or so.

'*You* gave me these?'

Gilbert nodded, stepping out onto the top landing, absurdly proud of himself.

'I did,' he said.

'Why? What have I done to deserve them?'

He smiled at me, indicating the other present. I was to take it inside and open it. He was sorry about everything that had happened. He hoped we'd be happy now.

The latter phrase, an echo of a Gilbert I wasn't keen to remember, confused me. What did he mean? I took the flowers through to the kitchen and laid them in the sink. When I opened the present, I found myself looking at a tin of DIY stuff called Permafil. According to the instructions, this was ideal for stopping up holes in plasterwork, partitions, and other damaged surfaces. It needed minimal preparation and could take umpteen layers of paint. I looked up at my poor ceiling, wondering what this funny man was trying to tell me. Had he been listening to me and Gary this morning? Had he heard us talking about Brendan? About the shambles of my private life? Had he put two and two together and come up with an answer to why I was so suddenly back in residence?

I concluded that he had and I spent the rest of the afternoon perched on a chair, bunging layer after layer of Permafil into my hole in the ceiling. The stuff was putty-like and at first it just fell out but I managed to find a little piece of plywood to wedge in the gap and after that it was pretty easy. By six o'clock, with the help of the remains of the white emulsion, the ceiling looked as good as new.

Upstairs, I presented Gilbert with the tin.

'Done,' I said. 'And thanks for the thought.'

Gilbert shook his head. I was to keep the tin. Just in case.

'Just in case what?'

'In case it happens again.'

'But it won't, will it?'

He returned my look and then – quite suddenly – burst out laughing. I was so totally unprepared that it made me physically jump. He put a restraining hand on my arm. To my surprise it felt warm and reassuring.

'Keep it,' he said again.

As I turned to go, I remembered the LP I'd found.

'Tell me about that record of yours,' I said. '*Montparnassse*. You never mentioned you were famous.'

'I wasn't.'

'You were,' I insisted. 'You were released. You were in the shops. You must have been. That's where I found it.'

He shook his head.

'I was a fool,' he said, confirming what I'd learned about Palisade. 'I thought you could take short cuts, you know, cheat. You can't, though. They won't let you.'

'Who won't?'

He fixed me with one of his long, earnest stares.

'Them,' he repeated darkly. '*Tu comprends?*'

I didn't understand, but it wasn't something that bothered me any more. Leaving Doubleact, and Brendan, had been such an enormous bump in my road that every other obstacle just fell away. Real madness was Brad Pitt, I'd decided. Compared to him, and what he represented, Gilbert was sanity incarnate. He'd welcomed me back. He'd bought me flowers. He'd even, to my face, said sorry. If I was looking for a new start, and I was, then here was the opportunity.

I spent the weekend with my mum in Petersfield. I knew I'd been neglecting her since moving up to London but I'd always told myself it wasn't my fault. To make amends, I took her across to Winchester and we spent an idle afternoon browsing through the shops. She has a passion for a tweedy kind of look and we managed to track down a rather nice skirt and jacket for her winter wardrobe. Even I liked it, which probably signalled the onset of middle age, and over a Hampshire cream tea my mother gave me the opportunity to take the thought a little further.

'You've put on a bit of weight, dear. The rate you've been working, I somehow thought you'd be thinner.'

The waitress had just arrived with the cream tea. My mother wasn't overfond of cream but strawberry jam had always been her favourite. I watched her loading the spoon.

'I'm pregnant,' I announced casually. 'I meant to tell you.'

The spoon wavered over the waiting scone. Despite the size of me, she obviously thought I was joking.

'Honestly,' I said. 'Seventeenth December, to be exact.'

My mother was flabbergasted. She wanted to know everything. She never touched the scone. After I'd finished, she put a hand on my arm. Had my father been alive, all this would have been extremely difficult. As it was, mum was a brick.

'It must have been terrible,' she said. 'You should have phoned.'

'Nothing to say, mum.'

'It doesn't matter. That's what I'm there for. Now then, what are you going to do?'

The question, I realised at once, was a declaration of intent. Without a job, things could get just the teensiest bit tricky. I'd be needing help. Lots and lots of it.

'You can move back,' she said. 'It'll be nice to have a baby around.'

I fought the urge to laugh. The thought of landing my mother with an infant was a joke. The thought of landing her with me was even funnier.

'I'll be fine,' I said airily. 'It's lovely of you to offer but I'm sure things will work out.'

'Work out where? Where will you be?'

'In London.'

'That same place? That flat of yours?'

'Of course.'

'But I thought you told me you were trying to sell it? Get rid of it?'

I refilled our cups, desperately trying to remember how much I'd told my mother about the problems at Napier Road. As ever, she saved me the trouble.

'That neighbour of yours upstairs. Mr Gilbert.'

'He's fine.'

'But I thought . . . ?'

'No.' I shook my head firmly. 'He can be a bit odd sometimes, a bit funny, but no . . . he's perfectly harmless. Nice man, actually. And talented, too.'

I told her about the flute music and finding the LP. She quizzed me further but when I told her the name – Gilles Phillippe – it meant nothing.

'How old is he?'

'Forty-five?' I guessed. 'Fifty?'

'Was he married?'

'I've no idea.'

'Does he work at all?'

'Not as far as I know.'

She pressed me with more questions, and the fact that I was able to tell her so little made me feel slightly ashamed. If I was really going to stay in Napier Road then I'd make it my business to find out a great deal more about the man I shared the house with. That, I thought, would be a real challenge, a chance to play Sherlock Holmes and keep my brain cells alive while the nights drew in and yours truly got fatter still.

My mother, newly indignant, was asking again about the baby's father. So far, I'd only mentioned his name.

'This Brendan,' she began. 'You say he's run out on you?'

'Not exactly. It's mutual, really.'

My mother was looking grave. I suppose I should have spared her the news but I didn't see the point. The last seventy-two hours, since I'd talked to Andi on the phone, had hardened me a great deal. Nothing good ever comes from hiding from the truth. I told her Brendan was married.

'And did you know that when you . . . you know . . .'

'Oh yes, his wife was my boss.'

'*Julie!*'

My mother looked round, horrified. There were obviously limits to her sympathy and I'd just breached them, though I had a shrewd feeling that bad news is better swallowed whole. Let's get this over with, I thought. Then we can be friends again.

'He left her for me,' I told her. 'We lived together for a couple of months then he . . .' I shrugged, '. . . went back.'

'Went back where?'

'To his wife.'

This time I laughed out loud. If anything, the news that Brendan had abandoned his mistress for his wife was even more shocking.

'How could he?' she said. 'What kind of man does that?'

'I don't know. But he did.'

'Did you love him?'

'Yes.'

'Badly?'

I think she'd got the wrong word but, although she hadn't meant to, she'd rather summed me up.

'Yes,' I admitted. 'Badly's about right.'

Afterwards, she insisted on a tour of Mothercare. It felt hugely presumptuous to be looking at nappies and baby gear when we were still months away from

December but I took it as a vote of confidence and we left with a bag full of Pampers and a rather sweet Babygro that my mother had fallen in love with. She'd wanted to buy a teddy, too, but I'd spent most of the previous evening rummaging in bedroom cupboards, looking for my own, and I was determined to pass it on.

Being at home, pregnant, made me realise what a magical childhood I'd enjoyed. With my father away at sea most of the time, the credit for that had been almost entirely due to my mother and as the rest of the weekend slipped by I became more and more aware of how my little piece of news had drawn us together. I don't think my mother was hurt by my decision to try and cope alone. On the contrary, I think she may have been quite relieved. But by the time she dropped me at Petersfield station on Monday morning, we were closer than we'd been for years. At last we had something in common, something to look forward to, something to protect.

'Find out about that neighbour of yours,' she sang out as the train drew slowly away. 'But no more falling in love!'

My quest, as I liked to think of it, for the real Gilbert began with a major windfall. It was Friday of the same week. The weather had broken with a vengeance. Big, fat clouds had been building over London since mid-morning and by three in the afternoon it was practically dark. The lightning, when it came, brought the rain sheeting down. Out shopping, I sheltered under the canopy of the supermarket until it stopped. Cars and buses had their lights on. It might have been ten o'clock at night.

I was home, soaking wet, an hour or so later. My shopping included a couple of items for Gilbert and I was putting them on his stairs when I saw the note on the doormat. It was written on the back of an envelope, backward sloping handwriting, a little smudged from the rain but perfectly legible. *'Gillie . . .'* it read. *'Mama's back home in one piece. Best give me a ring. 0831 306708 (new toy!!). Yrs. Tom.'* I lingered in the hall for a moment or two, reading the message again. Was this Gilbert's father? Favourite cousin? Whoever it was certainly sounded like family. I fumbled rather guiltily in my bag and made a note of the number. 0831 meant a mobile phone. Hence, presumably, the comment about the new toy. I returned the envelope to the mat and let myself into my flat.

Since I'd come back from Petersfield, at my mother's insistence, I'd invested in an answering machine. She was sick of ringing an empty flat and after such a lovely weekend, I thought an electronic message pad was the least I could offer.

The little window on the top of the machine told me a message was waiting. I dumped the shopping in the kitchen and returned to the front room. The moment I respooled the tape, I recognised the voice. It was Brendan. 'Lovely to hear you, Jules,' he began. 'Since when have you had one of these?' He paused for a cough here and I wondered whether he was back on the Camels again. Then the voice returned. 'Listen,' he said, 'I know I'm the last guy in the world you want to see just now but I'll be in Latino's at half past eight tonight. If, just if, big if, you could be there, I'll know there's a God in heaven. I love you, believe it or not.' The message came to an end and I was left standing by the phone fighting the temptation to go through the message again. What I wanted to feel was anger. How dare he call like this and invite me out? After everything that had happened? And just say I went? Just say I joined him at that table at Latino's, the one we'd practically rented, right at the back, beneath the rubber plant, what then? Would he apologise? Tell me he'd made a big mistake? Tell me we could wind the clock back and pick up where we'd left off? And just say I was foolish or pathetic enough to believe him? What then?

I shook my head, genuinely angry now, not that he'd phoned but that he'd so cleverly ambushed me with all these questions. He knew me inside out. He'd set me a little trap, baited with contrition, and he was probably over at Doubleact now, sprawled behind his desk, visualising exactly this scene. My big mistake, I realised, was ever letting him inside my head.

Nikki was at home when I phoned her. I told her I needed moral support. I told her I'd bought a present for the cat, and something ultra-yummy for her, and how would it be if I came over for the evening? A couple of hours later, after yet another visit to the supermarket, I was safely inside Nikki's flat. The cat demolished the offcuts of salmon, we gorged ourselves on a huge chocolate gateau, and when Nikki suggested I stay the night, no one could have been happier than me. The last thing on my mind before drifting off to sleep was Brendan. If he'd been silly enough to turn up at Latino's, I hoped he was still there, sat alone at our table, pining. Stupid man.

I was home by nine next morning. Nikki dropped me off on the way to work. Inside the door, I found a letter with my name on it. I opened it in the hall, recognising Brendan's handwriting. Inside was another cheque and one of the lovely paper coasters Latino's have printed specially. The cheque was for £500. On the coaster, above a single kiss, Brendan had written 'Missed you.'

I let myself into the flat, glad I'd slept over at Nikki's. The last thing I needed just now was a late-night doorstep confrontation with Brendan. Trying to cope at arm's length – letters, phone messages – was bad enough. Face to face, I just didn't know how I'd react. I circled the flat with water for my plants, wondering just how long Brendan would sustain this little campaign of his. His attention span was notoriously short – one of the reasons he'd done so well in television – and real life without yours truly was obviously a tougher proposition than he'd expected. Life doesn't come more real than Sandra and I was curious to know just how much rope she'd be allowing him. She knew Brendan better than anyone, better – certainly – than I did. Was she really silly enough to let him out for the evening? Or might they both have been waiting in Latino's?

To either question, I knew I didn't really want an answer. Between us, Nikki and I had agreed that icy indifference was by far the best tactic. Rekindling an old affair, especially one as intense as this had been, was one of the worst ideas in the world, and my sole responsibility just now was to turn my back and walk away. The fact that I missed him didn't matter. The fact that he could easily do it again – more damage, more hurt – most definitely did. Not only that, of course, but there were now two of us to think about. After what he'd done to me, would I really be daft enough to trust Brendan with my baby?

The phone began to ring. I looked at it for a long time, wondering whether it was wiser not to answer it, but the machine took over and the caller's voice came on at the end of my message. It was Nikki, bless her. She wanted to know whether I was OK. She wanted to be sure I hadn't weakened. I picked up the phone. I still had Brendan's cheque in my hand.

'He keeps giving me money,' I told her. 'Poor fool.'

*

Next morning, the builders arrived. They came in a battered old van and thumped up and down the stairs, carrying stuff in. I watched them from the front room, wondering what Gilbert could possibly be up to. On the side of the van it said 'Hackney Construction'.

Pretty soon afterwards, the house began to shake. The hammering went on and on, heavy blows. Alarmed, I went out into the street, looking up at the roof. A hole had appeared amongst the tiles, halfway between the guttering and the top ridge line, and as I watched, one of the guys appeared, head and shoulders through the hole. He peered around him, testing the tiles with his hand, then he began to pull them away, one by one, letting them slide down the roof. The tiles were heavy and one of them shattered on the low front wall. I stepped back, shouting at him to stop, and he looked down, seeing me for the first time. He yelled a cheerful apology and disappeared inside. A minute or so later, Gilbert stepped out through the front door. He was terribly, terribly sorry. He hoped I hadn't been frightened. Maybe it would be better if I came back inside.

He took my hand and I followed him into the hall. What I really wanted to know was when the work was going to stop. Pregnancy, I'd noticed, makes you very aware of your physical security. The simplest things begin to matter a very great deal. Were the guys upstairs replacing the whole roof? Was it leaking? Or was there some other problem?

Gilbert shook his head, unusually voluble.

'Good Lord, no. It's a little panel they're making me, a window, a porthole if you like. They'll be doing one or two other things, too, but nothing terribly fancy. Just some floorboards up in the loft and a light or two, and a couple of bits of insulation. Just enough to give me a bit of comfort up there.'

'You're making another room? A proper conversion?'

'Oh, no, no.' He shook his head again, emphatic. 'Just a perch, that's all.'

The thumping had started again. One of the china ornaments on the hall table was threatening to topple over. I moved it, just in case.

'Why?' I said. 'Why do you need a perch?'

'I'm installing an observatory,' he said at last. 'I thought I'd mentioned it.'

The building work carried on all day. My knowledge of the lease was pretty sketchy but I thought, at the very least, that I should have been consulted about something as major as this. The guys upstairs looked like cowboys. What would happen if they wrecked the roof and it all went wrong? Were we insured? Could we claim damages? And what about the local authority people? Weren't you supposed to get planning permission for something this big?

At lunchtime, I phoned poor Nikki again. One of her many virtues was a worldliness I lacked. She seemed to have been living in flats for most of her life. What, I asked her, should I do?

'Talk to the landlord,' she said at once. 'Before it goes any further.'

I'd had similar advice from Mark, the estate agent, but I'd done nothing about it. This time, I told myself, I had no choice. I rummaged around for the file I'd kept from the purchase and phoned my mother's solicitors down in Petersfield. The one who'd represented me was the senior partner. I'd found a name on the lease and he confirmed that Webb, Clewson were indeed the freeholders. They had a Sherborne address. Sherborne is in Dorset.

'Why down there?' I asked him.

'God knows. They're solicitors.'

'And they own this place?'

'Yes, though they may be fronting for someone else.'

He explained that leased properties were often made over to firms of solicitors by the freeholders. When I asked why he said there were dozens of reasons but sheer convenience was the most common. Shielded by the solicitors, the real owner could be protected from the attentions of anyone from the Inland Revenue to angry lessees.

Throughout this conversation, the building work was audible in the background. More thumping. Another shudder.

'So the guy upstairs would have needed their permission?'

'Of course.'

'And mine?'

'Not necessarily.'

'But definitely theirs?'

'Yes,' he laughed as a particularly loud crash shook the whole house. 'Why don't you give them a ring if you're worried?'

I was, and I did. The first time I got though, the person I needed to talk to was still out at lunch. Forty minutes later, Mr Clewson was back at his desk. I gave him my name and explained the situation. The moment I mentioned Gilbert, he became slightly defensive.

'Is there a problem?' he asked at once.

I repeated my line about the builders. The fact that they were there at all was obviously news to Mr Clewson.

'You don't know about any of this?'

'As it happens, we don't.'

'But shouldn't someone have asked you first?'

'Not necessarily, no.'

This answer made no sense. My own solicitor had told me exactly the reverse. Wasn't Gilbert obliged to ask for the landlord's permission? Wasn't that the real legal position?

Mr Clewson wouldn't give me a straight answer. He still wanted to know what the builders were up to. I did my best to describe progress to date. Half the roof was in pieces in the street and non-stop Radio One pounded through the floorboards above my head. Over the phone, I could hear Mr Clewson chuckling.

'I'd better give him a ring,' he said at last. 'Just to make sure.'

'Make sure what?'

'He knows what he's doing.'

I put the phone down and – on cue – the builders reached for their hammers. I listened hard for the sound of Gilbert's phone ringing but, given the other noises, I was hopelessly optimistic.

It wasn't until the evening that I remembered the note I'd found in the hall, the one about Mama from some relation of Gilbert's who'd signed himself Tom. My phone call to Mr Clewson hadn't filled me with confidence. Supervising major structural alterations from 100 miles away seemed less than satisfactory and his willingness to let Gilbert get on with it frankly baffled me. I thought there were procedures here, hoops we lessees had to jump through? How come my eccentric friend upstairs was simply allowed to get on with it?

Before I made a decision about getting in touch with the mysterious Tom, I went out in the street again. The builders had left at five o'clock, sweeping the shattered tiles into a neat pile against the cemetery wall, and now I stood in the middle of the road, peering up at the roof.

The ragged-edged hole had been covered with an old tarpaulin. The tarpaulin was secured with ropes threaded through eyelets at each corner, and every time the wind got underneath, it billowed up like a poorly-set spinnaker. Across the tarpaulin, in faded white letters, it read 'Property of Leyton Orient Football Club'. Gilbert had already told me that the work should be finished by the end of the week but his indifference to things like rain were making me more than nervous. What would happen if these builders of his didn't turn up to finish the job? What if they got a better offer from some other lunatic with equally grandiose plans?

I returned to the flat. I needed help now, an assurance that Gilbert really did know what he was doing. The mobile phone number I'd found on the doormat was still on the mantelpiece. I picked up my own phone and dialled the number. It took ages to answer. At last I heard a voice. It sounded quite old, and not at all sure of itself.

'Hallo?'

I introduced myself. I explained that I was living in Napier Road and that I was a neighbour of Gilbert Phillips.

'Who?'

'Gilbert. Gilbert Phillips.'

I waited for the name to register. It felt like a fairground game. I had my hand in the bran tub and I hadn't a clue what I was about to draw out.

'Ah, you mean Gillie?'

'Yes, Gilbert, Gilbert Phillips.' I tried hard to remember exactly what the note had said. 'He's a friend of yours, I think.'

'My brother, actually.' The voice was stronger now, more sure of itself.

'Your *brother*?'

220

'Yes, my brother. There are two of us.'

He inquired what he might do for me. He sounded cultured, refined even, recognisably from the same stock as Gilbert.

'Your brother's having some alterations done upstairs,' I said carefully. 'It's quite a big job. I just wondered whether you might know anything about it.'

'Good Lord no, why on earth should I?'

I'd half anticipated this. Next he'd want to know why I was interested. And after that, he'd probably ask why I didn't go and talk to Gilbert himself. I could, of course, but I wasn't entirely sure I'd get a coherent response.

'Your brother can be a bit . . .' I frowned, '. . . evasive at times.'

'You mean he's not all there?'

I smiled. It was a remarkably apt description of Gilbert, though saying so wouldn't make this conversation any the less awkward.

'No.' I tried to make light of what I had to say. 'It's just . . . he can be a little vague.'

'Vague?' I heard him laughing. 'That's very kind of you, my dear. Extraordinarily kind.'

'What would be your word for him then?'

'Gilbert? You mean Gilbert?'

'Yes.'

'He's barking, dotty, cuckoo, always has been. That's the authorised version, anyway, though I imagine it depends who you talk to. Some people say there's absolutely nothing wrong with him. Upstairs, I mean. Me? I think he's potty. Frightfully nice, terribly nice, but potty.'

It was my turn to laugh. I hadn't come across such frankness, such irreverence, yet such affection in quite this combination before. It was, in a very exact sense, the voice of sanity. Tom considered his brother was a lunatic, and yet he obviously loved him.

I thought of the note on the mat again.

'Do you see him a lot? Gilbert?'

'Good Lord no. Popped round the other day, first time for months. He wasn't in, of course. Typical.'

'You live in London?'

'Work there. Very occasionally.'

'I see.' I paused, wondering whether to own up about reading the note he'd left. So far, Tom hadn't asked how I'd got his number.

'I happened to see your mobile number on the envelope you left,' I said lightly. 'I hope you don't mind me ringing like this.'

'Not in the least, my dear. Now then, these builders. What can I do to help?'

I explained again about the work Gilbert had commissioned on the roof and about the landlord, Mr Clewson, down in Sherborne. He'd been no use at all.

'Never are. Bloody lawyers, all the same. Take your money, tie you in knots, leave you out for the wolves.' He paused for breath. 'Is it urgent? Or is that a silly question?'

I found myself telling him about the baby. In three months' time, it would be nice to know that the roof was in one piece. I hoped I wasn't making a fuss but what I'd seen today had made me nervous.

'I'm sure.' Tom had gone abruptly quiet and I wondered whether I'd ventured too far. Saddling a stranger with bits of my private life was, at the very least, an imposition. I began to say so, as apologetically as I knew how. There'd be another way around it. I was sorry to have wasted his time.

'Not at all, not at all, I was just having a think, wondering what I might suggest. Why don't I give Gillie a ring? Find out what the daft bugger's up to? Wouldn't do any harm, would it?'

I broke in. The thought of him telling Gilbert about the baby was a little premature. I'd have to break the news sooner or later, but not just yet.

'Good Lord, no. Though he's very good with babies, you know, always has been. Babies and animals. Loves 'em, just loves 'em. Same wavelength, I shouldn't wonder. Probably born a rabbit, poor old Gillie. Now listen, just give me your number. I'll have a chat with him. Ring you back. How's that?'

I thanked him, absurdly grateful, and hung up. I stayed in the front room for the rest of the evening, listening to the slap-slap of the tarpaulin against the roof, but I didn't hear the phone go upstairs.

Next morning, even earlier than usual, the builders were back. I awoke to Chris Evans on the radio. The volume was so loud, the trannie must have been directly above my head. I fled to the kitchen, shutting the door and making myself a pot of tea. Expecting a letter from my mother, I tried to edge into the hall but the path to the front door was blocked by a pile of sawn timber. It wasn't a good sign.

Back in the kitchen, I made myself a couple of slices of toast. I was loading the second with Marmite when the door opened. I looked up. It was Brendan.

'Your door was open,' he said at once. 'I knocked twice but nothing happened.'

I was still staring at him. I must have left the door on the latch. Shit, shit, shit.

Brendan was eyeing the teapot. I pulled my dressing gown more tightly around me. I didn't invite him to sit down.

'What do you want?'

'A cuppa would be nice.'

'It's cold, stewed.'

'OK, then,' he shrugged. 'No tea.'

I wanted him to go, badly. Letting him see me like this was a nightmare, not at all what I had in mind for the eventual settling of our accounts.

'How are you?' he said.

'Fine. You?'

He didn't answer. He was wearing a light tan polo-neck sweater under a leather jacket I hadn't seen before. I wondered whether he'd got it in Singapore but I didn't ask.

'I'm back with Sandra,' he said. 'I thought I should be the one to tell you.'

'What makes you think I'm interested?'

'Nothing. It's just that I wanted you to know.' He ducked his head, as melodramatic as ever. 'I have to tell you something else, too.'

'What?'

'It's the biggest mistake I ever made.'

'Going back to Sandra?'

'Letting you go.'

'I agree.'

He looked up again. He desperately wanted me to smile.

'You *agree*?' he said, 'You mean that?'

'Yes,' I nodded. 'It was a crazy thing to do, and cruel, too. You hurt me, if that's what you came round to find out. And it still hurts.'

'I know.'

'Yet you still did it.'

'Yes.'

'Well, that makes you very foolish, doesn't it? Throwing something like that away? Something that good?'

'That brilliant.'

'Quite,' I nodded. 'And then going back to your wife.'

Brendan began to talk about Sandra again. He'd been under immense pressure. Things weren't as simple as they'd looked. When it came to fighting dirty, she was the all-time expert.

'You could have stayed with me,' I pointed out. 'We could have talked about it.'

'I had no choice,' he insisted. 'None at all.'

'I don't believe you.'

'You don't? You want to know why?'

'Not especially.'

'You don't want me to tell you?'

I could taste the anger inside me. This man had walked into my life and helped himself to whatever had taken his fancy. Emotionally, sexually, any way you like, his was the worst kind of smash and grab. And now here he was, doing it again, uninvited, blatant, and – in some curious way – wronged.

'Tell me,' I said wearily. 'And then get out.'

He hooked a chair towards him with his foot, turning it round, sitting down. When we'd first met he and Sandra had been on the point of agreeing terms for the flotation of Doubleact. I nodded. I could even remember the sums involved.

'£3 million,' I said.

'Yes. And that was just my share.'

I shrugged. The arithmetic was irrelevant. You can't put a figure on betrayal.

Brendan ploughed on. When he'd started to see me, Sandra had put the flotation on hold. When he'd bailed out completely and moved into De Beauvoir Square, she'd cancelled it.

'Cancelled it,' he repeated, staring at me, wide-eyed.

'Am I supposed to ask why?'

'Because of you. Us.'

'So what?'

'So *what*? Ten years' work down the khazi? Ten years grafting my arse off? Ten years wanking around with crap quiz shows? So *what*?'

I half-smothered a yawn. I felt, quite suddenly, monumentally tired. Giving in to his emotions, to his better self, had cost Brendan £3 million. So what?

Brendan was explaining about the joint shareholding, himself and Sandra, in Doubleact. I, like everyone else, had always assumed it was a 50/50 partnership. Now, it seemed, that wasn't the case at all. Sandra had come to the party with money and the organisational skills, Brendan with talent and programme ideas. Sandra being Sandra, the money had won. It was she, not the pair of them, who effectively owned the business.

I had a sudden vision of Brendan on his knees, his head between my legs.

'I'm sure you have a say,' I suggested. 'I'm sure she needs you.'

'Yes, but on what terms?'

'You're a grown-up, Brendan. Whatever terms you make, you live with. That's one of the glories of capitalism, isn't it? Taking control? Keeping it?'

'I never took control. I've never had control.'

'Tough shit. You should have thought of that earlier. Besides, I'm still not with you. We were in love, my darling. Love's different. It's got nothing to do with any of this.'

'It's got everything to do with it.'

'How come?'

'Because that's the money we were going to use to launch. That was the three million quid we needed.'

'Who? Who needed?'

'You, Jules. You and me.'

I began to laugh. He looked so earnest, so fervent, he might have been back in his teens again, the passionate adolescent, all promise.

'You're telling me you expected Sandra to give you £3 million? So we could go off and make films together? Is that what you're saying?'

'She'd have to.' Brendan had the grace to blush. 'At least that's what I thought.'

'And it turns out you were wrong?'

'Yes.'

'So you went back?'

'Yes.'

'For the money? To get the money?'

'Yes.'

'For who? For me?'

'Of course.'

'And you really think that'll fix it? Kiss and make up? You, me, and three million quid?'

He stared at me, baffled, and I thought of the cheques he'd been sending. Same logic. Same medicine. Money cures all.

'It wouldn't have worked anyway,' Brendan muttered. 'She's got everything tied up in big, fat knots. Even my brief says it's hopeless. But that's why I went back. That's the truth of it.'

'And you never thought of discussing it with me? Talking it over?'

'No.'

'Why not?'

'Because I didn't want to burden you.'

'*Burden* me? You think splitting up is better than burdening me?'

'I never wanted to split up.'

'Then we should have talked. Like real people do.'

'*Real* people?' He gazed at me, expecting me to go on.

When I didn't, he got to his feet, returning the chair to its little slot beneath the table. 'I want you back, Jules, before the baby comes. Fuck the money. Fuck the flotation. She can have it all.'

'Even Brad Pitt.'

'Especially Brad Pitt.'

'Whose idea was that? As a matter of interest?'

'Hers.' He looked rueful. 'And mine, too. Bottom-line, it's shaping to be a fantastic deal. Not that I expect you to agree.'

'I don't. As a matter of fact I don't even believe you. Brad Pitt doesn't get out of bed for less than ten squillion quid. Do you have that kind of money?'

Brendan didn't answer me. Instead, he reached out a hand to touch my face. Instinctively, I withdrew. I didn't want to get in any deeper. I wanted him out.

'I love you, Jules. I waited three hours in that fucking restaurant. Me? Three hours?' He shook his head, scarcely believing it.

I stood up, signalling that our little chat was at an end. My bump was visible now, though I did my best to hide it under the folds of the dressing gown. When Brendan asked me again whether we couldn't give it another go, pick up the threads, I shook my head.

'It's over,' I told him. 'It was your decision. You made it. It's finished. It's gone.'

'I'm not hearing this.'

'You'd better, my love, because I mean it. And no more phone calls, either.'

He shook his head, as stubborn as ever, refusing to concede an inch. His sperm, he said. His baby. His rights. I took him by the arm, angry again, but a different kind of anger, quieter, calmer, more resolved. By the front door, desperate, he made one more lunge at what he'd come to tell me. He'd learned a great deal. It would be different this time round. And I was right, dead right, about the money. The three million quid didn't matter a fuck. Not compared to us. Not compared to me.

I had the door open. The biggest of the builders was sawing a length of timber in the hall. Brendan stepped around the pile of sawdust, looking back at me.

'It's my baby,' he said. 'I've got rights here.'

My hand was behind the door, feeling for the deadlock.

'I'm not a programme idea,' I smiled. 'You have no rights.'

Tom phoned back that night. It was nearly ten o'clock. I settled on the floor beside the receiver. Tom was talking about Gilbert. He'd called his brother, as he'd promised, and he'd learned what he could about what he termed 'the works in hand'.

'Meaning?'

'Your roof,' he chuckled. 'It turns out Gillie wants to put a big telescope up there. Foolish boy, he's always had his head in the clouds.'

'He wants what?'

'He wants to build himself an observatory. Actually, it's something he's always been after. May I ask you a question?'

I was still thinking about the roof. Gilbert had used exactly the same word, 'observatory'.

Tom was waiting for an answer.

'By all means,' I said. 'Ask away.'

'How well do you know Gillie?'

I pulled my dressing gown a little more tightly around me. Tom was a stranger. How candid was I supposed to be?

'I know him moderately well,' I said. 'As you would, sharing a house with someone.'

'You're friends?'

'Yes, I'd say so.'

'Good friends?'

'Er . . . yes.'

My hesitation drew another chuckle. The next bit took me by surprise.

'I expect you've had your little upsets,' he said. 'Most people seem to. Gillie isn't always the easiest person to live with.'

I thought at once of Kevin Witcher. I told Tom what I knew, based on what Frankie had told me. Had Gilbert really put him in hospital?

'I believe there was an . . . ah . . . altercation,' Tom said carefully. 'Some unpleasantness.'

'Why?'

'Do you really want to know?'

'Yes . . . please.'

'I understand this man . . . Witcher . . . made advances to Gillie. Physical advances. Gillie wouldn't have liked that. Not at all. In fact he was very upset.'

'So he hit him?'

'My dear, I've honestly no notion of what happened. I don't believe Witcher went to the police, if that's what you're saying. It's inexcusable, of course, physical violence, but I suppose you have to draw the line somewhere. Gillie's lines have always been a little different to ours, that's all.'

I frowned, wondering quite how far to push my curiosity. For whatever reason, Tom seemed to trust me.

'Has Gilbert ever been under treatment?' I asked.

'For what?'

'For any kind of upset. Mental upset. Maybe a breakdown of some kind.'

'What makes you ask that?'

'I just wondered. Sometimes . . .' I drew a deep breath, trying to gauge how long my credit with this man would last, '. . . you're right, he can be difficult. I don't think he means it, I don't think he's wicked, or evil, or anything like that, but just sometimes he's been a little . . . strange.'

There. I'd said it. There was a long silence at the other end. Then Tom again. He'd had to see to the dog. She was wrecking the tassels on one of the chairs.

'Now, my dear, where were we?'

'Your brother,' I repeated. 'I was just saying he can be odd sometimes. Not altogether . . . normal.'

'You mean loony? Go on, say it.' He roared with laughter. '*Veritas vincit omnia.* Truth conquers all. A spade's a spade, my dear, and we do Gillie no favours by pretending he's normal. He isn't.'

For a moment I didn't know quite how to respond. Tom's language, to say the least, was picturesque. It somehow conjured images of a big country house, with huge sash windows and vast views. There'd be stables, and horses, and a long curl of gravel drive, and over the front door, in fading gilt, would be the family crest. *Veritas* whatever. Truth conquers all.

I smiled, visualising this chocolate box vision of an England that had passed most of us by. Was this where Gilbert belonged? And if so, what on earth was he doing in N17?

'Going back to your roofing, my dear,' Tom was saying. 'I get the impression it's not quite as dramatic as you think. Gillie says he's taken advice. That could mean anything, of course, but let's hope he's seen someone useful. Like an architect. Damn.' The dog again. The curtains this time. Tom returned to the phone. 'I really must go, my dear. I do hope I've been of some use. Was there anything else?'

Quickly, I mentioned the freeholder again. This time, the name made an impact.

'Peter Clewson? You talked to Peter?'

I blinked.

'Yes,' I said. 'Do you know him?'

'Good Lord, yes. Peter's an old chum. He's been representing the family forever. He and the bloody dog go back years, generations probably.'

I pictured him reaching for the dog. Probably a spaniel, I thought. Probably liver and white.

'But he's our landlord,' I said. 'Or that's what I thought.'

'You're probably right. He very probably is. The old man wouldn't leave the bloody house to Gillie, not in a million years. Oh no, get the lawyers involved, keep poor Gillie in line. I can hear him saying it. Typical.'

'He's dead? Your father?'

'Heavens, yes. Years back.'

I wondered whether I ought to be taking notes. Each fresh answer triggered a new question in my head, taking me an inch or two closer to the man upstairs. I thought I could hear the dog in the background now, though it might have been my imagination.

'If I phoned again,' I said quickly, 'might that be OK?'

'Good Lord, yes, whenever you like. What was the name again?'

'Julie. Julie Emerson.'

'Phone any time, Julie,' he chuckled. 'It'll be a pleasure, an absolute pleasure.'

The roof was fixed by the end of the week. To the naked eye it was simplicity itself, a long glass panel set in a rather nice wooden frame, much like any rooflight. The following week a United Parcels van delivered something long and bulky which I took – correctly – to be the telescope. Within an hour, Gilbert had it up in the loft and, when I next checked from the road, the glass panel had slipped back to reveal a big glass eye on the end of a long, black barrel.

It was dusk, still light, but Gilbert must have been up there getting himself ready for the first twinkle in the night sky because the telescope moved from time to time, traversing left and right on some kind of tripod. Watching him, before returning inside, I thought again about the contents of the audio cassette he'd left under my pillow, the weekend he'd slept in my bed. The gist of the message was simple: we were all facing oblivion, either economic, or spiritual, or – most likely of all – as a result of some enormous onrushing asteroid. I remembered, too, Gilbert's strange obsession with what he called The Dark. Was this why he'd installed the telescope? To get on closer terms?

Later that evening I shared the thought in another conversation with his brother, Tom. I'd phoned out of courtesy to say that my earlier fears had been entirely misplaced. It was, I thought, the very least I owed him.

'He gets terribly involved, doesn't he?' I ventured. 'And terribly upset, too.'

I mentioned Gilbert's convictions about impending disaster. His brother agreed at once. He said he knew exactly what I meant, not simply about Gilbert's pessimism but the sheer effort he put into believing that everything, sooner or later, would go wrong.

'Obsessive, some of it,' he said.

'It takes him over,' I agreed. 'You can see it happening. He loses touch, loses perspective.'

'Exactly. Then the bloody thing gets the better of him,

and then we've *all* got a problem. Dear God, you're very shrewd, aren't you?'

I told him that was the last thing I was. Shrewd people can spot a problem a thousand miles away. Me? I opened the door and invited it in. In Gilbert's case, quite literally.

'Hasn't disgraced himself, I hope?'

'Not really. I just . . . it took a bit of getting used to.'

'Good, good. Trusting girl like you . . . doesn't do, does it?'

He mentioned the baby and hoped I was keeping fit. He was far too polite to be explicit but when he asked whether the flat would be big enough for the three of us, I knew exactly what he really meant.

'Two of us,' I said. 'Just me and the baby.'

'Oh dear, I am sorry.'

'No need.'

'Is it a joint decision? Do you mind if I ask?'

'Whose?'

'Yours and the father's? Not to live together?'

I began to warm to this man even more. When he chose to, he could be very direct indeed.

'Not really,' I told him. 'It was more my decision than his.'

'May I ask why?'

'Of course.' I hesitated, realising the importance of the answer, not just to Tom but to me as well. 'It's to do with courage,' I said. 'And priorities. We faced a kind of test, I suppose.'

'And you're saying you failed?'

'Yes.'

'Personally?'

At this, I began to withdraw. When it came to the test, I certainly hadn't failed but the question of blame was quite separate. That, we had to share. I tried to explain it

234

as best I could to Tom. He said at once that he understood.

'Might he come back? The father?'

'No.'

'Might he try?'

'I've no idea.'

'Would you want him to try?'

That was a very perceptive question. I'd hated having Brendan in my kitchen. I'd hated the way he'd provoked me, aroused me, made me angry. Yet he'd cared enough to come and that, I suppose, was a kind of compliment.

'It's over,' I told Tom for the second time. 'You get one chance in life, one chance to make it work, one chance to find out whether it's real or not.'

'And after that?'

'You have the answer.'

'My thoughts entirely, my dear.' I could hear the smile in his voice. '*Veritas vincit omnia*.'

Out of the blue, the following week, I got the offer of a job. It was nothing permanent, a couple of months at the very most, but it would nicely bridge the autumn months, put money in the bank, and return me to Napier Road just in time to give birth.

The company I was to join ran a cable news operation from a converted warehouse in Rotherhithe. They'd acquired the funds to expand and they wanted someone to sort out a production schedule that would give them as much crew time as possible for their money. It was a one-off job – hence the short contract – but mine was one of the names that had come up at the execs meeting and because I happened to be by the phone that morning, yours truly was first to appear for interview.

The latter, as so often in television, was a formality. I

turned up in time for coffee and Danish. The Head of News was nursing a hangover and his PA, who clearly ran the show, had a sister who was nearly as pregnant as me. Over a second helping of pastries, we discussed the merits of breast feeding and by noon the job was mine.

I started the following week, joining the early morning queue at the bus stop at the head of the road. On a good day, the ride across to Docklands took forty minutes, plenty of time for me to absorb the lighter articles in the paper and brace myself for the frenzy of snatched interviews, ten-second sound bites, and longer featurettes on three-legged dogs that masqueraded as hard news.

Over the weekend I'd had a chance to sample the feed from Metro, and I had absolutely no illusions about what I was in for. The stuff I watched, in pretty much every respect, was truly dire: underfunded, under-resourced, and horribly tacky when it came to content. On most of the stories, they even had a problem with focus, something I put down to a decision to operate without lights. Even at university we'd always had access to a couple of redheads, or a hand lamp, but at Metro, all too obviously, the emphasis was on natural light. Natural light, in the upside-down world of telly, is what you rely on when you can't afford the real thing. To make up for the soupy look of the pictures, you normally bang on about 'grittiness' and 'realism' and – on a really dark night – 'ultra-realism'. At Metro, the technical coverage had got so bad that even the technicians had started talking about 'Bat TV'.

It was fun, though, over in Rotherhithe and I settled in behind my computer, trying to unpick the tangle of scheduling arrangements that had taken root since the station had been transmitting. Like weeding, it had its compensations and it was nice to sit on the bus home, knowing that I'd at least made a start in teasing some kind of logistical sense into Metro's news gathering. Best of all, as I spaded deeper and deeper, I began to suspect that I could come up with cost savings that might – just might – make it possible for each news crew to carry a decent set of lights. This proposal, dangerously radical at management level, gave me hero status amongst Metro's army of young cameramen, and it was over coffee with one of them – a dry New Zealander called Angus – that I caught up with events at Doubleact.

Angus had only just joined Metro. Before that, he'd been pushing a big Sony at the studios used by Doubleact. *Members Only* was two programmes into its second series, and rumours on the studio floor suggested that Doubleact was in trouble.

'How come?'

'Seems they were after a flotation, you know, cashing in the chips.'

I said I knew about that. It had been on the cards for a while. Angus shook his head.

'Cancelled,' he said flatly. 'No can do.'

'Who says?'

'The City boys. Doubleact's a partnership. His and hers. Mummy and Daddy have fallen out. The merchant bankers don't like it.'

'You mean they've split up? Brendan and Sandra?'

'Finito.'

'Since when?'

'Last week.'

'You're sure about that?'

'Yeah. The marriage is history. Ditto the company.' He grinned, drawing a finger across his windpipe. 'They've kissed goodbye to nine million quid. Can you believe that? Not toughing it out? Making a go of it? Just a couple more months?'

I agreed it sounded incomprehensible. While Angus fetched more coffee from the machine, I rubbed thoughtfully at the stains on the formica table top, wondering about Brendan. Had he precipitated this wild act of commercial suicide? Or had Sandra finally had enough?

Angus returned with more news.

'She's suing him for everything,' he said. 'And vice versa. Isn't it fun when the rich fall out?'

I was still thinking about Brendan.

'They're getting divorced?' I said. 'Is that what you're saying?'

'Sure,' he nodded. 'And it's one of those times when you can actually put a figure on the grief. Nine million quid's worth of marital fucking guilt? Can you imagine that?'

As it happens, I could but I didn't let on about Sandra. Working with her was enough for most people. Having to sleep with her was obviously a seven-figure nightmare.

'Singleact,' I mused fondly. 'Doesn't quite have the same ring, does it?'

By now, we were close to the end of October. The nights were drawing in and I was more than happy to spend my evenings at home in Napier Road. The installation of the telescope in the attic had effectively put an empty floor between me and Gilbert, and it was odd to be without his music, and the back and forth pacing of his footsteps overhead. He'd somehow fixed a camera to his telescope and sometimes he came down with handfuls of the photos he'd taken. The quality wasn't brilliant but a month at Metro had revised my expectations to the point where anything in focus was a real treat.

I was admiring the latest nightscape when the phone went. It was Tom, Gilbert's brother. Gilbert had disappeared back upstairs only minutes earlier.

Tom sounded cheerful, if slightly out of breath. He was phoning, sweet man, to check on my well-being.

'I'm fine,' I told him. 'Just fine.'

'And baby?'

'Kicking for England.'

'Marvellous, marvellous.'

I told him a bit more about how things were going. Twice a week I took the afternoon off for ante-natal classes at the local sports centre. I'd thought I was reasonably fit but some of the exercises were finding me out.

'I ache,' I told him, 'in the most extraordinary places.'

Tom thought that was very funny and I elaborated a bit, describing some of the conversations we had afterwards, us mothers-to-be. A lot of the girls were black and some of their personal circumstances made my own situation seem very tame indeed.

'How's all that going?' Tom inquired.

'All what, Tom?'

'Your partner, the father.'

'I haven't heard a word, not for at least a month.'

'Is that good?'

'It's very good.'

I meant it. Back in September, just the mention of Brendan's name made me practically seize up. I dreaded him coming round or phoning. I dreaded another scene. Now, though, much of the angst had simply dropped away. Snug and safe in Napier Road, mention of Brendan Quayle would arouse, at most, feelings of mild curiosity. Had I really wasted so much of myself on a forty-five-year-old cokehead? Someone else's husband? Was that really me in all those fading mental snapshots?

Tom, for some reason, still needed persuading.

'Won't baby be a problem?' he asked. 'Won't that bring him back?'

'It might,' I conceded. 'But I'm sure we'll work something out.'

'What kind of thing, my dear? Won't it be terribly . . .' he paused for emphasis, '. . . awkward?'

'Not at all. Every baby has a father and I suppose fathers are allowed to take some kind of interest.'

'You mean financial? Money?'

'Yes, but other stuff, too. I shan't lock him away.'

'Who?'

'The baby.'

'You know it's a him?'

'No,' I laughed. 'I'm afraid that was Freudian.'

It was, too. I was always saying him, eyeing little tiny Arsenal kits in the local sports shops, planning the rig for his first sailboard, nagging my mother to dig out my brother's old Dinky toys. Not once had it occurred to me that the baby would be anything but male and when the nurse at the clinic had offered me a confirmatory test, I'd turned it down.

'No point,' I'd told her. 'It's going to be a boy.'

Tom was inquiring about Gilbert. How was his dear brother getting on? I was still looking at the print that Gilbert had brought down. The pattern of twinkly little dots made absolutely no sense but I did my best to describe the shot to Tom. The fact that Gilbert had got as far as taking photos impressed him.

'You know, I think it's a good sign,' he said. 'I truly do.'

'Why?'

'He's always been crazy about the night sky, the stars, all that malarkey, but there was always something, I don't know, not quite *real* about it. He'd talk about the dark a lot, the black wind, that kind of nonsense.'

'The black *wind*?'

'Yes, he'd carry on about what went on up there. It was as if he'd actually been, actually visited. He was quite proprietorial, I must say. His space. His planets. His moons.' He paused. 'Ring any bells?'

I was still inspecting the photo. The most that Gilbert had ever said to me about the night sky was that it was so cold, and formless, and empty. He liked that, he'd told me. He liked what he called 'the bare interstellar spaces'.

I repeated the phrase to Tom, admitting that it had stuck with me at the time.

'Exactly.' I could visualise Tom nodding. 'Absolutely spot on. I think he sees a logic there. You and me? We'd probably go for somewhere sunny and hot and nice to wake up to. Gillie? He'd be up there with the asteroids. He's very austere, you know, personally. Gets by on practically nothing. Always has done. Maybe he should have been a monk. I did suggest it once, as a matter of fact.'

'And what did he say?'

'He laughed at me. He was in his acting phase then. God's gift to the theatre. Major talent in the making. All that moonshine.'

I thought of the sleeve notes on Gilbert's LP, and the rather self-conscious pose on the front. Listening to Tom, it was the first time that I realised that the yearning to become an actor had been real, not the work of the Palisade copywriter.

'How far did he get?' I inquired. 'As a matter of interest.'

'Not that far, as I recall. I think he tried for RADA and one or two of those other places but none of them would have him. I knew he wanted to go into rep but there was some problem with the ticket. Equity, isn't it?'

'Yes,' I smiled, trying to imagine Gilbert treading the boards. The range of parts available to him wouldn't have been vast. Too distinctive. Too idiosyncratic. Too Gilbert. 'Did he give it all up in the end?'

'He did, my dear, as we all said he would.'

We ended the conversation soon afterwards and I spent the rest of the evening tidying up in the kitchen, wondering where else Gilbert's talents might have taken him. The better I got to know Tom, the warmer the glow that this strange, intermittent relationship shed on his brother. I'd been right not to lose patience with Gilbert; I knew I had. He'd been odd, and occasionally scary, but behind his occasional mumbles about the dark, I'd never once glimpsed anything truly evil. With his long, awkward body and his big, troubled face, he didn't quite fit with the rest of the human race. But that was our fault as much as his, and if the last six months had taught me anything then it had taught me the importance of making space in my life for a little more than deadlines, and schedules, and million-dollar programme ideas.

Before I went to sleep, lying in bed, I heard Gilbert overhead again. He must have come down from the attic. He must have put his precious stars away for the night. The dark, I thought fondly, reaching for the light.

My birthday falls on November 5th. How Gary ever got to know is a mystery but he phoned that morning, telling me to get dressed and ready. A car would be at my door at ten o'clock. We were off to an undisclosed destination. As it happens, this was the first week of freedom after my stint at Metro. Though Gary, being Gary, probably knew that too.

He was, as ever, early. By now I was very visibly pregnant, much to Gary's amusement. He'd borrowed a decent car from somewhere, a big, black Jaguar, and as we glided south through Putney he kept extending a reassuring hand. His years in the SAS had included an emergency childbirth course. Should our trip extend beyond a month, he'd be delighted to do the honours.

I told him he was welcome to have it himself but he said that didn't appeal much. What interested him more was the identity of the father. Was it really Brendan's? As everyone was saying? I told him it was, partly because I saw no point in denying it, and partly because I was curious to know the latest at Doubleact. By now, Brendan and Sandra's divorce had become the talk of the trade press and though there'd been no official word from Islington, it was an open secret that the company was on the verge of closure.

'So where's Brendan?' I inquired, 'in all this?'

The fact that I should even have to ask the question was obviously a shock to Gary. Once I'd confirmed who was the baby's father, I think he'd automatically assumed that Brendan and I were, as they say, still *à deux*.

'You don't know what he's been up to?'

'No idea.'

'America? Australia? All that?'

'Pass.'

We were on the A3. Gary slowed to 85 m.p.h. and brought me up to date. With Sandra serving divorce papers, and threatening to wind the company up, Brendan had been circling the globe, trying to secure Doubleact projects he could properly claim as his own. The crown jewels in this bundle of programme rights was undoubtedly *Celebrity Home Run*, and he'd spent the best part of a month commuting between Sydney and Los Angeles, making sure the money was rock solid. Gary wasn't privy to all the details but word in the

Celebrity Home Run production office suggested that this first series, at least, was safe.

'But what's he going to do?' I insisted. 'Start a new company?'

'Something like that.'

'Has he got a name? Premises?'

'A name, yeah.'

'What is it?'

Gary sniggered. Deep-down, I think he'd always regarded Brendan as a bit of a prat. Clever guy. Mega-talented. But a prat.

'Solo Productions,' he said at last. 'I think it's supposed to be a joke.'

Solo Productions. I gazed out at the blur that was Esher. If Gary was right about Brendan's wanderings, then it certainly explained why he'd left me alone for so long. Not even Brendan would pop back to N17 for coffee. Not when he was in mogul-mode.

'When's he back?'

'Next week, as far as I know.'

'And the show? The programme?'

Gary patted my arm, a gesture of reassurance. Underneath the action man affectations – the thin-lipped smile, the unwavering gaze – I think he was infinitely more sensitive than I'd ever imagined.

'It's going fine,' he said. 'That's all you need to know.'

'But what about you? Are you enjoying it?'

'Loving it.'

'That's bullshit.'

Gary said nothing for at least a mile. Then he yawned.

'You might be right,' he admitted. 'But the money's fucking wonderful.'

We were heading, of course, for Portsmouth. I gave my

244

mum a little wave as we sped down the Petersfield by-pass. Fifteen minutes later, we were climbing Portsdown Hill. On the crest of the hill, beside one of the sprawling Victorian forts, there's a pub called The Churchillian. Gary knew it because I'd taken him there a couple of times when we were working with the kids. It served decent beer, and the food was OK, and from the big picture windows at the front you could get a sensational view clear across the city to the Isle of Wight.

We parked the car. It was a blustery, rain-washed day, perfect after the drizzle and traffic fumes we'd left behind in London. I stood in the car park a moment, feeling the wind in my hair, remembering days like this that I'd spent on Hayling Island, way over to the left. Thanks to a friendly sandbank, Hayling offered some of the best windsurfing in the country, and it was there that I'd first sensed that I was good. Not just averagely good, but exceptionally good. That particular year – 1992 – was the summer I'd caught the eye of one of the national coaches but it had taken another couple of seasons, and some of the hardest physical work I'd ever known, before I made it into the British team.

I was still warming to the memories when I felt the touch of a hand on my arm. It was Gary. He was gesturing at one of the big picture windows in the pub. Behind it, looking out at us, were the kids he and I had chosen for *Home Run*.

We went inside. The kids cheered. One of them started singing 'Happy Birthday'. Even the barmaid joined in.

I waddled across. A youth we'd always called Wrigleys couldn't take his eyes off my stomach. I might have just landed from Mars.

'You never,' he said at last. 'That's well out of order.'

'I did,' I told him. 'Does it upset you?'

'Yeah.' He offered me a stick of gum. 'It does.'

I think the others felt pretty much the same way. They didn't actually say so but they'd never been over-keen on spontaneous conversation and to begin with it was Gary and I who made most of the running. Gary had arranged food – eighteen variations on pastie and chips – and as the kids fought over the sachets of brown sauce, he told them how the new series was shaping.

Little bits and pieces had already been in the local press and the name on everyone's lips was Brad Pitt. Had Gary met him? What was he like? For my part, I still didn't believe he'd have anything to do with the series but that wasn't the point. The point was the kids and their attitude to what we'd planned together. Not once was there any mention of the training session up north, or regrets that their own part in Gary's little adventure was over. On the contrary, I got the impression that they were rather glad to be back in Portsmouth, basking in a limelight they hadn't really earned. Gary was right. That one taste of the real thing, five wet nights on Skye, had convinced most of them that watching Brad Pitt on a Saturday night was infinitely preferable to dangling on a rope, scared witless, with nothing but the prospect of more terror to come. In a way, I suppose I didn't really blame them. Pregnancy seemed to have robbed me of some of my own thirst for physical challenge. Maybe they were right, I thought. Maybe it's better watching it than doing it.

The serious baby gear arrived that same week. I stood in the front room, watching two men unloading a cot from the back of a van. With the cot came a playpen, a collapsible pram, a set of yellow plastic ducks, a changing mat, and sundry other goodies. I'd been planning to pick up most of these items over the next few weeks, taking my time, and the fact that someone had robbed me of this pleasure wasn't an altogether wonderful surprise. There was no card with the delivery, no clue to the sender's identity, and my suspicions fell at once on my mother. Forgetting to add a tag of any kind would have been completely typical but when I phoned her she denied all knowledge.

'*What* did they send?'

I went through the list again. In all, as my mother pointed out, it would have cost hundreds.

'Who could it have been?' she wondered aloud. 'Who'd do such a thing?'

My heart was already sinking. If my mum hadn't sent the stuff then it had to be Brendan. He was the only other suspect, the only other interested party. He must have returned from Los Angeles, or Sydney, or wherever he'd been, and lifted the phone to Mothercare and told them to get on with it. Staying anonymous was his style, too. A gesture like that would earn him the right, at a time of his choosing, to spring another little surprise. Like appearing in person to claim the credit. That's what he'd do. I was sure of it. He'd turn up tomorrow, or the day after, and invite himself in, just like the last time.

I'd piled the stuff in the front room. The big items were still boxed. I toyed briefly with sending them back, then decided against it. There was another option, altogether bolder. I'd go and find Brendan myself, seize the initiative, turn the tables. I'd be very polite, very cool. I'd say thank you and then bring the conversation to a rapid end.

I rang the Doubleact number. Brendan wasn't there but I managed to talk to Andi. She confirmed that Brendan and Sandra had split for the second time and that everyone was prepared for the worst. Accountants had been crawling over the books for weeks and it now looked like a take-over was in the offing. As for Brendan, she thought he was back in the flat at De Beauvoir Square. He still had the tenancy and the flight schedule he'd left on the office computer indicated that he'd returned to the UK this very morning. That seemed a bit on the tight side for the Mothercare pressies but when I told Andi the story she said that he often snuck back on an earlier flight. Give him a ring, she suggested. Wake the bugger up.

I rang but there was no answer. When Brendan's voice came up on the pre-recorded tape, inviting callers to say something witty, I hung up. By now I was convinced that the initiative really did – for once – lie with me. Hopefully, he'd be jet-lagged. After a month's non-stop negotiations, he'd probably look a wreck. What better chance would I ever have for establishing that surprise gestures like the Mothercare delivery were strictly off-limits? Our relationship was well and truly over. Nothing would revive it.

It had started raining again and I took a cab to De Beauvoir Square. The sight of Brendan's Mercedes outside the flat made me wobble for a moment or two but I was well and truly psyched up and I didn't falter on the steps down to the basement door. After the third ring, I'd concluded that no one was in. Then I heard footsteps and a hacking cough. Brendan, when he finally opened the door, was naked except for a pair of boxer shorts. The shorts were patterned with little black scorpions. Wholly appropriate.

The moment he saw me, Brendan scowled. It wasn't, somehow, the reaction I'd anticipated.

'What do you want?'

'I've come to say thank you.'

'What for?'

'The presents. That's all. Just thank you.'

He stepped back, inviting me in with a jerk of his head. The flat smelled of joss sticks. Brendan never used joss sticks.

'I'm intruding,' I said at once. 'I'll give you a ring.'

Brendan was halfway down the hall, fetching his dressing gown from the bedroom. He returned, belting it at the waist.

'There's no one here.' He gestured at the sofa: 'Make yourself at home.'

I was trying very hard to put my finger on this mood of his. It was something new; something I'd never seen in him before. He seemed preoccupied, serious, business-like. Whatever his priorities just now, they certainly didn't include me.

'What are these presents?' he said.

I told him about the morning's delivery. When he said it had nothing to do with him, I suspected he was probably telling the truth.

'Why would I go to all that trouble,' he asked, 'when I'd only just got off the bloody plane?'

'I didn't know that,' I lied. 'I thought . . . I'm sorry.'

He shrugged, turning away. When I caught up with him in the kitchen, he was laying out two cups beside the kettle.

'It's instant, I'm afraid.' He reached for a jar of Nescafé. 'I haven't been around too much.'

We sat next door, waiting for the kettle to boil. He told me a little about the bail-out he was organising from Doubleact. As Gary had described, he was making off with a programme or two, storing nuts, he said grimly, for the winter.

'It's hard out there,' he scowled again. 'Hard like you wouldn't believe. You can't afford to give an inch. He who bleeds last, wins.'

Brendan had always gathered a little moss in his journeyings, a trace of an accent here, a mannerism there, little personality tics he picked up en route from meeting to meeting. You could generally tell from the way he behaved exactly what kind of company he'd been keeping, and on this particular occasion, my money was on some pretty hard-nosed business types. He seemed impatient, dismissive, wound-up. It was nothing to do with me but I hoped, for his sake, that the change wasn't permanent. Maybe Sandra was getting the better of the legal battles. Maybe Solo Productions wasn't quite the gig he'd expected.

The kettle was boiling. I could hear it.

'This baby,' he said. 'I still can't believe you're just getting on with it.'

'What else do you suggest I do?'

'Be reasonable, for a start. It's our baby, Jules: yours and mine. We were both there. We both made it. You can't just take it away and pretend I never happened.'

I didn't want to go through all this again. Talking about Brendan's so-called rights simply wasn't on the agenda. I found myself making coffee in the kitchen. For one.

'Sugar?' I called.

'No thanks.'

I took the coffee into him. I was still wearing my anorak. Unzipped, I looked like some cartoon character. Big Julie. For the first time, a smile ghosted across Brendan's face.

'Come here.'

'No.'

'I said come here.'

I stared at him. This, too, was new. No please. No thank you. No gentle change of gear. Just the curtest of commands. My flat. My space. My bloody rights.

'Come here,' he said for the third time.

I was nearly at the front door when he caught me by the hand. I was far too heavy for him to spin round but that had clearly been his intention and it was my wrist that suffered. I began to rub it. Brendan's face had reddened, pure emotion.

'Don't do that again,' I hissed. 'Ever.'

'You're carrying my baby.'

'Fuck off.'

Our faces were very close. I had an enormous urge to make some kind of gesture, underlining my resolve, but there was another part of me that sensed we were very close to physical violence. This is how it happens, I thought. This is how women get hurt.

The blood had left Brendan's face as abruptly as it had come. He was chalk-white, shock or anger, I didn't know which.

'I'm back for a while,' he said softly. 'And believe me, we have a lot of talking to do.'

'About what?'

'Napier Road. That flat of yours.' He touched me lightly on the cheek. 'I'm going to have you out of there. No matter what.'

I think I was still trembling when Gilbert knocked on my door, several hours later. I was sitting in the front room. Most of the stuff from Mothercare was still boxed. I'd stopped even thinking about who might have sent it.

I invited Gilbert in. He gave me a folded sheet of plain white paper.

'Someone from United Parcels knocked and gave me this,' he said. 'I think it must be for you.'

I took the paper and unfolded it. I'd never seen the handwriting before. The message had to do with the person who'd paid for the baby things. He'd phoned in with the order. His name was Tom Phillips. He hoped I'd find houseroom for the stuff.

I looked up. Gilbert had obviously read the note. Tom Phillips was his brother. I didn't know what to say. Sheer exhaustion made me stick to the facts. *Veritas vincit omnia.*

'I came across your brother recently,' I said lightly. 'We've become friends, sort of.'

Gilbert, typically, seemed unsurprised.

'Oh?'

'Yes, we talk on the phone sometimes. He's a lovely man, isn't he?'

Gilbert was still looking at the pile of packages on the carpet. It had been obvious for a while that I was pregnant but I still wondered whether he'd put two and two together.

'Your brother,' I prompted. 'A very nice man.'

'Yes.'

'And generous, too. Extremely generous.'

'Yes.'

Gilbert stood there, his long, bony hands hanging limply down. I wondered briefly how the star-gazing was going then I remembered the rain. He was bored. This, God help us, was the opportunity for a little chat.

'As a matter of fact,' I said, 'where exactly does he live?'

'What?'

'Live. Tom. Your brother.'

Gilbert had at last finished with the Mothercare boxes.

'Dorset. That's where they both live.'

'Who?'

'Tom and Mama.'

I looked up at him. Sherborne was in Dorset. And

Sherborne was where I'd found Peter Clewson, our landlord.

'Whereabouts in Dorset?'

Gilbert cocked an eyebrow as if he hadn't quite heard the question. I asked him again.

'Hasn't Tom told you?' he queried.

'No. But then I haven't really asked.'

'Well he must, he absolutely must. He's the one who lives there, after all.'

I heard a tiny quiver in his voice and I looked up again in time to see one bony finger intercept a falling tear. Tears, as far as Gilbert was concerned, were a giveaway. What nerve had I touched now? And where might it lead next? I thought of the nice, sane, predictable conversations I'd had with Gilbert's brother. Quite suddenly, I wanted to go to bed.

'I'll ask Tom about the address,' I said gently. 'I don't suppose he'll mind, will he?'

I struggled to my feet, accepting Gilbert's hand, and then showed him to the door. After he'd gone, I picked up the note he'd brought in, knowing I really ought to phone Tom. Quite why our conversations had produced such a generous present, I didn't know, but it would have been churlish not to say thank you.

Tom answered on the second ring. He's probably been waiting all evening, I thought, visualising the spaniel at his feet.

'Filthy night,' he boomed at once. 'Filthy, filthy night.'

'It's Julie,' I said.

I thanked him for the presents and said what a surprise it had been. He dismissed my protests about going over the top.

'Absolute pleasure old thing, the very least we could do.'

'We?'

'The family. After all the fuss with Gillie.'

I paused. Had I been that frank about my little run-ins with Gilbert? I rather thought not.

'He's a bit vague about family stuff,' I said casually. 'He doesn't even seem quite sure where you live.'

'Live? Mama and I, you mean? God, I'm not surprised.'

Gilbert, it seemed, had been on his own for most of his life. Every family has its skeleton and theirs was Gillie. He didn't go into detail but there'd obviously been a bust up of some kind and the one to suffer was now my neighbour.

'Does he ever get down to see you?' I asked.

'Never.'

'You never invite him?'

'God, no. The odd meal, maybe, when I'm in town with time to kill, but Gillie down here? Frightening the animals? My dear, the very thought . . .'

I remembered Gilbert leaving, a couple of minutes earlier. Something I'd said had upset him. Something to do with the family.

'Do you think he misses it?' I asked.

'Misses what?'

'Home? Dorset? Wherever it is you live?'

'To be frank, my dear, I haven't the foggiest. My poor old brother has a number of endearing qualities but confiding in the likes of me isn't one of them. You probably know him better than I do. Why not ask him? Make friends? I'm sure he'd welcome you with open arms.'

He barked with laughter, obviously amused by the prospect, and I felt a deep rush of sympathy for Gilbert. Tonight, for some reason, Tom Phillips was fed up with Gillie. The thought of his brother, even at 100 miles' distance, was getting on his nerves.

'Actually, it's not such a bad idea,' he was saying. 'Gillie's damn protective, once he makes his mind up. Loyal, too. You could do a lot worse.'

'Worse?'

'Yes. Try him out. Best pals. Why don't you?'

For the second time in a couple of hours, I was losing my bearings. Was he serious? My telephone friend? This stranger who'd just bought me several hundred quid's worth of baby gear?

'He's a very nice man,' I said carefully.

'Damn right.'

'And I can't say thank you enough for the presents. We're both very lucky.'

'Both?' He was onto the word like a shot.

'Yes,' I nodded, 'Me and the baby.'

Brendan started laying siege to me within days. He was coldly polite, even formal, unrecognisable from the man I'd fallen in love with. He'd phone from the office in order, he said, to make an appointment. He'd fix a time and tell me he'd be round and, whatever I said to the contrary, he'd turn up in the Mercedes and sit in the car until I relented and opened the door to him. On the first couple of occasions we talked on the doorstep, or on the pavement beyond the gate, but the third time he came round it was pouring with rain, and my front room was infinitely preferable to the intimacy of his car.

It was on this occasion that he produced the document from his lawyer. It was a deed of some kind, a draft legal agreement, and our joint signatures would give him agreed access to the baby. Talking like this about a child who hadn't even been born was the oddest experience but I told myself that negotiation was a huge advance on slapping each other around, and in any case it seemed totally in keeping with Brendan's new persona. There was obviously no more room in his life for something as unbusinesslike as emotion. Whatever I produced on 17th December would be strictly a question of legal entitlement. In return for access to the baby, I'd receive regular monthly payments way in excess of anything imposed by the Child Support Agency. Beyond that, by signature of the deed, I'd formally waive any other claims I might want to pursue against him. It was cold-blooded but – like I say – it was preferable to confrontation.

Brendan stayed, that morning, for more than an hour. I'd got all the baby gear out of the boxes by now but his only real interest was in the donor. Who'd sent this stuff? Who'd paid for it? When I told him about Tom, Gilbert's brother, mention of my neighbour triggered another carefully-tempered lecture. Staying in the flat was completely unacceptable. He knew what a trial living beneath Gilbert had been and there was no way he was entrusting any child of his to the mercies of the loony upstairs. I resented this description and told him so. Since I'd parted company with Doubleact, Gilbert had been nothing but helpful. We were back where we'd started, the very best of neighbours, and in my little head, having someone as kind and as helpful as Gilbert around was a huge bonus. Besides, moving flats at this late stage was unthinkable. I was knackered enough as it was. Why on earth would I want to put everything at risk for no good reason?

'Risk?'

'Yes.'

I pointed out the physical consequences of moving my goods and chattels halfway across London. After my ante-natal classes, I was word perfect on the perils of overdoing things.

'We're fine here,' I told him. 'We're staying put.'

'You're not. You can't.'

'Of course we can. It's got nothing to do with you. It's my decision.'

'Our baby.'

'Sure, but my decision. You have to accept it. You haven't got a choice.'

It was the latter phrase that really got to Brendan. I'd never said it quite this way before but I could tell from the expression on his face that he hated being told he didn't pull the strings any more. In retrospect, I understand this all too well. Control was Brendan's speciality. At Doubleact, and with me, he'd always decided exactly the way things would be. Now, that control was a thing of the past and I think he was beginning to realise that no amount of fancy legal drafting could ever bring it back. Doubleact had gone. I'd gone. And the baby, when he arrived, would emphatically be under my care.

Brendan left towards midday. At the door, buttoning his new Burberry against the rain, he gestured up towards Gilbert's flat.

'One of you has to go,' he said. 'Maybe it should be him.'

In a way, it was a declaration of war, though I was blind to the fact at the time. Late November was busy for me. I was laying in supplies, squirrelling away nappies and wipes and even a shop-bought Christmas pudding in case the baby and I had to spend the festive season alone. Providing everything went well, my mother was insisting we go down to Petersfield for at least a week with her – Christmas Eve through to the New Year – but my faith in other people's arrangements was at an all-time low and I was becoming increasingly attracted to the notion of the baby and me against the world. It was like a call to arms. Life hadn't been easy. The baby, by some strange ante-natal whispers, would know exactly what the score was. One way or another, we'd battle on through.

I spotted the water in the kitchen in early December. My nine months were nearly up and the last thing I needed was a problem around the house. The water seemed to be coming through the ceiling and seeping down the back wall where the previous owner, the luckless Mr Witcher, had fixed his cupboards. The plaster above and below the cupboards was wet to the touch and when I looked up I could see a dark stain where the ceiling met the wall.

My first thought was that Gilbert's plumbing must have sprung a leak. I hadn't heard or seen Gilbert for days and when I struggled upstairs and knocked at his door, I couldn't get any reply. Back in the kitchen, I took a towel to the walls and mopped up the moisture. I'd keep an eye on it, I told myself. And if it kept on happening, I'd contact the water board.

Brendan came round again that night. He was as cold and cautious as ever and because I found that easy to cope with, I didn't altogether mind him coming in. He'd bought himself a new attaché case, a big, boxy thing in black leather, and he produced a thick wad of details from half a dozen estate agents. Some of the properties were flats, others were whole houses, and when – out of interest – I asked who'd be footing the bill, he said it wouldn't be a problem. After all the traumas at Doubleact, Sandra had evidently found an interested buyer. Prospects for her estranged husband weren't as bleak as he'd once imagined.

Brendan had obviously been through the properties already because he'd ranked them in order of priority. His favourite was an attractive terrace house in a

Barnsbury square. A flight of steps led to an imposing front door. The door looked newly-painted – a deep red – and the house had tall sash windows, and tiny little dormers at the top. On the back of the details was the price.

I laughed.

'£290,000? Who's got that kind of money?'

'I have.'

'For me?'

'For both of you.'

'You're not serious.'

'I'm perfectly serious.'

I studied the details again, looking for the catch. Brendan helped me out.

'I'll live in the basement,' he said. 'There's plenty of room.'

We laboured once again up the foothills of the old, old argument. Sharing a house together, no matter how platonic the arrangement, was putting back the clock. That wasn't going to happen. Not now. Not ever. I'd made up my mind. For the immediate future, while I and the baby sorted each other out, we'd be staying here. If we really had to move, it would be on my terms and at my bidding.

Brendan gathered the stuff from the estate agents and left it in a pile by my chair.

'Fine,' he said. 'I'll put some more details through the door.'

He did. Most of the following day I was out with Nikki. We had lunch at an Italian place in South Kensington and afterwards we walked in Hyde Park. The weather was glorious – cold, sunny, sharp – and she dropped me back in Napier Road an hour or so before dark. Pushing at the front door, I could scarcely get it open. Inside, you couldn't move for yet more bits and pieces from various estate agents. This was a gesture I recognised from the old Brendan: excessive, out of proportion, totally over the top.

I was still leafing through this latest batch of details when I drifted through to the kitchen to make some tea. Opening one of the cupboards, I remembered the problem with the water. The walls were wet again, glistening in the light. Water had pooled on the working surfaces beneath the cupboards, and when I looked up at the ceiling I was certain that the stain was spreading. There was also a smell, slightly sour, that I took to be damp. It wasn't a serious leak, nothing actually dripping, but I knew I had to get something done before it got much worse.

Gilbert, once again, was out. Coming back downstairs, it occurred to me that he might be down in Dorset, visiting his brother. Tom had told me that Gilbert was the last person he'd invite but I wondered whether our little conversations hadn't mended some of the family's fences. I decided to phone him and find out.

Tom, once again, was in a bleak mood. No, Gilbert wasn't there. Yes, to be honest he was terribly busy just now.

'I'm sorry,' I said at once. 'I shouldn't have phoned.'

'Not at all, my dear.' He paused, more conciliatory. 'You've caught me at a bad time. Mama's ill again. I don't know whether I mentioned it.'

He hadn't, but I remembered the note he'd left for Gilbert, the one he'd posted in through the door. *Mama's back home in one piece,* it had read.

I inquired after Mama's health. She had a heart condition, Tom said, and when she got upset things could get tricky.

'She's upset now?'

'Very.'

I wondered why but didn't ask. Tom was talking about the possibility of a bypass operation. Problem was, you could never tell when the old ticker might pack in. They'd had a couple of scares already. And Christmas wouldn't help.

'How about you?' he said. 'Must be nearly due.'

'Eight days,' I told him.

'A week. Good Lord, is it really that close? Seems no time at all since you were flying around, thin as a rake.' I stared at the phone. To my knowledge, we'd never met. What on earth was he talking about? 'Figure of speech,' he chuckled, reading my thoughts. 'Time just gallops by, especially when you're my age.'

I told him about my problems in the kitchen. Did he happen to know where Gilbert might have gone?

'Haven't a clue, old thing. Is it bothering you? This water?'

'Not really, but I ought to get something done.'

'What about that job he had done on the roof? Wouldn't be anything to do with that, would it?'

I hadn't thought of Gilbert's new skylight. I closed my eyes, trying to visualise the van. Hackney Construction. I'd put money on it. Tom was warming to his theme.

'Bloody cowboys, they're everywhere. Can't find a decent tradesman for love nor money. I bet that's it. Rain penetration. Dear old Gillie, show him a perfectly good roof, he'll have it ruined in minutes. And I'll bet he paid the earth, too. Damn fool.'

I found Hackney Construction in *Yellow Pages*. I phoned them the next day. A harassed-sounding woman took the call and as we talked I gathered that she must be the wife of one of the roofers. I could hear kids in the background and what I took to be the grumble of a washing machine. At her suggestion, I phoned again at lunchtime. The men were still out on a job. Why didn't I call round after six? She gave me the address and said her husband would be back by then.

I spent the day, off and on, checking the kitchen. There was more water seeping through the ceiling and down the wall. The smell, too, was stronger, damp of a kind I'd never come across before. I looked out of the window, thinking about the skylight again. It hadn't rained since the weekend.

The address the woman had given me was actually in Clapton. I recognised the big guy who opened the door. He'd been the one sawing lengths of timber in the hall. He invited me in, introducing me to his wife with a grin I didn't entirely trust. I did my best to explain about the water in the kitchen. Not quite a leak, more a seepage. Might it have come from the attic? A problem with the skylight, maybe, or a pipe they might have damaged during the installation? Neither suggestion cut much ice, though he did promise to give Gilbert a ring when he had the chance and maybe drive over and take a look. Meantime, he agreed it would be best to contact the water board. He took the trouble to look up the emergency number in the phone book, scribbling it down for me on the back of an old betting slip.

On the way out of the house, I passed his wife again. She was working through a huge pile of ironing.

'What's it like then?'

'What's what like?'

'This windsurfing?'

I stared at her, lost for words. Then I looked at her husband. He was standing by the front door, visibly embarrassed.

'Them pictures,' he mumbled. 'In the old bloke's flat.'

'Pictures?'

I was still struggling. Then I remembered the photos

262

Brendan had taken down in Jaywick, the day I'd tried to teach him how to windsurf.

'You've seen them? Those shots of me?'

'Not me, love, him.' The wife was nodding at her husband. 'Made a bit of a name for yourself round here. The lads couldn't stop talking about it. Old boy like him. Young girl like you.' She looked me up and down. 'Still, no accounting for taste, eh?'

Her husband had opened the front door. He wanted me out before his wife made things even worse.

'Take no notice,' he told me as we stepped into the street. 'She's only jealous.'

Back home, I mopped up in the kitchen. The walls were wet again, the stuff running down behind the cupboards. I was almost glad when I heard the bell at the front. Brendan was waiting for me on the doorstep. He was swaying slightly and it took me several seconds to realise that he was drunk. Not just drunk but paralytic.

'Cracked it,' he beamed at me. 'Fucking cracked it.'

I stepped aside. How he'd got the Mercedes round here in one piece was beyond me. I guided him along the hall and into the flat. The door to the front room was open. He headed for the sofa but missed. I helped him to his feet and he clung to me a moment, swaying again. Jaywick, I thought. The roles reversed. Brendan drowning. Me there to help.

I made him tea. He wanted Scotch. I had none.

'What happened?'

'Got pissed.'

'I can see that. Tell me why.'

He was lying full-length on the sofa, his Burberry still on. Every time he tried to focus, his head fell forward and it took him an age to get it up again. I wondered whether he was going to be sick but decided that appearing with a bowl might be premature.

'I love you,' he muttered at last. 'The rest of it is shit.' He lifted an arm and made a floppy, encircling gesture. 'Shit,' he repeated.

I tried to make him drink the tea. He wouldn't. He'd come to tell me he loved me, tell me he was crazy about me, tell me he'd changed, tell me everything would be all right.

'It's fine,' I said as gently as I could. 'You'll be better in the morning.'

'I'm better now. Much better.'

'You've been drinking.'

'You're right.'

'Something must have happened.'

'It's all happened. Everything's happened. Everything's . . .' with an effort, he sat up, '. . . shit.'

He ran a hand over his face then peered at it as if it belonged to someone else. The sale of Doubleact had gone through. He was a rich man. And he was out from under.

'Mother hen,' he giggled.

'Who?'

'Sandie.'

It was the first time I'd ever heard him call his wife Sandie. It sounded like someone else, someone I didn't know. Brendan was trying to stand up. I didn't think that was such a great idea. The moment I touched him, he collapsed backwards onto the sofa, his hands reaching up for me, exactly the way he'd fallen off the windsurfer.

He'd upset the tea. He watched blearily while I cleaned it up.

'I don't care,' he said very carefully, 'about the money.'

'Of course you do.'

'No I fucking don't.' He waved an admonishing finger very slowly in front of my face. 'And I don't care about the baby, either. I just care . . .' he frowned, trying to concentrate, '. . . about us. I mean you. You down there. Missus.'

I ignored the comment. Getting him out of here wasn't going to be easy but I was buggered if I was going to listen to this all night. I went to the kitchen to fetch a cloth and bowl of cold water for the carpet. When I turned the taps off I became aware of a dripping noise. I looked up. The stain was spreading in front of my eyes, water running down from the ceiling. I watched, wondering quite where to start, then Brendan appeared in the doorway. He was clutching the door jamb very tightly, like a man contemplating a long jump. When he finally got the words out, it occurred to me he was trying to say sorry.

'It's no problem.' I gestured at the bowl of cold water. 'It'll wash out.'

'I meant the baby . . . all that . . .'

'Ah.'

That was something no amount of scrubbing in the world was going to shift. Soon enough there'd be two of us.

'Three,' Brendan insisted. 'Three.'

I began to shake my head but I knew there was no point. He was beyond argument. I tried to change the subject.

'I've got a problem.' I pointed at the wet patch on the ceiling. 'As you can probably see.'

Brendan nodded, emphatic. His eyes never left my face.

'And I love you too.'

He gave me a lop-sided smile and then took a little

265

half-step forward, abandoning the door jamb. For a moment, he wavered. Then, with a long sigh he collapsed face down, asleep at once, his face cradled in the towel I'd used to mop the walls. Hours later, when I finally tracked down the key to my bedroom door, he was still there, snoring gently, oblivious to the soft drip of water through the ceiling.

By the time I woke up next morning, he'd gone. A note on the gas stove told me how much he loved me. Instead of the usual sign-off, the distinctive 'B' he always used, he'd scrawled a single kiss.

I phoned the water board at eight o'clock, as soon as the office opened. I explained about the leak, and about my neighbour being away, and when I mentioned how pregnant I was, they promised to get someone round straight away. I stayed in all morning, waiting. At noon, the phone rang. I thought it might be the water board. It wasn't. It was Tom.

'How's tricks?'

'Bloody awful.'

'Why?'

I told him about Brendan staying the night, about the state he'd been in, about the things he'd said. I had to get it off my chest and telling Tom was oddly risk-free, like phoning one of those help organisations. Nikki, bless her, would have insisted on coming round and just now I didn't want that.

'He's gone?'

'Who?'

'That Brendan chap?'

'Oh yes, he went hours ago, before I even got up.'

I explained about him passing out. He'd spent the night on the kitchen floor, I said, unconscious.

'When's he coming back?'

'He's not.'

'Just as well, old thing. Best forgotten, eh?'

I heard him laughing. Then, without saying goodbye, he hung up. I returned to the kitchen, mystified. Why the interest? Why the questions? I shook my head, bewildered. My eyes kept straying to the damp patch on the ceiling. It was like a spot I couldn't leave alone. It represented decay, things falling apart. I felt completely powerless, utterly vulnerable, waiting for an engineer who never came, fielding calls on the phone from the wrong people, answering my door to an ex-lover who'd probably be back within hours. It was a nervy, out-of-control feeling, horribly close to panic.

I was on the point of returning to the front room and shaking up the water board with another phone call when there was a huge crash. I heard myself screaming. It was so loud, the noise, so physically close, I thought the ceiling had collapsed. There was dust everywhere. I looked up, my hand to my mouth, coughing. The ceiling was intact but where the cupboards had been there was nothing but bare plaster, scabby and pitted around the holes drilled for the supporting screws. The cupboards had been full of crockery – plates, cups, saucers – and I reached for the table, supporting myself, staring down at the wreckage.

There were shards of china, much of it my mother's, all over the floor. I backed slowly towards the door, feeling behind me for the handle, swaying on my feet, trying to keep the room in focus. My pulse was beginning to slow again but I felt physically sick. The smell, quite suddenly, was overpowering.

In the bathroom, I bent over the toilet bowl, retching. Then I turned round, lowering myself onto the seat, forcing my head between my knees. This was far from comfortable but it was the best I could do. I was close to fainting, and I knew it. Minutes passed while I fought fresh waves of panic. What had happened? What had I done? Why was everything disintegrating?

I reached for a flannel, turning on the tap in the handbasin, sponging my face. The cold water made me feel a little better. I washed my mouth out, then walked unsteadily back towards the kitchen. The last ten minutes, I seemed to have lost touch with reality. Had I really been there in the kitchen? Or was I in some fantasy world? A nightmare of my own making?

The kitchen was a mess. A big bottle of olive oil had smashed and the floor was slippery underfoot. I knew I had to get a grip on myself. I knew I had to cope. I owed it to myself, to the baby. Breaking down, giving up, just wasn't an option.

I hunted half-heartedly for the dustpan and brush and I was on my hands and knees, working clumsily around the edges of the wreckage, when I heard a knock at the front door.

It was the man from the water board. I stood in the hall and reached sideways to the wall for support. He was old, as old as my dad would have been. He took one look at the state of me and when I gestured wordlessly back up the hall, he found his own way to the kitchen. I told him about the leak from upstairs, gesturing feebly at the stain on the ceiling, but he was over where the cupboards had once been, examining the plasterwork. At length, he ran a finger across the wall then lifted it to his nose. I was still talking gibberish about Gilbert's skylight. The roofers must have upset the pipework, I muttered. There was definitely a leak.

The man from the water board glanced back at me. It was obvious he didn't believe a word.

'Begging your pardon, miss,' he said, 'but someone's been pissing through your ceiling.'

I had the baby that night. I went into labour shortly after six and Nikki drove me to the hospital. The contractions went on until the small hours and the baby arrived around half past three in the morning. Nikki was there to hold my hand and all the nurses said how marvellous I'd been. The baby was a little girl. I called her Billie.

I stayed in hospital for five more days. Something had gone wrong with my end of the umbilical cord and it took a minor operation to sort it out. Nikki came to see me every day and my mum took the train up from Petersfield. I got visits from mates at Doubleact and from Metro as well, and my corner of the four-bedded ward ended up looking like a flower shop. I tried to get hold of Tom a couple of times, to tell him the news about Billie, but his mobile wasn't answering. Of Brendan, to my intense relief, there was absolutely no sign.

Gaynor came on the third day. I'd phoned the police station from the ward and we'd had a brief chat but she'd been too busy for me to go into real details. Now, she settled herself beside the bed. She'd brought a big box of chocolates as well as her notepad. Billie was asleep in a cot beside the radiator. Gaynor thought she looked smashing.

I told her about the cupboards falling down, and what the engineer had said. I gave her the water board's number, and the key to the house. No one would have touched the kitchen. She could take a look for herself.

She came back next day. She'd been round to Napier Road with a colleague whose job it was to collect samples for scientific analysis. He'd scraped away at the plasterwork behind the cupboards and with luck the results should be back within twenty-four hours. She'd also phoned a couple of lads she knew who owed her a favour and they'd be in first thing tomorrow to tidy the place up. When I tried to thank her, I found myself in floods of tears. She fetched some Kleenex from the nursing station out in the corridor and sat with me for an hour or so, just chatting. The smell in the kitchen, she agreed, was dreadful.

By the time the results came through, Billie and I were down in Petersfield, tucked up with my mother. It was obvious from the moment we arrived that she was out to make a tremendous fuss of us, and it was equally obvious that the arrangement wouldn't survive more than a week or so. My mum was kindness itself but I felt hopelessly claustrophobic. Billie was the new start I'd been praying for. The sooner we were out on our own, the better.

On the phone, Gaynor came to the point at once.

'Urine,' she said. 'Definitely.'

I asked her what would happen next.

'I've already been up there. Talked to him about it.'

'What did he say?'

'He admitted it. He said he'd had a little accident.'

'Really?' My heart sank. 'How many little accidents?'

'Just the one. Though he was a bit vague.'

'But he'd been up there? All the time it was happening?'

'Probably, but we can't prove it.'

I half-listened to her explaining the legal situation. Technically, Gaynor could arrest him for criminal damage but to do that she had to establish intent. Gilbert's little accident proved no such thing.

'What about these stalking laws?'

'It's still tricky.'

'Why?'

'He's not really done anything, not on purpose, anyway. Nothing we could stand up in court.'

'He's barmy,' I said. 'Isn't that enough?'

'No, I'm afraid not.'

I heard my mother returning from the garden. Billie was beginning to stir. I thanked Gaynor for everything she'd done, especially cleaning up the kitchen. She said it was no problem.

'There's one other thing,' she added.

'What?'

'I phoned your old number. That one you gave me in De Beauvoir Square? I thought you'd be there.'

'And?'

'I talked to your partner, boyfriend, whatever he is. Brendan.'

I could feel the blood thudding in my head. This wasn't Gaynor's fault at all. When we'd last been in touch, back in the summer, Brendan and I were practically glued together.

'What did you tell him?'

Gaynor hesitated a moment, unusual for her.

'I mentioned the kitchen,' she said. 'You know, what had happened.'

'And what did he say?'

'He sounded very interested.' She paused again. 'I got the feeling he was hearing all this for the first time. Bit late, I know, but it's better I tell you.'

I thought about it for a second or two. Then I shrugged. What's done's done.

'Fine,' I said. 'And thanks again.'

The baby and I returned to London in the New Year. Christmas had been a non-stop succession of relatives queuing for a glimpse of my beloved Billie, and what little time I had to myself was wholly devoted to being a mum. Nature, I'd concluded by now, was truly miraculous. In three short weeks, Billie had transformed my life. The bond between us was quite extraordinary. We slept together, awoke together. I had no trouble breast-feeding and afterwards she'd lie peacefully in my arms, making gummy little noises that signalled the purest contentment. Now and again she'd yawn, and flex her little fingers, and smile a private smile and, watching her doze off again, I came to the conclusion that – despite the traumas of the last few months – I was the luckiest woman alive. In every respect I could think of, she was perfect. Just looking at her made everything seem possible.

Nikki loved her. She'd already agreed to be god-mother (my brother was godfather) and she drove down to pick us up. That night, at her insistence, we pitched our tent at her flat. Next day, we'd go back to Napier Road.

The evening at Nikki's was a riot. Billie was on her best behaviour, farting softly when we took it in turns to serenade her, and the three of us had Christmas all over again. We ate turkey, opened presents, drank loads of wine. Afterwards we had mince pies and brandy butter, neither of which would do much for what had once been my figure. That night, all three of us slept in Nikki's huge double bed, and when Billie needed changing, it was Nikki who did the honours.

The baby and I were back in Napier Road by ten o'clock next morning. I carried Billie around the front room, showing her the bits and pieces that Tom had sent her from Mothercare. Three weeks in Petersfield had given me plenty of time to think. Tom's gesture had been wonderfully generous but the time had now come for him to take some kind of responsibility for his brother. If he didn't then I'd bloody well find someone who would. Gilbert, this time, had gone too far.

To my surprise, though, when I finally ventured into the kitchen, it looked immaculate, completely untouched by last month's disaster. Not only had the mess disappeared but someone had taken the trouble to put the cupboards back up. I opened them one by one. New plates, new cups, even a new litre bottle of extra virgin olive oil. I transferred Billie to my other arm and opened the little card waiting for me on the table. It had come from Gaynor. She'd been talking to Gilbert again. He'd insisted on paying for the work, and for all the replacement crockery, and all the other bits and pieces that had come to grief. He'd left the choice of dinner plates to her, and Gaynor hoped I approved. I heard myself laughing and I looked up to check the ceiling. Sure enough, the stain had gone.

I bent to the note again. At the end, Gaynor wished Billie and me a Happy New Year. I knew the number to phone if there was any more hassle but she truly hoped it was sorted. She'd signed off with two kisses, one for me and one for Billie. Lovely thought.

Later that day, we ran into Gilbert in the hall. He made a great fuss of the baby and when he asked to hold it I saw no reason why not. Billie was our new start, I kept telling myself, our slate wiped clean. Nikki, who knew about everything that had happened, thought I was barmy staying anywhere near him but I had a thousand reasons for wanting to hang onto Napier Road. It was quiet. It was a perfect size. And, most important of all, it was ours. Maybe all the stuff through the ceiling really had been an accident. Maybe it was time to forgive and forget.

All three of us stayed in the hall, chatting, for nearly

half an hour. Gilbert and Billie seemed to have taken a shine to each other. They made exactly the same kinds of noises, halfway between a kiss and a gurgle, and watching Gilbert cradling Billie I was reminded of what his brother had told me. Good with babies and animals, he'd said. Hopeless with the rest of the world.

I tried to phone Tom that night. I dialled the number three separate times but got the same recorded message. The mobile phone I was calling was switched off. First time ever.

Failing Tom, I decided to go to the Social Services about Gilbert. My knowledge of what they actually did was pretty sketchy but I knew it included something called the At Risk register and I thought it was a reasonable bet that I might qualify. We were a single-parent family, for God's sake. And human beings don't come more vulnerable than a month-old baby girl.

The local Social Services department was a bleak suite of offices just up the road from the police station. The waiting room reminded me of the thousand and one documentaries I must have seen about inner-city deprivation. Men lolled against the walls. Most of the women looked utterly defeated. Their kids were either silent and tight-lipped, or raging around, totally out of control.

I waited an hour and forty minutes. Finally, I found myself explaining my problem to a young social worker. He had a neat pony tail, John Lennon glasses, and a grey collarless shirt. He listened politely to everything I told him about Gilbert but not even the stuff dripping through the kitchen ceiling counted for very much after my earlier admission about the keys.

'You actually lent them to him?'
'Yes.'
'And he made himself at home?'
'Yes.'

'Knowing you didn't mind?'

'Of course not. Not then.'

I recognised the nod and the weary smile from my encounters with the police and when I inquired what he might be able to do, I think I knew what was coming next.

He gestured towards the door. The waiting room outside was full to bursting.

'You've had a shock,' he said. 'But no one's dead. No one's even hurt. That's rare, believe me.'

I nodded, feeling guilty for wasting his time. When I apologised, he glanced down and shrugged. His list of appointments was on the desk in front of him. They went on until 7.15, name after name, each one a little pocket of someone else's grief. At length, he helped me towards the door. To be honest, he said, there was nothing they could do. Technically, Gilbert might be mad but it would take two independent psychiatrists to certify him. As long as he stayed at home, tucked up with his telescope, he was one less case to worry about.

He opened the door. Two kids were on the floor, fighting over the remains of a can of Coke.

'Maybe you were the crazy one,' he said gently, 'to lend him the key.'

I went back to Napier Road, feeling faintly disloyal. I was determined to give Gilbert a fighting chance and the more we saw of him, the more complete was the transformation that Billie's arrival seemed to have wrought.

By far the most useful of Tom's presents was a carrycot that doubled as a pram. For a brief spell in the middle of January the weather was glorious – unbroken sunshine from eight until four – and the three of us began to make regular expeditions to the local park. Gilbert and I took turns to push the pram and Billie gazed up at us both, swaddled in her quilted papoose, her bright little eyes just visible beneath the woolly cap my mother had run up over Christmas. Gilbert had a special way of tickling her face and Billie responded like the musical instrument she undoubtedly was. Gilbert had the knack of playing tunes on her, almost literally, and she loved it.

Afternoons when we didn't visit the little café in the park for hot doughnuts or sticky buns, we'd have tea at home instead. I'd hang our coats on the back of the kitchen door and toast crumpets for Gilbert and myself. Not once did we mention what had happened before Christmas and I was absolutely convinced that I had Billie to thank for this heartening transformation. Watching the gummy, toothless smile that spread across her face the moment she laid eyes on Gilbert, I found myself believing that everything, finally, had come right. Maybe Billie and I should go into mental health, I thought. Maybe the pair of us had stumbled on a treatment that had nothing to do with drugs.

It was during one of these little picnics that Brendan appeared again. Gilbert was the one to answer the front door. By the time Brendan got to the kitchen, I could hear Gilbert's footsteps retreating upstairs.

Brendan was dressed for the city. I hadn't seen him since the night he'd turned up paralytic and the suit and the subtly patterned tie did him more than justice. I introduced Billie. It should have been one of those deeply profound moments but somehow it wasn't.

'Girl or boy?'

I thought Brendan was making a joke. Evidently he wasn't. He'd been away again, Japan this time.

'Girl,' I said, removing a smudge of Marmite from her cheek. 'So what do you think?'

He didn't say anything. He didn't even want to hold her. He just looked round, as if he was drawing up some kind of list.

'I'm thinking about moving on one of those properties,' he said. 'I thought I'd keep you up to date.'

'Oh? Which one?'

'The Barnsbury place.'

I remembered the one with the steps and the red front door.

'Isn't it a bit big?' I said. 'For one?'

Brendan had crossed the kitchen. The window over the sink looked out on the back garden.

'Mind if I take a look?'

He was at the back door now. I shrugged, pointing out the key on the hook by the gas stove. He was out in the garden for quite a long time, looking up at the back of the house, and I stood at the sink, watching him. When he returned, he locked the door and put the key back on the hook.

'Chilly,' he said, buttoning his coat again and disappearing up the hall. Seconds later, he'd gone, but it took Gilbert more than an hour to venture back for the rest of his crumpet.

Billie and I took the train down to Dorset several weeks later. It was another glorious day and the pair of us sat beside the window watching the bare, shadowed fields roll by. At Salisbury, we were joined by an elderly lady with a beautiful red setter and by the time the train stopped at Sherborne, she and Billie were firm friends. As we got ourselves together in the aisle, she pressed a pound coin into Billie's little hand.

'That's for good luck,' she whispered.

The meeting at the solicitor's office was at noon. I'd phoned the previous week and explained that I wanted to talk to him about the house. He didn't seem the least bit surprised and it occurred to me that he might have been in contact with Tom.

Mr Clewson turned out to be an amiable, rather tweedy man in his middle fifties. His office smelled of the brand of pipe tobacco my grandfather used to smoke and everything about the way he'd decorated it spoke of treasured possessions and a life well spent. He seemed to me to be one of those rare human beings who are truly happy. He radiated contentment.

He gave me coffee and offered to organise some warm milk for Billie. It was a kind thought but I'd fed her on the train and I knew she'd last out until we found somewhere for lunch. Clewson had a little mobile on his desk, one of those clever executive toys that react to sunshine and go round and round, and Billie couldn't take her eyes off it. I'd brought her because I thought it might concentrate Clewson's mind. She was, to me, the very best evidence that he ought to take my story seriously.

I told him everything about Gilbert. I went right back to the early days when I'd just moved in and I took him round all the bends in the road between then and now. I explained about how kind he'd been, and how helpful, and how I'd been trusting enough to lend him the key to the flat. I told him about the liberties he'd taken – sleeping in my bed – and about everything that had followed from that April weekend. I admitted at once that I was no expert but the longer I spent sharing a house with Gilbert, the more convinced I became that he'd been through some kind of trauma. He was certainly damaged. Of that, I was absolutely sure.

Clewson had produced a pipe. He began to fill it with tobacco from a lovely old leather pouch.

'Do you view him as a threat?'

It was a question I knew he had to ask. I tried to explain about how erratic Gilbert could be, how his behaviour could veer wildly from total coherence and genuine kindness to the craziest excesses. The latest, of course, was the stuff through the floorboards.

'The what?'

'Urine.' I nodded at Billie, asleep on my lap. 'Wee-wee.'

I described the events that had probably triggered my labour. The cupboards falling down. The kitchen floor awash with olive oil and shattered china.

Clewson was looking thoughtfully at Billie.

'What do you think made him do it?' he asked at last.

I'd spent a great deal of time over Christmas tackling exactly this question and I answered it as truthfully as I could. I told him a little about Brendan, about my own circumstances. Gilbert, I suspected, had been jealous. Every time Brendan had made an appearance, he assumed the worst.

'The worst?'

'That we were together again.'

'And did he ever talk to you about it?'

'Never. I don't think he's like that. I don't think he can. It's beyond him.'

'So he expresses himself in a different way? Is that what you're saying?'

'Yes, that's exactly what I'm saying. There are some things he just can't handle.' I frowned, trying to put this conviction of mine into words. 'Life just gets too much for him.'

'You're sounding sympathetic.'

'I am,' I nodded. 'He's a nice man. With Billie, he's

wonderful. I don't want to see him hurt, nothing like that. I just want to be sure that we'll both be . . .' I smiled rather bleakly, '. . . safe.'

Clewson tamped the tobacco and lit a match. What I really wanted was some clue to his firm's relationship with Gilbert. I'd got enough from Tom to be reasonably certain that he wasn't just another tenant. On the contrary, his family seemed to own our little house.

I put this to Clewson. There wasn't much point in leaving it unsaid. He looked at me through a cloud of blue smoke.

'It's the case that I represent the family,' he nodded. 'That's certainly true.'

'Gilbert's family?'

'Yes.'

'So you'd know about his problems already?'

'I know . . .' he frowned, '. . . that he has his upsets. Frankly, some of what you've told me is, to say the least, a surprise.'

'He's not done this kind of thing before?' I was thinking of his previous neighbour, Kevin Witcher.

Clewson shook his head.

'Certainly not. As far as I'm aware, he's always coped. I've absolutely no evidence to the contrary.'

'But you do believe me, don't you?'

'Of course.'

'And you think something should be done about it?'

He didn't answer. Billie was stirring. Her little arms went out and Clewson smiled, watching her.

'Of course,' he said at last. 'Of course it should.'

He took us for lunch at a pub across the road. We sat in an alcove at the back, waiting for a waitress to arrive with the menu. I was determined to find out more about the family. Where they lived seemed a good place to start.

'Tom says the family come from round here,' I ventured.

'Who?'

'Tom.' I paused. 'Gilbert's brother.'

Clewson was looking at Billie again. Eventually he reached out, tickling her under the chin.

'I think it's wise to clarify our interests in all this,' he said at last. 'The firm represents the family. You'll understand that.'

'Of course.'

'That imposes certain duties. One of them is a duty of confidentiality. They are our clients. You wouldn't expect us to break that confidentiality.'

'No, absolutely not, all I'm asking—'

Clewson held up both hands, a gesture that produced a gurgle of applause from Billie.

'I know what you're asking,' he said. 'You're asking me to help you. And you have every right to do that. Indeed you have a duty to do that.' His eyes were still on the baby. 'Have you thought of moving?'

'I've tried that already.'

'And?'

I told him about my adventures with Mark. Gilbert had done his level best to wreck the sale and he'd been a hundred per cent successful. Now, though, Billie and I were nicely settled in Napier Road. Just as long as Gilbert behaved himself.

'You're saying he didn't want you to leave?'

'Yes.'

'Why would he want to do that?'

This, of course, was the heart of it. The waitress had arrived with the menu. I took Clewson's advice and ordered steak and kidney pie. The waitress disappeared again. Clewson returned to Gilbert. Was I implying some kind of obsession?

'I think he's in love with me,' I said simply. 'Not that he's ever said it.'

'In *love*? You mean . . . ?' His elegant gesture encompassed the baby.

I shook my head.

'Nothing physical. Nothing like that. I just think he has . . . a thing about me. It's not threatening. It's more protective than anything else. As far as he's concerned, I think I'm almost family.' I nodded, pleased with the phrase. 'It's almost as though he's responsible for us. You can see it when he's with Billie. He dotes on her. He's like a favourite uncle.'

'And Brendan?'

'Brendan's a threat. Brendan's the one who wants to take us away.'

'And does he? Is Gilbert right?'

I looked down at Billie for a moment, thinking about all the literature from the estate agents.

'Yes,' I muttered. 'I think he does.'

The meal, when it arrived, was a bit of a disaster. Billie got fractious and in the end I had to retreat to the loo to feed her. When I got back, Clewson was sitting in front of his empty plate, his raincoat folded on his lap.

'I've been thinking,' he said. 'And I suspect there's a way round all this. It needs me to talk to the family, of course, and I can't possibly pre-judge what they may come up with, but I'd hope to have a proposal for you within, say, a couple of days.'

'A proposal?' I was lost. 'What do you mean?'

'I mean, and this of course is extremely provisional, that there may be options we can pursue.'

'What kind of options?'

'I can't say. Not until I've had a word.'

'But what about Gilbert? What would happen to him?'

'Gilbert?' Clewson stood up, putting on his coat. 'Gilbert, I'm afraid, would be out of my hands.'

He offered to drive us back to the station but I said we were planning to look around town. We said goodbye on the pavement outside the pub and, when he asked for it, I gave him my phone number. When he'd gone, we walked down the street until we found the post office. They had a local phone directory but when I looked under Phillips, trying to find an address, there were so many entries it was pointless trying to pinpoint anyone in particular.

There was a phone outside the post office and I tried Tom's mobile number. If he really lived nearby perhaps, at long last, we could meet. He might be a good deal more frank than his solicitor.

'Long time, no hear,' he said. 'I've been away a bit. *Hors de combat*. How's the baby? He? She?'

'She. And she's brilliant. Wonderful. The best thing ever.'

I told him all about Billie. Then I said we were down in Sherborne. There were plenty of trains back to London. We could delay our departure a couple of hours. Might there be time for a get-together?

'Extraordinary,' he said at once. 'The one day you make it down here, I'm off the plot.'

'You're what?'

'Indisposed, otherwise engaged. In fact, old thing, it's even worse than that.'

'Oh?'

'Yes, you've caught me in bloody London. Hell's teeth, you should have phoned earlier. Yesterday maybe. I'm sure we could have sorted something out.'

I said I was sorry I hadn't. I checked my watch. It wasn't three o'clock yet.

'We could be back in London by six,' I suggested.

'Why don't you pop round for a drink before you come back down here? It would be nice to meet you. Billie, too. She loves all those things you bought her.'

'She does?'

'Yes.'

There was a long silence. I wondered whether he was looking for excuses to turn the invite down. Meeting after all this time would, for both of us, be a strange experience.

'What do you think?' I said at last. 'Nice idea?'

'Very nice.'

'You'll come? Eight o'clock, say? Have something to eat?'

'Of course I will.'

He checked the address and mumbled something about having to be away before the last train out of Waterloo. Then he rang off.

Billie and I were back in Napier Road by seven. I'd bought a bagful of stuff from the local deli, and two bottles of good Rioja. I strapped Billie into her little rocker in the kitchen and she watched me while I found bowls for the various dips. I was polishing the glasses when it occurred to me that I ought to ask Gilbert, as well. The two of them were brothers, for God's sake. One social evening a year wouldn't over-stretch the family ties.

I went into the hall, meaning to call up to Gilbert, but then I had second thoughts. One of the reasons I wanted to talk to Tom face to face was to try and sort something out about this brother of his. Things between us were fine just now but if anything happened again it would be nice to know that Gilbert had somewhere to go to. Better, therefore, to keep Tom to myself for an hour or so and then invite Gilbert down afterwards. That way, I told myself, it would be a nice surprise.

Tom was due around eight. By half past, Billie was asleep and there was still no sign of him. I'd already been to the window twice, peering up the street. I was about to try his mobile number when I heard a light tap at my door. It made me jump. I got to my feet and crossed the room. It was Gilbert. He was carrying a wicker basket.

I invited him in, knowing that he'd seen the food and glasses already. With Tom due any minute, I could hardly pretend I was expecting anyone else.

'Have a drink,' I said, stepping back.

Gilbert put the basket on the floor. Already I could see something fluffy moving around inside. Gilbert was looking down at the carrycot. Billie was still asleep.

'May I wake her up?'

'Why?'

'I've got a little present.'

I could see the kitten now, tiny little paws reaching out through the wickerwork. Gilbert knelt on the floor, undoing the straps that secured the flap at one end. He reached in, extraordinarily gentle. The kitten was the sweetest thing you ever saw, tabby with a white blaze on its face. Gilbert was looking at the bottle of wine I'd uncorked beside the gas fire.

'You could call it Rioja,' he suggested thoughtfully.

Gilbert stayed for the rest of the evening while we waited for Tom. Billie was entranced by the kitten and Gilbert hovered over the pair of them, making sure that neither came to any harm. When Tom didn't turn up, we piled hummus and taramasalata onto biscuits and ate our way through the egg and anchovy rolls I'd prepared. Gilbert was even quieter than usual but when I asked if anything was wrong he said no. Around ten o'clock he fetched his flute from upstairs and played some of the lullabies I remembered from that first night I moved in. One in particular, Billie seemed to love. Gilbert played it again and again, drawing the notes out longer each time, a strange, far-away look in his eyes. He said it was his own favourite. He said it was called *Nocturne*.

Finally, past midnight, I tried Tom's number. Gilbert was still watching over the baby, the kitten curled in his lap. Billie, by now, was fast asleep. I keyed in the last of the numbers for Tom's mobile. This time there wasn't even a recorded message. Just silence.

Clewson phoned two days later. As soon as I heard his voice I could smell the tobacco in that office of his. He asked me about Billie. I said she was fine.

'I've been talking to the family,' he said. 'As I expected, they want to put a proposal to you.'

He mentioned an intermediary. For reasons he wasn't prepared to discuss, they were insisting on keeping themselves at arm's length from anything, as he put it, 'pertaining to 31 Napier Road'. Halfway through trying to change Billie, I was trying to prevent her rolling off the mat.

'I thought you were the intermediary,' I said. 'Isn't that what solicitors do?'

He told me he was too busy to make it up to London. There was someone else they were happy to use, a name he thought I'd recognise.

'Who?'

Billie had caught the corner of her soiled nappy. She began to drag it towards her.

'Morris Fairweather,' I heard Clewson say. 'I believe he's an MP.'

*

Fairweather arranged for us to meet at the House of Commons. My days on *Members Only* had given me a working knowledge of the geography of the place and I had no problem finding the big Central Lobby where the public can mill around, waiting for a word with their MP. I gave my name to one of the policemen on duty at the desk. He winked at Billie and made a phone call. By the time Fairweather came down from his office, we were sitting on one of the benches across the other side of the lobby.

I don't think he expected the baby to have come too.

'Name?'

'Billie.'

'*Billie*? I thought it was a girl?'

'She is.'

'So what kind of name is that?'

He was as bluff and direct as ever. I hadn't seen him since I'd tempted him onto *Members Only* but the intervening months hadn't changed him at all. We agreed that the lobby was a lousy place to talk. Getting us passes for his office might be a pain so I suggested a turn or two around St James's Park. At first, he looked horrified. Like most MPs, he had a deep mistrust of physical exercise but he fetched his coat, and a funny little pork pie hat, and when we got outside he even volunteered to push the pram.

St James's Park was a trailer for early spring. There were drifts of snowdrops and crocuses, white and mauve against the pale grass, and I propped Billie up in the pram, giving her a chance to see the ducks on the lake. Fairweather had recently made a return appearance on the first of the new series of *Members Only*, and he amused me with a couple of behind-the-camera stories. Brendan, it seemed, had just added the programme to his private collection, another of the office goodies he was smuggling out to his new life.

'He was always crazy about you,' Fairweather said. 'You know that, don't you? I always told him he had no chance. I said you had taste.'

He was looking rather pointedly at Billie. I told him that Brendan and I were no longer together.

'So I gather.' He brought the pram to a halt beside a bench. 'Does that mean I was right all along?'

I smiled but said nothing. I wanted to know what the family planned for Gilbert. And I wanted to know why on earth they'd chosen Morris Fairweather to pass the message on.

'Old friends,' he said briskly.

'Is that the only clue I get?'

'Dead bloody right.'

'But you know them well?'

'Well enough.'

'So why didn't you let on before?'

'When?'

'When I first told you? That night we went to the Caprice, and then the club afterwards?'

Fairweather shot me a sideways look. He'd obviously spent less time preparing for this conversation than I had.

'You gave me a name,' he said carefully. 'Maybe I didn't recognise it.'

'You're telling me Gilbert Phillips isn't Gilbert Phillips?'

'I'm saying nothing of the sort. I'm merely speculating.'

It was a political answer and try as I might I couldn't budge him an inch further. The implication was pretty clear – that Phillips wasn't Gilbert's family name at all – but Fairweather hadn't come here for anything as helpful as a candid chat. On the contrary, as he kept pointing out, he was only the messenger boy, the bearer – he hoped – of good news.

'They want to make you an offer,' he said. 'And frankly you'd be daft not to say yes.'

I had Billie in my lap. We were surrounded by ducks now and I wished I'd brought some bread.

'What is it?' I asked.

'They'd like you to move out.'

I'd already told him about last time, with Mark, but he shook his head.

'They'd buy it,' he said. 'Take it off your hands.'

'They would?'

'Yes. Decent price, too. I managed to get them up to £65,000.'

I glanced sideways at him. He was looking pleased with himself.

'But what about Gilbert?' I asked.

'Bugger Gilbert. It's you you should be thinking about. You and little Willie here.'

For the first time he tried to touch the baby. She watched his big fat finger waving in front of her face.

'He needs help,' I said. 'That's what I thought this was all about. I thought they were going to get him treatment of some kind. I don't know, drugs, counselling, whatever it is he needs.'

'You really think that would help?'

'Of course I do. He's in a real mess sometimes. You can see it coming on, once you get to know him.'

Fairweather had a packet of fruit gums. He tossed one to the nearest duck. The duck ignored it.

'Clewson was right,' he frowned. 'He said you were naive, very nice but very naive. Gilbert's not your problem, it's theirs, the family's.'

'But they've done nothing, absolutely nothing, not

even that brother of his, Tom. They won't come round, they won't even invite him down. They just leave him there, stewing in his own juices. What kind of family's that? To just abandon him?'

Fairweather looked unimpressed.

'Happens all the time,' he said. 'Families splitting up, fathers, mothers . . .' He nodded at Billie. 'Christ, girl, you should know.'

I objected to that. Very strongly indeed. Billie, as far as I knew, was normal. She'd grow up strong, protected, ready to make her way in the world. Gilbert, on the other hand, was completely adrift, hopelessly vulnerable to the next passing squall. His attempts to make a name for himself – like the LP he'd paid the earth for – had come to nothing, and he'd ended up with half a house in N17 and a telescope to keep him company on cloudless nights.

My outburst stung Fairweather into defending himself.

'I'm told he's happy enough.'

'Who says?'

'His father, for one.'

'His *father*?' I stared at him. 'But his father's dead.'

'Really?'

'Yes, Tom told me, his brother. You don't believe me?'

Fairweather gave himself a moment or two to compose his thoughts. Then he put a gloved hand on mine.

'It's a good offer,' he said. 'I'd take it. I'd find another place, move out, forget all about Gilbert. Clewson told me about what happened to your kitchen ceiling. If that doesn't make your mind up, God knows what will.'

I looked down at Billie, wondering whether to bother with my little speech about causes and effects, about the pattern I'd detected behind Gilbert's wilder excesses, about what it was that tipped him into madness. Fair-weather, like Clewson, didn't want to know. They thought my concern and my sympathy were quaint, and wholly wonderful, but their sole responsibility was to get me out of Napier Road. Gilbert could look after himself. Always had. Always would.

Fairweather was still watching me, still waiting for an answer.

'In the nicest possible way,' he said, 'they're giving you a deadline.'

'Oh?'

'Yes.' He stood up, looking at his watch. 'They want a decision within forty-eight hours. I make that Wednesday.'

As good as his word, Fairweather phoned me at home two days later. All three of us had taken the bus over to Whipp's Cross and walked around the ponds across from the hospital. Gilbert, unlike me, had thought to bring nuts for the squirrels and Billie had been entranced. Now, still in his duffle coat, he was out in the kitchen making us tea.

I took Fairweather's call in the front room, tip-toeing to the door and closing it.

'Well?' he said.

He wanted an answer. I did my best to postpone the decision. Two days' thinking had led me to certain conclusions.

'He's an MP,' I suggested. 'Like you.'

'Who?'

'Gilbert's father.'

'How do you make that out?'

I told him I'd been asking around, using the contacts I'd made on *Members Only*. It wasn't true but I thought it was a reasonable guess. Politicians, like any caste, tend to mix amongst themselves.

'He's quite well known,' I went on. 'And I expect he wants to keep the skeletons in the cupboard.'

'What skeletons?'

'Gilbert, for a start.'

Fairweather's voice was beginning to harden. The bonhomie had gone. He was getting irritated.

'Who he is doesn't matter,' he said. 'All he's after is a bloody decision. Do you want the sixty-five grand or not?'

I heard Gilbert's footsteps falter outside the door. I visualised him trying to juggle plates and a tray of tea. I got up to open the door.

'I'll phone you later,' I said to Fairweather. 'I'm still thinking about it.'

I didn't phone, not that night and not next day either. Partly because I objected to being backed into a corner, and partly because I simply hadn't made up my mind. Of course a move had its attractions. Of course the money would come in handy. But there were other factors, too, and I judged them equally important. For one thing, we were happy in Napier Road, all three of us, and for another I felt very sorry for Gilbert. Moving out would be a gross betrayal. He had very serious problems, no question about it, but just now I'd never seen him happier.

At the end of the week, after non-stop rain for two days, the weather cheered up again. After lunch, I slipped Billie into the papoose and settled her in the pram. When there was no answer at Gilbert's door, we left without him, walking the mile or so to the park off Lordship Lane.

It happened to be half term and the place was full of kids. I parked the pram outside the café, as usual, and went in to get a sticky bun and a can of Diet Coke. I always left Billie where I could see her, but this particular afternoon the heat of all the bodies inside the café had misted the windows. To be honest, as well, I probably spent a second or two longer than usual in the queue for the cash till.

I paid for the bun and the drink, then picked my way out between the bodies. I remember the air being cold on my face as I pushed out through the door. I'd left the pram a couple of paces to the left. It was empty.

I dialled 999 from a phone in the café. The police were there in minutes, two men and a woman. I was hysterical by now, howling my eyes out, and the woman did her best to calm me down while they tried to get to the bottom of what had actually happened. It's incredibly hard to be rational when you've just lost the most important thing in your life, ever, but they were very patient, coaxing the facts out of me, and afterwards we all drove back to Napier Road where I found some photos that Nikki had taken around Christmas. Handing over those photos triggered another flood of tears. It was as if I'd lost her twice. My fault. My baby. Gone.

Nikki came round and stayed with me that evening. I couldn't stop talking about it, going over those minutes I'd spent in the café time and time again. Why had I ever developed a taste for sticky buns? Why had I ever dreamt of leaving Billie, even for the time it took to go into the café, and point at the cabinet, and take the paper bag, and pay? Didn't I know about the world outside? The kind of monsters who lurked round every corner? Where on earth had I been all my life?

Nikki, of course, was all sympathy, telling me I shouldn't blame myself, telling me it could have happened to any mother, but I knew this was nonsense. I'd lost her. It had been my fault. I sat by the phone, my hand ready to snatch it up, and all the time I was wondering where Billie might be, whether she'd be hungry or not, fed or not, changed or not, whether she'd even realise what had happened. A couple of times, journalists rang up or came to the door. They wanted to talk to me, to find out how I felt, but Nikki chased them away. She'd brought a bottle of vodka from her flat. Just looking at it made me feel physically ill.

At length, I summoned the energy to go upstairs and break the news to Gilbert. When I told him that Billie had gone, been stolen, he stared at me. At first I thought he hadn't understood but as soon as I started the story again he reached out, putting his hand on my arm, appalled. The park had been a place of safety, our place, Billie's place. There was no room in this little corner of Gilbert's world for news like this.

Around midnight, Nikki went home. She'd offered to stay but I'd said no. I was cold by this time, colder than I've ever felt in my life, and I didn't want to talk to anyone. Losing Billie had walled me off. I was a hopeless mother. The fault was all mine. If she was hurt, if she was dead, then I'd as good as killed her.

I lay in bed that night, waiting for the phone to ring. By the time the police broke in, evacuating the street, I'd lost track of how late it was. They took us in buses to the local library. Most of me had ceased to relate to the real world, to the offer of a cup of coffee, to the invitation to help myself to a mattress and a couple of blankets. All I could think about, all that mattered, was Billie.

Somehow, exhausted, I must have slept for an hour or so because it was Gaynor who woke me up. We left the library, stepping over the rows of sleeping bodies, and she drove me to the police station. I asked her about Billie, what news there'd been, but she said she didn't know. Once so friendly, she looked wary, guarded, even cold.

Someone much older was waiting for me at the police station. Judging by his face, he'd had about as much sleep as I had. He and Gaynor took me to an interview room. He said he was a Detective Chief Inspector. He asked me whether I'd had anything to eat.

'You've found her,' I said dully. 'And she's dead.'

His face softened a little. He said he knew about Billie and he said he was sorry. My photos had been circulated. Officers were making inquiries. But so far there were no solid leads. He looked at me with some sympathy, then produced a pad, checking his watch.

'This Gilbert Phillips . . .' he began.

He wanted to know everything about Gilbert and I heard myself telling him what I knew. I hadn't a clue why he was interested and I didn't bother to ask. Whatever had happened overnight was madness, more evidence that the world had finally toppled from its axis. Gilbert had been right all along. The Dark.

The Chief Inspector was watching me.

'We had a call,' he said carefully. 'A tip.'

'About Billie?' My heart leapt.

'About Phillips. The flat. The call came with a recognised codeword. We had no alternative but to take it seriously.' He frowned. 'The caller said there were explosives at number 31A.'

'*Explosives?*'

'Specifically Semtex. And timing devices.'

'So what happened?'

'The caller was right.' He nodded. 'That's exactly what we found.'

I looked helplessly at Gaynor, quite lost. First Billie had gone. Now my mad neighbour was some kind of terrorist. Gilbert? Making bombs? In Napier Road?

'I don't believe it,' I said quietly.

'You don't believe we found the material?'

'I don't believe he was involved.'

'Why not?'

I did my best to pull myself together and concentrate. Gilbert was a child, I explained. He was under-developed, a little simple, easily hurt, but there wasn't an ounce of malice in him. He wouldn't know one end of a bomb from another.

'We found a target list as well,' the Chief Inspector pointed out, 'and supporting material. The search isn't over, by any means. We may find more.'

'A written list?'

'Yes.'

'May I see it?'

The Chief Inspector studied me for a moment. Then he nodded at Gaynor. When she returned, the photocopy was still warm from the machine. I studied the list. Individual names had been blacked out but there was enough scrawl left for me to be sure.

'This isn't Gilbert's handwriting,' I told the Chief Inspector. 'It's completely different.'

'That proves nothing. Someone else may have drawn up the list. Possession is what matters. And intent.'

I was still looking at the list. There were lots of blacked-out names.

'You really think Gilbert would blow these people up?' For the first time I ventured something close to a smile. The idea was absurd.

The Chief Inspector's gaze didn't waver.

'It's a possibility,' he said. 'One amongst many.'

'There are others?'

'Of course.'

'Like what?'

There was another silence. The Chief Inspector was still looking at me. Gaynor, too.

'Tell us again about Gilbert,' he said at length. 'Start where you did before.'

I stared at them and began to cry. The Chief Inspector glanced at Gaynor, plainly uncomfortable.

'Would you like a break?' Gaynor got to her feet.

I shook my head, then nodded and buried my face in my hands.

'I'd just like my baby back.' I sobbed. 'Is that too much to ask?'

The interview ended soon afterwards. I'd done my best to pull myself together. I'd confirmed various bits of information they seemed to have gathered about Gilbert. I'd even given them Morris Fairweather's name in the hope that they could get more out of him than I ever had. Then, all of a sudden, I spotted the uniformed policewoman out in the corridor. I could see her through the little square of wired glass. She was signalling to Gaynor. She had important news. I caught Gaynor's eye. She went to the door. The two women had the briefest conversation, then Gaynor was back again.

The Chief Inspector glanced up at her but she was looking at me.

'We've found Billie.' She was grinning. 'She's safe and well.'

Gaynor drove me to Billie. Bits of Barnsbury slipped past. Finally, we stopped outside a tall, handsome house, part of a terrace looking onto a square. The house had a red door. I recognised the Mercedes at the kerb.

Brendan took us down to the basement. Billie was asleep on a big double bed. I gathered her in my arms. I lifted her up, burying my nose in her Babygro, smelling her, like an animal. She began to stir, and I held her tight, tighter than I've ever held anything in my life, and the gulping noises I made when I started to cry again woke her up. She rubbed her eyes with the backs of her little hands. Then she reached out for me.

When I was back in control of myself, I asked what had happened. Brendan said he'd found her on the doorstep. I called him a liar.

Gaynor intervened.

'She's back,' she pointed out. 'And she's intact.'

True. Gaynor and I left with Billie minutes later. Billie didn't seem the least bit hungry, and I was already convinced that a search of the house would turn up feeding bottles, Ostermilk, the whole gig. Brendan stole my baby. I'm sure he did. I put the thought to Gaynor, outside on the pavement. Wasn't the theft of a baby a criminal offence? Wasn't Brendan guilty of third degree harassment? Couldn't she march back into the house and arrest him? Gaynor gave me a funny look and held open the car door while Billie and I ducked inside.

'Where to?' she asked, eyeing me in the rear-view mirror.

For the next couple of days we were back with Nikki, exactly where I started. She, as ever, was quite brilliant. She promised to help me hunt for a flat and when the time came, she said she'd be there to help with the move as well. Staying at Napier Road, we both agreed, was out of the question. Nikki made a huge fuss of Billie, who seemed quite unharmed by the whole experience, and on the second night we celebrated with champagne and a small mountain of smoked salmon.

I was still hungover, the following afternoon, when Gaynor phoned. The boys from the Anti-Terrorist Squad had nearly finished at Napier Road. She knew I'd never been upstairs into Gilbert's flat and she wondered whether I'd like to take a look.

After some thought, I said yes, and she drove round and picked us up. Since the reunion at Brendan's house, Billie and I were inseparable. I wouldn't let her out of my sight.

At the far end of Napier Road we found a white van that evidently belonged to the forensic people. We got out of the car and crossed the road. The front door to number 31 was still hanging off its hinges from the early morning raid and I stood by the gate for a moment or two, staring at the splintered panels with their broken grin. Had I really lived here for more than a year? Was this the house where – for most of the time – I'd been so happy?

We mounted the stairs, Billie in my arms. I was aware at once of an overwhelming smell, deeply chemical, which Gaynor blamed on the forensic people. They'd spent a day and a half tearing the place apart. Out on the top landing, there was no floorboard unlifted, no pipe unexposed. Even the residues in the kitchen soakaway, Gaynor said, had been carted off for analysis.

We went into the flat to find more chaos. The main room looked like one of the blitz photographs my father used to show me when I was a child, the ribs of the house plainly visible, and I stepped very carefully from joist to joist, raising dust as I went. The murals caught my eye at once, huge purple planets, hand-painted, cratered, wreathed in cloud. Dominating another wall was a line of colour photos, beautifully framed shots of a girl windsurfing on a choppy grey lagoon. I stared at the photos, one by one, my throat tightening with the dust and the memories. That's me, I told Billie. That's Mummy.

I gazed around at Gilbert's few sticks of furniture, the handful of items that must have softened this bleak, cold world he'd made his own. The chairs had been torn apart, their stuffing ripped out, and the cheap MFI sofa had been mauled as well. Beside the audio stack, abandoned, was his flute. I asked Gaynor if I could pick it up. She called out to the man we could hear working in the kitchen and he appeared in a dirty blue overall, his hands clad in latex gloves.

When I asked about trying the flute, he nodded. Gaynor took the baby. I tried to coax out a note or two but nothing happened.

'It's a real art,' the man grinned ruefully. 'We've all had a go.'

He'd been here throughout the search and I asked him what else he'd found. He glanced at Gaynor who said it was OK to show me round. I followed him through into the narrow hall. Wherever we walked, there were empty egg boxes underfoot. At the end of the hall, I found a small lavatory. The door was open. The forensic man gestured inside.

'That's where the egg boxes came from,' he explained. 'And this stuff as well.'

He stooped in the gloom and picked up a length of felt. It was the same material Gilbert used for his curtains: thick, absorbent, heavy-duty. Gilbert had spread layer after layer of it on the floor.

'And the egg boxes?'

'Glued to the walls.'

'Why?'

He looked at Gaynor again. Gaynor nodded. With the

door closed, he said, the loo would have been virtually soundproof, an acoustic cell, utterly sealed off from reality. He thought the guy must have had a thing about privacy, about shutting himself away. That's where they'd found the mobile. That's where he'd taken his phone calls.

Phone calls? We returned to the wreckage of the main room. Underneath a pile of bedding, the forensic man found the mobile phone he'd been looking for.

'The guy had two phones,' he said. 'One on a socket, and this one.' I stared at it. I'd just noticed the Mothercare catalogue, half-hidden beneath a pile of old newspapers.

'What's the number?' I asked him.

He glanced at Gaynor again and then disappeared towards the kitchen. When he came back he was carrying a clipboard. He began to look for the number, his finger working down a typed inventory. When his finger stopped he looked up.

'0831?' I asked him, '306708?'

'That's right.'

Gaynor was looking surprised.

'You used to phone him? When you lived down-stairs?'

'Yes. Sort of.'

'What do you mean, sort of?'

I was still looking at the phone.

'He had a brother,' I faltered. 'At least, I thought he did.'

It was nearly a month before I saw Brendan again. He called me at the new flat, a sunny, top-floor conversion in Chiswick two streets away from the Thames. A carpenter was still busy putting up cupboards in the kitchen, hammering and sawing, and I had difficulty making sense of what Brendan was saying. Something about his new company. Something about a project. Something about the need for us to meet.

'Tomorrow morning,' he said. 'Ten o'clock. I'm sending a car.'

The car arrived at the appointed hour. Billie and I settled into the back of a dented Shogun which delivered us to a newish-looking building in a street off the Tottenham Court Road. Brendan had rented a suite of offices on the third floor. The logo of Solo Productions was a lone sail. Sweet.

We waited for several minutes in the little reception area. The place felt exactly like Doubleact – the framed production stills, the pile of bagged video rushes on the desk – and I was half-tempted to gather Billie up and run. Even the sound of Brendan's voice on the phone had upset me.

At length, a rangy American redhead took us to Brendan's office. He was sitting behind a huge desk, looking pleased with himself. The redhead didn't leave.

'This is Varenka,' he said. 'She's from LA.'

Varenka and I exchanged wary smiles. I began to wonder about their relationship but Brendan spared me the trouble.

'I've asked Varenka to sit in,' he grinned. 'There's not much we don't discuss.'

'I'm sure.'

Brendan ignored me. He was looking at the baby. It was the first time he'd seen Billie since I collected her that afternoon from Barnsbury.

'We must fix some kind of schedule,' he told Varenka. 'Weekends or something. You're supposed to be good with babies.'

I pointed out that Billie was a bit young to lead a life

of her own. Did Varenka breastfeed? Brendan and Varenka exchanged looks. He'd obviously warned her about how difficult I could be, and the sight of her trying to rouse a smile from Billie made my blood run cold. These people are beneath contempt, I thought. Brendan owed me some answers, and I wanted an undertaking that he'd leave us both alone, but after that Billie and I were out of there. Just being in his office, just looking at him, soiled me.

'Gilbert's been released,' I said. 'Did you hear about that?'

'Yes.'

'Seems he wasn't a terrorist after all. Surprise surprise.'

Brendan returned my icy smile.

'You're saying he's normal now?'

'No, I'm saying he was framed. Someone dumped all that stuff in his flat. Someone with an interest in getting me out.'

Varenka butted in, trying to change the subject, but I'd spent nearly a month getting this far and I wasn't going to stop now. Brendan motioned to Varenka to shut up. He was looking interested.

'Go on,' he said.

'My point is that someone wanted Gilbert and me apart. You know about the family, Fairweather, the offer to buy me out?' Brendan nodded. 'And you know I didn't give them the decision they wanted?'

'Yes.'

'How come?'

'Morris told me.'

'OK,' I shrugged. 'So there you have it.'

'The family? Gilbert's family?' Brendan was grinning now. 'You think Gilbert's family planted the explosives?' He began to laugh.

303

'Yes,' I said, trying not to sound defensive. 'They obviously have money, connections, power. The one thing they couldn't buy was me.' I was starting to lose my temper. He still had the knack of getting under my skin and that angered me even more. 'You think I've got it wrong?'

'I know you've got it wrong.'

'Really?'

'Yes,' he nodded. 'Try looking at motive.'

'I just did.'

'Look harder.'

I stared at him. What was he telling me here? What had I missed? Who else wanted Gilbert and me apart?

'You?' I queried softly. 'You did it?'

Brendan looked briefly pained, chiefly I think because I hadn't got there earlier. He always loved taking the credit, even for something as serious and as bizarre as this. I was thinking hard now. Would he really have gone to such lengths? Semtex? Target lists? Code words?

'I don't believe you,' I told him. 'I think you're fantasising again.'

'Why?'

'Because it was so elaborate. And so . . .' I frowned, hunting for the right word, '. . . crazy.'

'You think I wouldn't take the risk?' He was looking at Billie. 'Given what was at stake?'

I couldn't take my eyes off his face. I remembered now. I remembered that last time he came to the house. That chilly afternoon when he spent so long in the garden, looking up at Gilbert's flat. Was he casing the joint? Looking for ways in?

'You'd need access to explosives,' I pointed out. 'And you'd need the codeword. To make them take you seriously.'

'Of course.'

'You had all that?'

He didn't say anything. He was still looking at Billie. Finally he leaned back in the chair, his feet propped on the desk, the old pose. I might be here for an interview, I thought to myself. We might have never met.

'Who Dares Wins?' He was grinning now. 'All that special forces shit? You know how these guys operate, surely?'

I blinked. Of course I knew. Of course I bloody did. It was Gary. Faithful old Gary. With his SAS contacts, and his black balaclava, and his empty bank account. Brendan was right. Why hadn't I got there first?

'So what did it take?' I asked softly, 'Money?'

'Interesting question,' Brendan sighed. 'What does it ever take?'

I stared at him, for once robbed of a reply. I was back in the park, that terrible afternoon when I lost Billie. I felt the panic again, and the fear. And then I felt the anger. This man had taken my baby. By bragging about the rest of it – the Semtex, the codeword, the target list – he'd given himself away. If he could do that, he could do anything. He was pitiless. He was psychopathic. It was Brendan, not Gilbert, who belonged with the insane. How come I'd ever let him so close to me? How come I'd believed a single word he'd said? How come he wasn't in a lunatic asylum? Or a prison cell?

At this point, a secretary intervened with coffee and biscuits. While I crumbled chocolate digestives for Billie, trying to control myself, Brendan treated me to what was obviously his standard pitch for Solo Productions. How many projects he had in the pipeline. The backing he'd raised abroad. The huge potential of the US market. Then, quite suddenly, he was talking about a specific programme idea. It was about power, he said. About love. About insanity. Two brothers, one successful, one not. Brother number one becomes a politician. Brother number two's half-mad.

'So they bury him,' he explained. 'They put him in a little flat with a pension from a trust fund and they leave him to get on with it. This is an idea that travels. It could be any city in the western world. London. New York. Melbourne. The guy's mad, crazy, a non-person.'

'Gilbert?' I inquired coldly. 'You're talking about Gilbert?'

Brendan ignored the question.

'Brother number one makes it big time. Becomes a minister. Sits in Cabinet. Brother number two goes from bad to worse. Problem is, we need a POV.'

POV means Point of View.

'This is a documentary?'

'Drama.'

'*Drama?*'

'Yes, a series. Six hours. Maybe seven.'

Billie's face was smeared a rich, dark brown. I moistened a finger, wiping away some of the chocolate. Brendan, I finally realised, couldn't keep his hands off other people's lives. First it was me. Now it was Gilbert. Cuckoo Productions, I thought bitterly.

'How much do you know?' I heard myself saying.

'About Gilbert? Quite a lot. About what it's been like for you? Not very much.'

'Is that why I'm here?' I looked up at him. 'Am I the POV?'

He smiled at me, not answering, completely shameless. Even Varenka, I sensed, was startled.

For a moment or two I was tempted to surrender to what I really felt, to tell him what a monster television had turned him into, but that would bring this conversation to a close and there were certain questions to which I still needed answers.

'Where's Gilbert?' I asked.

'Dorset somewhere. They've put him in a home.'

'Who have?'

'The family.'

I nodded.

'Did Morris tell you that as well?'

'Yes.'

'And he's told you everything else he knows?'

'He's told me enough.'

'In return for what? A series of his own?'

'Of course. What would any politician want?'

He smiled, happy at the thought of the webs he could spin, and I sat back, making Billie more comfortable in my lap, waiting. Hatred is too weak a word for what I felt for this man but in spite of everything I still wanted the rest of the story.

I'd been a spectator at this play for far too long. I'd even struck up a relationship with Tom, Gilbert's so-called brother, the voice at the end of the telephone. The fact that Gilbert had fooled me over the course of all those conversations was a tribute to his acting skills. He should have stuck with the stage, I thought. I'm sure he'd have made it in the end.

Sipping his coffee, Brendan began to fill in one or two of the gaps that had been preoccupying me for most of the last four weeks. Gilbert, he said, was the only child of his father's first marriage. The marriage had ended with his wife's suicide. At the inquest in Dorchester, she was judged to have taken her life while the balance of her mind was disturbed. Gilbert, at the time, was nine years old. Mother and son had been inseparable. Within months, the father remarried. Another child, a boy, quickly followed.

'So there *is* a brother?'

'A step-brother, yes.'

'Just the one?'

'Yes.'

'And you're saying he's now a politician?'

'Yes.'

'Well-known?'

'Household name.'

'Are you going to tell me who he is?'

'No.'

'Is his name Tom?'

'No.'

'Is it Morris?'

'No.'

'But Morris knows him?'

'They keep the same political company.'

'Like minds?'

'Yes.'

'Cabinet minister?'

'Yes.'

'Who is it, then?'

Brendan didn't answer me. I shrugged, not bothering to argue, no longer wanting to give him the satisfaction of pleading for the name. Numbed by the exchange, I didn't want to hear any more about drama projects, about points of view, about international sales projections. I didn't even flinch when Brendan taunted me with the working title he'd come up with for the series. He wanted to call it *Trickledown*, he said. He thought it was rather witty.

I ignored him. All I could think about was Gilbert and the makebelieve world he'd probably inhabited for most of his waking life. A world where his precious mother was still alive. A world freed from the shadow of the father he hated. A world where – when the going got truly unbearable – he could seek a kind of solace by pretending to be his step-brother. Soon enough, with the little word processor I'd just bought, I'd be able to re-run all those phone conversations in my head and try to understand the way things really were. I'd get everything in order, exactly the way it had all happened, and see what sense it made. For now, though, I'd had enough.

I got to my feet and brushed the crumbs from Billie's Babygro. Brendan was looking up at me. He said he hadn't finished. He'd got more to tell me, more trumpets to blow, more ways of pointing out just how much I was missing by no longer being part of his busy, busy life. I shook my head. I'd heard far too much already.

'You're either crazy or inadequate,' I said softly. 'And you're not crazy.'

The word inadequate stopped Brendan in mid-flow. It was the one accusation he couldn't handle, the one home truth that seemed to get through.

'What do you mean, inadequate?'

'You copped out,' I said savagely. 'You copped out then and you're copping out now.'

'Then?'

'With us. When we were together. The little lies. The big lies. The not facing it.'

'Facing what, for fuck's sake?'

'Life, Brendan. You could have been honest with me. I'm glad now that you weren't but it was there for you, there on a plate. I trusted you completely. God knows, I even loved you. You took it all, didn't you? You took it all, and you played your little games, and when you'd had enough you ran the fucking credits.'

Varenka blinked. The last bit seemed to have impressed her.

'It was over,' Brendan muttered. 'It was finished.'

'That's not what you said later.'

'That was different.'

309

'How?'

'You were pregnant. You were going to have a baby. I had rights. Responsibilities.'

'Responsibilities?' I held Billie a little tighter. 'What would you know about responsibilities?'

'Quite a lot as it happens.' Brendan had composed himself now, pulled himself together. 'Are you saying I was wrong to get Billie out of there? Out from under that loony upstairs?'

'He's not a loony.'

'He's not? He watches you? Follows you around? Breaks into your flat? Pisses through your ceiling? Have I been away too much? Has the language changed? Am I missing something here?' He'd raised his voice again, letting his anger get the better of him.

Billie was beginning to stir.

'So you did take her,' I said quietly.

Brendan didn't answer, just stared at me. I stepped towards the desk, came very close. On top of the pile of scripts was a glossy presentation brochure. *Celebrity Home Run*, it said, *Japanese Edition*. I bent towards him, cradling Billie in my arms.

'You'll never see this baby again,' I said. 'Not if I have anything to do with it.'

'Really?'

'Yes.'

'And you think you can do that?'

'I know I can do that.'

'How come?'

I glanced down at Billie. Her Babygro looked bulky enough to conceal one of those tiny audio recorders.

'I wired Billie,' I lied. 'And I made some good friends in the police. So just leave us alone, eh?'

I looked him in the eye. He didn't flinch. By the door, on the way out, I paused.

'Life's not a game show, Brendan.' I glanced at Varenka. 'Not quite yet.'

Billie and I visit Gilbert as often as we can. His room looks south, over the soft green hills towards Charmouth, and we spend the afternoons chatting, or playing with Billie. Gilbert has acquired a huge library of children's books and Billie sits on his lap gazing up at him while he reads her stories. For each of the characters, he puts on a different voice. The one she loves best of all is Pinocchio, at which Gilbert is very good indeed. He's had enough practice, bless him.

At four, the staff at the home serve afternoon tea. We generally have scones and little glass bowls of Dorset cream and home-made strawberry jam. Billie adores the strawberry jam and since the New Year Gilbert has been giving her big jars of it to take away. We carry them back to London with us, trophies of our expeditions to see Uncle Gillie, and once the jar is empty we know it's time to go back. Lately, the jars have got smaller and smaller but I think that's because Gilbert misses the company and wants us back again sooner.

As a special treat for Billie he'll sometimes play the flute. With Gaynor's help, I managed to rescue it from Napier Road and Gilbert dances awkwardly around the room, inventing little jigs, pursued by Billie. She's only just learned to walk but I know she's really determined to catch him. One day, if she's as lucky as her mother, she will.